PAINT ME MIDNIGHT BLUE

A NOVEL

BRUCE COLBERT

Paint Me Midnight Blue
Copyright ©2022 Bruce Colbert
Cover Photo: Nancy Basinger, 2021

ISBN 978-1-7374758-3-5

Published by:

Blue Jade Press, LLC

Blue Jade Press, LLC
Vineland, NJ 08360
www.bluejadepress.com

For Woodstock, where it all started

Prologue

The woman's labor was long and hard. The doctor working that night knew that it was up to him to deliver this baby and he somehow would.

She told him in her delirium that she was a country music singer and wrote her own songs. She'd learned to play music while living in one of those rural hollows that pepper the Kentucky border above Clarksville. Her grandpa had been a banjo player and a darned good one, she whispered to the young physician between painful gasps.

He didn't ask about the child's father. He assumed, like so many young pregnant women who came to this hospital to give birth, that the father either left, or simply didn't care what happened. Either way, his absence was conspicuous.

The doctor missed the East Coast, well, the mesmerizing energy of New York anyway. He yearned for its concrete and the bustle, and the sophistication too. He was specializing in pediatrics, but all the interns in that specialty did birthing too, as was expected. He'd be finishing his long residency here soon.

His father-in-law, a Wall Street investment banker, had bought them a nice Tudor home in the Riverdale suburb where he had his own spacious house only blocks away. The young couple would move there within the next three months. However, the banker hadn't bought it outright. Instead, he had lent them the money for the down payment, and then had taken on the hefty mortgage which he'd pass on in time. It was a gracious wedding gift.

His mother had lived in New York for over forty years, moving there with his father, at the end of the Second World War. But at heart, she remained a southern belle. The doctor wanted to live in the same town where his mother had grown up, so, he went to Nashville for medical school. He was welcomed into the bosom of his mother's family there in the Old South. Earlier, he had graduated from Cornell with a degree in biology but soon tired of those frigid Ithaca winters. The doctor had married his college sweetheart. He would finish Vanderbilt Medical School with ease, and through personal contacts, the young doctor joined Columbia St. Luke's hospital in Manhattan. He'd devote his practice to pediatrics because he enjoyed the expansive feeling of making a difference with young children.

The gentle young man told the woman in the delivery room to think of something that might calm her such as a sunny meadow, or even a birthday party she had as a child. She confessed she never had a birthday party. But maybe she'd sing to herself, some of the songs she'd written and soon hoped to record for the Grand Ole Opry. The doctor said he'd very much like to hear them. She began to sing one, softly almost like a whisper, and the pain of her contractions seemed to lessen.

He encouraged her to tell him about her girlhood, about the euphoric moments she treasured, not about the drunken abusive father or rural poverty and the meanness of hard backwoods life. He told her about his close boyhood friends, and how as children they built a cardboard box fort in the woods. They visited it every afternoon in the summertime, and had secrets they only shared with each other, never their parents.

"A new life," he said with sweetness in his voice, "is a gift we're given from God, and it's such a wonderful thing." He held her hand in his to calm her further. His attentiveness and caring manner allowed her to relax.

The woman couldn't help but smile as he talked, despite the labor pains. There was a kindness about this man, and he would be the perfect children's physician because in his heart, they all held a special place. In a funny accent, he mimicked the children's comedian Pinky Lee he had seen on an old black and white Saturday television show as a kid. The young woman laughed hard until she had to grab her distended stomach.

The time passed and the birth moved forward. Those long hours slowly ticked by. The contractions became more frequent now and the time for delivery of this baby was almost at hand.

She couldn't help it, the pain made her scream, but the doctor told her that was alright. Go ahead and cry out. It was natural. His own mother had done that too when he came into this world. He sang a country song that he knew and she sang along. She said he had a beautiful voice and he laughed when he heard that.

The time was near, and he gently prodded, "Push hard, push. You can do it, and tonight you will have a beautiful baby, I promise."

The young girl pushed. It happened as he said it would, and the baby slipped out into the world. It was a healthy boy and when the doctor slapped his backside, he cried loudly in opposition. The doctor congratulated her as he placed the baby on her chest and asked her if she might already have a name for the boy. She told him she did, it is the same as her younger brother who died as a child from leukemia.

With a toothy smile she looked up happily into the young doctor's face as he held her sweaty hand, "My son's name is Eddie, like my brother. Eddie Reece."

The young doctor looked at the girl with his tired eyes. In his imagination, he envisioned her journey ahead as a single mother as a long and arduous one, wishing for her that it might have a happy ending.

He was a decent man, and he had chosen medicine as a vehicle to help the less fortunate, not as a moneymaker or to achieve some secure future for himself. He wished the best for the young woman lying in front of him who had drifted off into a drug-induced slumber. She'll have a difficult life ahead of her, and for the child, he thought to himself, as he gently peeled back her fingers that gripped his hand.

At the nursing station, he signed the hospital birth certificate. The morning shift nurse would complete the form later after sitting down with the mother when she awoke. He smiled as he relaxed for a moment with a hot coffee. In his exhaustion, the doctor glanced out at the skyline where he could see the large garish billboard that announced: *Welcome to Music City*.

How many of these children born to single mothers in this city end up single mothers themselves, or would-be guitar players trying to break into The Grand Ole Opry, and miserably failing? This world can be a cruel place and it often was. He wanted to help people. That was the only reason he had suffered through the rigors of medical school, internship, and his residency.

After he finished his coffee, the young doctor allowed his mind to drift. A wave of furtive sleep came over him following his draining shift despite the caffeine. Fortunately, there were few complications, and mercifully, no still births.

He thought about the birth of his own child someday. He dreamed that he would have a daughter and he'd deliver her himself. He imagined holding her tiny body in his strong hands, thanking God for the marvelous gift of life. In his momentary dream state, he saw the cameo face of his unborn daughter. It was the color of fine ivory and with the same piercing dark eyes of his beautiful wife, her small mouth would pucker when she was angry.

The doctor was deep into his sleep when he was awoken abruptly by one of the nurses. She needed his help with a patient who had developed complications from the medications given her. Forced out of this slumber in the lounge chair, he bolted up in perfect wakefulness. Clearheaded again, he was poised and ready to address the patient's pressing needs.

He hurried down the corridor, and the vision was instantly forgotten as he entered the hospital room with a troubled young mother. Her breathing had become strained, and her blood pressure was dropping. He quickly instructed the attending nurse to administer an adrenaline shot. It provided her otherwise young body with the immediate strength to move forward with its natural healing. In less than three minutes, the mother's breathing and blood pressure had normalized.

Once in the empty hallway, he removed his surgical mask, looking at his wristwatch. It was well past the end of his regular shift, though he wasn't in a hurry to leave the maternity floor. The doctor noticed his replacement saunter down the corridor giving him a ready smile. He then shrugged his shoulders and called out, "Another day in paradise." It was an inside joke among the young residents at Vanderbilt taken from a popular song on the radio. They employed it for almost every trying situation they encountered at the large hospital.

On his way out, the doctor greeted the new mothers he knew on the maternity floor. Putting his head inside the room of his last delivery, he called out to the mother who was holding her newborn infant, asking her, "How's Eddie?" The young woman looked up and gave the doctor the most engaging of smiles.

She said, "I think he's going to be a musician. He just laughs when I sing to him."

The doctor moved quickly into her small room. He urged her further, "Sing to him for me. I'd love to hear it." He sat quietly on the edge of her bed in his green wrinkled scrubs as she began to sing to the newborn. It was one of her own songs. As she sang the lullaby to the infant, the doctor thought of when he'd see his own child's first toothless grin.

Instinctively, he knew his first child would be a girl although he was uncertain exactly when it might happen. He'd name her Elizabeth after his mother. Everyone would then call her Lizzie, as his mother had been called by all those who had loved her.

The doctor adored the idea of a large family of boisterous, joyful voices because he had been an only child. As much as his parents had tried for another child, there was only his own birth early in their marriage. Lizzie will be the greatest of gifts, he thought to himself.

The young doctor walked along the broken sidewalk in the early morning, the air pristine in the Tennessee city. He breathed the freshness deeply into his lungs. His apartment wasn't far, so he was able to quickly walk the four blocks to his squat building as dawn approached. The southern sky reminded him of an impressionist painting streaked with rich purples and yellows.

He always checked his mailbox before he climbed the stairs to the tiny apartment. Inside, he found a handmade postcard from his wife living in the New York suburbs where he'd soon be. She had recently started her first year as a second-grade teacher. She made a large greeting card out of her class portrait, and he couldn't stop laughing at all the silly grins.

* * * * * *

Unfortunately, they had been frustrated as a couple during the first five years they tried without success to start their family. But then the miracle came in time. A lovely baby girl was in fact born, and they named her after his mother who would have the opportunity to hold her granddaughter a few times before she died.

They named their baby Elizabeth, though everyone always called her Lizzie. Lizzie Connelly, this beautiful Irish lass with dark, shiny hair.

The doctor often looked back on his daughter's christening at Holy Name Cathedral as perhaps the most important event in his life. Lizzie was christened by his dear friend and fellow rower, the assistant rector Father Tim Dolan. The doctor was the only man in the parish to bring an infant to the early mass. Father Tim celebrated the mass holding Lizzie in his arms at the Communion rail, and it had raised some eyebrows among the staunchest of Catholics. But the fiery priest had defended his actions as they were in line with the present Vatican changes in the liturgy which sought to make the church more accessible, more human, of more relevance.

During late summer, and particularly into the early fall months when the Hudson River is framed in a breathtaking penumbra of colored leaves, they'd row sculls together. He and the muscular priest would row two Saturdays a month in the Hudson League races against the likes of Columbia, Cornell, Princeton, and Fordham. These were non-conference races, with the older guys against the up-and-comers and potential Olympians. They kept their boats at the Riverdale Yacht Club where doctor had become a member and both would sit out on the terrace with a cold beer after practice talking about everything under the sun, and moon.

He wasn't afraid to talk about the faith with Father Tim. They often had heated, though friendly discussions. Since he was a physician, he felt he had a broader understanding of life and death than many others. However, they could never agree on abortion, although they came close, and since they respected each other, it was a subject that they didn't press. His innate love for children strove him to become a pediatrician, and his own daughter made him even more of an advocate for a purer, kinder humanity.

Lizzie had learned to swim in the club pool as it was the craze with newer mothers in those days. His wife would slip into the pool with Lizzie in her arms and let her go gently into the water, as he called out to her to come to him. He'd croon, "Sweet Lizzie. Come on, swim to me." She would look at him standing in the pool.

She was only a little over a year old, yet she was so alert that her face would light up with the sound of his voice. She would let out a high-pitched shriek of the purest joy and begin to swim directly toward him. She'd put her little head into the water and then in a second take it out for a breath, moving her little arms and legs feverishly with his wife an arm's length behind her in the pool, everyone cheering Lizzie on. With splashing

7

strokes, Lizzie would reach him, then leap into his arms and hug him as hard as she could.

They never pushed Lizzie to swim. A single lap was all they thought an infant should attempt, so they dried her off quickly and dressed her. Afterward they would have brunch on the terrace as she sat in a highchair eating her soft-boiled egg while they ate their omelets. It was their usual summer Sunday routine after mass with Father Tim.

The next summer when she was two, the doctor put Lizzie in a newfangled aluminum rod backpack, and he carried her on long walks all through the woods around Riverdale. They would go down to the river, walk along the trails, and up into town where they would sit at a café table and have hot chocolate together. It was a unique father and daughter bond that they shared, and none of the other fathers would spend the same amount of time with their children, only him.

One would often see the smiling young doctor in his shorts, or khakis and worn tennis shoes striding down the street, or in the park along the river. On his back would be the toddler girl with her black hair flowing in the breeze, laughing and singing, her hands resting on the top of his head. Lizzie would sometimes reach down and caress his face with her small fingers. And he would sing to her too, recalling some hiking song he remembered from the camp he'd attended in the Pocono mountains.

Can anything truly be called fate in this world? Or perhaps as the Quran proclaims... our lives have been written in their entirety already by God, set down meticulously in this indelible language of the unchanged and we're powerless to alter them.

Chapter One

In those earliest days, I would paint scenes of rock bands like The Rolling Stones on stage in London. After a while, these rock scenes took little effort and required scant imagination.

For inspiration then, I started to sketch my own dreams. I would wake up on freezing nights and sit across the narrow bed in my attic bedroom. The radiator would bang in our narrow apartment above the lumber store. Freshly awakened, I'd feverishly color these vivid dreams of elusive sirens and Godhead images with a box of dime store Crayola crayons. I'd color three, or sometimes four over several hours each night.

Then I'd sign my name *John Howard* with a flourish, in broad cursive strokes imagining my life as a famous painter. These dream state drawings seemed to be childish to me now. But, they weren't, and of course I hadn't heard of Jung then.

Not long afterward, I found myself studying at the Chicago Art Institute. Here, anything went in those heady days: sex, art, drugs and enough rock 'n roll to shake their concrete building walls. No one told you what to do, or what you couldn't do either. It was all free form, a pass-fail school of misfits and rebels.

We painted every night until midnight, or even later. Sometimes we'd work until early morning and were usually half drunk and high. It didn't matter which drugs. We would try anything we thought might take us to a mythical place of ultimate vision. We sought the uncharted and unknown paths. How I relish those fading memories. Art was the only thing that mattered to me then, as it is now.

I stayed in Chicago after art school and found an apartment in the Andersonville lakeside neighborhood. Uptown was only half safe most nights, and unfriendly every day. It had an enclosed back porch that became an art studio. On many cold nights, there would be a young woman there with me. I'd meet them in one of the few neighborhood bars and they agreed to become a model to sketch and paint. Looking back, they were all sweet women, maybe a year or two out of Michigan or Northwestern, working somewhere downtown. After a conversation and a beer at the nearby bar, they were readily available for the madness of the times. It was the late Sixties, and that extended Summer of Love.

Sex was our ready and facile communication method. It was a language we all spoke fluently, usually unencumbered by any sort of guilt afterwards, and this ultimate freedom we had rarely left us, or certainly not me. But it was always only the art that really counted at the end, and that never changed. It hasn't even today.

Shows were hard to get. All the art galleries were only interested in a group calling themselves Imagists, whatever the hell that meant. The canvases were filled up with a plethora of badly drawn cartoon characters. But they were hot. They sold to the few collectors who wanted modern art on their high-rise or townhouse walls. And most everybody starved, even the half successful painters in Chicago, so I found my way out to San Francisco, if more for the climate than the opportunities.

The whole Bay Area was a political hotbed and Berkeley had exploded. I located some dirt-cheap lodgings in a dilapidated warehouse in the Mission District south of Market. It was a dusty and drafty place with skylights and cracked concrete floors where I might paint in relative peace.

Sometimes I could even eat, if I were lucky, with the little money left over. Since I was an artist from the so-called East, I got into group exhibits with the few decent galleries on Geary Street that wanted non-figurative work. But truthfully, abstract painting wasn't the currency in this town, and that's what I did.

I had worked around sailboats on Lake Michigan most summers and found that I could make money varnishing wooden boats in nearby Sausalito. In those days, I worked for a French-Canadian woman who'd grown up in a rugged seafaring family in Nova Scotia.

She was the eldest of nine children, and she had worked the fishing boats alongside her father for years. What she didn't know about the sea, or below decks on most sailboats, wasn't to be learned. She was small, full-figured and bronzed from the sun. She was a woman with honest green translucent eyes.

Michelle liked me mostly because I wasn't from California. She taught me how to make the marine wood finish lustrous, and forever please those cranky sailboat owners. Michelle was a rather attractive woman, maybe ten years older than me, and over the few years on the Sausalito docks, she had her share of florid affairs. She finally settled in with a commercial fisherman turned yacht delivery captain. They lived together on his Japanese-made teak boat in the marina nearest the town square.

Thankfully, she found a thirty-five-foot yacht for me to live on for two years while the boat owner was away in Europe only a few docks away from her. Through her other contacts in town, I'd also met a few painters who reconverted a rickety boathouse into a rabbit warren of art studios. I took one for myself.

All the prairie darkness left my paintings. Now, most of my larger canvases were vistas of greens and yellows. The bright colors seemed to be swimming together in some delightful synchronicity, or so I figured. Collectors with money were well hidden in San Francisco then. It was a time when few galleries would display any of my abstract work, even the smallest pieces.

Frustrated I started to look toward Los Angeles. I met a British artist who was usually holed up in a converted brewery loft in Downtown L.A. that sat right on the border with gangland East LA. He said he'd put me up for a few bucks for weeks at a time. I could work the town at my leisure.

L.A. had its own art language. I made the rounds of the better galleries which were really places for the movie stars, or would-be film people. The more vulgar the paintings, the higher the prices were. One artist I saw used a dressing table mirror to view swollen boils on his buttocks and painted them in an ultra-realist manner. Perhaps this stuff was more fitting for clinical pathology textbooks than fancy ranch houses in Laurel Canyon, but the market was nevertheless edgy. Dismayed and without much encouragement, I found my way back to Sausalito, the waiting sailboats, and my small studio on the water. It cost fifty-four dollars a month.

Life wasn't unpleasant. I was young and didn't want for female companionship. I found myself in an arrangement we somehow called an affair with Lucy Fonseca, an architect who had a small residential practice in town. She had shiny black hair and piercing dark eyes. Growing up in southern California, she had been surfing before she started primary school.

True, Lucy could paint a little, but in this dull and stilted format that most architects other than Mondrian try when they leave their drawing boards for the fine arts. The woman didn't have a conceptual bone in her trim little body. Her watercolors were always of those ubiquitous square houses on the green rolling Marin hillsides. Lucy painted with this careful rendering of strict right angles. Geometry naturally was her master. She'd sometimes include a woman gazing out the window in them, imitating an impressionist masterpiece.

Although that addition always seemed like an after-thought. Put something in the living room, something human. Though usually her paintings were mostly about the building itself, the structure, and little else.

In her favor, she did understand light, and the rooms and figures in these paintings. They all had provocative shadows giving them some small taste of mystery.

We got along well enough for a few months, and occasionally talked about permanence, though I could see that it wasn't anything that I was ready to embrace.

12

Painting was the only future I thought about. Clearly, I didn't want a wife and two small children getting in the way. There wasn't enough room in my life for a family. Of course, Lucy wanted what I didn't plan to give her. We argued about it at first, then we let the mounting distance take over and that ended the whole thing.

She was an unfettered fiery Sicilian. When I told her I didn't want to continue, she stood up in a Thai restaurant on Caledonia Street, and yelled, "You bastard, you think you can sleep with me, and walk away?" In the blink of an eye, she reached across the small table and slapped me as hard as she could right across the face.

Furious, Lucy turned and ran out the door. Her sharp nails had caught the side of my nose, slicing it enough to emit a trickle of blood above my lips. Shocked, I picked up a napkin holding it long enough against the wound to stem the blood flow before I paid the check. Walking out the door, the eyes of the ten people in the restaurant followed me. Women whispered knowingly to the men with them at the tables.

The embarrassment was over at least. Outside on the Sausalito sidewalk, I just smiled, shrugging it off glancing once more through the restaurant window at the curious faces inside who'd gone back to their dinners.

That same night Lucy went to my sailboat and started to throw things from the dock onto the boat while screaming. Luckily, I had stopped off at the No Name Bar in town for a beer. Wrought up by my untimely absence, she started kicking the boat hull until she sprained her ankle and slowly limped away.

All this was duly reported to me later that night by the guy on the boat next to mine. He was supposed to spend a quiet night there with his wife. He'd prepared a marvelous candlelight dinner and they had just sat down when Lucy started her antics on the communal dock. For someone whose parents were both quiet and rather humorless medical doctors, she had a mouth like a barbary pirate and a shrill voice like a fishwife. I apologized to the dockside neighbor and his wife, though to no avail. His wife was finished with their untouched dinner plus the coarse behavior she'd witnessed and decided to drive back to their house in Mill Valley for the night. Lucy returned later much calmer and we tried to repair the damage. After this futile attempt, she could see that I had no real interest in the same future. We ended the whole affair if I could call it that without much rancor and I never saw her again.

Painting consumed my life. I painted a half dozen big abstract canvases that I managed to show in LA. However, they didn't sell though it did give me courage to continue. The gallery owner who took my art was originally from New York City. She told me that my painting style would never be successful in Los Angeles as it was too rough and abstract.

"The best thing you can do for yourself, is to go to New York," she confessed as we nursed white wines in the office at the gallery. "I like your painting, but it's because I'm from Chelsea."

Probably I could've slept with her if I'd tried, she seemed interested, but I never mixed business with pleasure, it didn't seem smart.

Not taking her opinion as gospel, I booked a few more LA shows, though soon enough I decided to give San Francisco a final try. With some dogged effort, I talked a decent gallerist into a two-man exhibition. The other painter in the show did large monochromatic lined female nudes. He wasn't much talented, but he sold half his canvases. I sold nothing. And that experience pretty much ended anything I might find in San Francisco.

I toyed with the prospect of going back to Chicago and did for a time. Yet, New York made more sense to me. When I wasn't bartending, with the snow falling outside in Chicago, I thought more about the New York move.

A friend at the Art Institute told me about the Whitney Museum deal. Each year they had artist residencies to offer to a few out-of-town painters. It was a cramped studio space located in the museum's basement.

All that was required was a single page application and a few photos of your artwork, easy enough to do. A committee sent me a return letter two months later. They would provide painting space in the museum for a year if I wanted. The only requirement was to meet a few times with museum donors at cocktail fundraisers. Talk about my own painting a bit, maybe smile, and shake a few hands.

I left for New York and quickly found a place with a friend's sister who lived in the city. She had recently divorced and rented me a bedroom in her rent-controlled apartment on 116th street at Columbus Avenue, right above Morningside Park.

This woman worked as an adjunct instructor at Baruch and FIT teaching students how to write professional business letters, or something like that. I stayed with her for a while all the time looking around for my own loft. We rarely spent any time together it seemed, and the few conversations we had in the tiny kitchen over coffee were pleasant enough. She lived her life, and I lived mine.

The Whitney worked for me, and people were nice. I could paint night and day hidden below the street in the bowels of the massive building. And there were a few galleries which would put your work in their large group shows based on the Whitney association. It was a feather in your cap in many New York art circles.

Two months before I left the Whitney, I moved into a loft on the Upper Westside, right outside of Spanish Harlem on 181th Street. There was a whole city block of white painters who had homesteaded there, and the local Dominicans accepted us because we were artists.

We could drink wine in their bodegas as long as we kept away from their women and most of us did. Although, one painter from New Jersey started going out with a Dominican woman. She had fights with her extended family about the guy though nothing violent ever came of it. In the end, they rented an apartment together.

I'd sometimes stop at the Dominican cigar shop in the neighborhood and buy two hand-rolled cigars. On sunny summer days I liked to sit out front on the chairs against the shop window and smoke one with the locals. They all called me Chicago, and they'd joke about Al Capone. It was a good time to be alive. All the women in the art world and the pretty Spanish women seemed interested and attentive.

My artwork started to please me, and I began doing large canvases. They somehow were invested with all the West Coast colors I saw living on the boat. Few of the other abstract painters around me ever used the same palette. It was pretty much mine alone and so it became a signature style. I was branded a California artist in New York. It was a label I didn't fight. At least it was a small recognition that separated me from the thousands of other guys and few women who were painting in this town.

I started to get exhibitions. Nina Johnson, who had worked for Peggy Guggenheim, took me on for a gallery opening. She wanted to feature five young artists to show new work at the gallery she created out of an old meat market. It was on the corner of 10th Street and 10th Avenue and, unsurprisingly, called Ten.

Ten was an immensely popular gallery in its first year. Even as it cooled, I started to sell large abstracts making some real money. The work began to interest collectors and Nina would steer them in my direction though sales were painfully slow. For those first few years, I lived a more or less hand-to-mouth existence. But painting was all that mattered anyway. Women, booze and drugs came too and life seemed alright.

One night a group of us went to a party in the early fall. That's when New York is at its best, with a fragrant smoky chill in the air. The leaves had started to turn into reds and oranges, and the sun was bright in the early evening as we walked up 1st Avenue to the three

16

flat. Inside, the music was deafening, and the room was filled to capacity with young men and women quite like us. They were all engaged in these flippant huddles about art and life itself. Some were smoking joints while others were swigging inexpensive red wine as the music blared.

Large canvases were hung on the walls. They were mostly figurative, self-portraits, nude, or half-clad. One stopped me. The figure was thin with ample breasts and had a half-depressed look on her abstracted mouth. I walked from canvas to canvas, and as I stood in front of the largest, I heard a woman's voice behind ask, "What do you think?" I answered without looking at who was speaking, "Strong color. I like the work." Then, a soft voice whispered into my ear, "Thank you." There was staccato laugh as I turned to look at the young woman.

She was the hostess, her dark hair cut short with bangs down her forehead. She had on a black sweater with cream-colored slacks which hugged her hips, and wore a headband with rhinestones. Her skin was flawless. Her deep-set eyes were almond shaped and surrounded by purple eye shadow. She held a wry smile on her face as she continued to speak in a mock whisper, and told me her name was Yvonne. She said her mother had named her after the Forties film star Yvonne De Carlo and continued to laugh.

I didn't speak right away. Instead, I looked closely at her bewitching face and traced her nose and chin lines with my eyes, drawing her quickly in my mind. Shading her high cheek bones, and the thick dark eyebrows. That night was the beginning for us.

Over the next few months, we would see more and more of each other and ultimately, she invited me to live with her. In less than a day after the invitation, I moved into her East Village studio. We became bohemians, painting and making love most nights. We found bartender and waitress jobs to pay the rent and eat. Somehow it all worked, but that first cold winter in New York, we almost froze with the lousy radiators in the

17

flat. We slept in our clothes and huddled together for warmth.

Her paintings got some recognition. She appeared in an exhibition in a women's co-op gallery which had opened downtown funded by women who were art faculty from Columbia and Pratt. I remember she sold a painting for a hundred dollars, almost unheard of at the time.

We treated ourselves to a feast at an Italian restaurant, putting the hot bread in our coat pockets for later. We even pinched the sugar packets the waiter put on the table with our steaming coffee. That first and only time, I was jealous of her talent and success with her paintings. But I knew that I was the better artist. The world later proved that, or so I thought, when my career in New York took off. Then, I left her behind without ever looking back. Art becomes a selfish profession, though most artists are open-hearted creatures.

It was the Seventies. We'd sometimes hang out at a restaurant/club called Max's where the big Abstract Expressionist painters who made it would drink. They were welcoming of new talent. In truth, they were far more generous than my own generation ever was, and not as greedy either. Maybe the Second War had done that to people in America, where Vietnam only polarized everyone and made them paranoid.

Warhol had become an art star in New York and had his entourage at Max's. They were a vulgar lot, even the musicians who trailed along. It was a cult, really, and his studio became like a factory of awful excess. He was a dynamic painter too, but he made celebrity more important than art. That had never happened before, and it wouldn't again. Maybe it was the 'fifteen minutes' he notoriously described as everyone's time in the spotlight.

Contemporary art gradually became more about money, magazines, newspaper headlines, and TV talk shows. Singlehandedly, Warhol put New York on the world artistic map once again while the LA and London played second fiddle.

Yvonne never liked Max's. She would be harassed by drunk men twice her age and the Warhol hangers-on who happened to like women. She was tired of pushing them off, so we stopped showing up on weekends. The crowd had changed anyway, and with it, the ambiance, and camaraderie among painters. It was all back room doping and anonymous sex, and garishness. It was Warhol's celebrity era, and his town.

The two of us painted feverishly. We showed wherever and whenever we could in the city. My own breakthrough came from old Whitney contacts. There were three women curators, all who went on to open thriving galleries that quickly became the alternative to the Warhol scene and the celebrity.

Joyce Coletta made my reputation in New York. Her gallery was the only one that took a chance on me. She went out on a limb with the New York Times and other critics and gave me my first solo art exhibition. She made certain it would be a success. She called in favors she'd already cultivated with art magazines, and the people who mattered.

In 1977 this art gallery was the premier space in New York, or even Europe. It drew the attention of the entire art world, and high-end collectors. Joyce doubled and tripled the prices that I asked for my paintings within a year. She'd sit beside me in any magazine interview and answer half the questions. I willingly let her talk to the journalists, mostly because she was adroit with that language. It was easier for me that way. I did the painting and that was my only métier.

Joyce had once worked at the Guggenheim. By that time, Peggy Guggenheim was almost senile. However, she still loved Joyce who was the only one of her former crowd of assistants who bothered with the irascible society matron anymore. The lasting connection gave Joyce the cache she needed in those moneyed circles that continued to fuel contemporary art in New York and throughout the world. Peggy was always her ace in the hole.

We found a large and luxurious loft in Chelsea, and moved there. We filled it with the amenities and comforts that two working painters might want or need, then we married. It was fast, unannounced, and not particularly well thought out by either of us. It seemed like the logical next step in our lives. We had been living together as a couple for almost four years, and were in our early thirties.

We didn't think of a family, a household of toddlers, or primary school children and soccer practice. We could only focus on art. Painting was a master, muse, and, perhaps, our continuing curse. Yvonne took birth control pills and we worked. We painted incessantly because that was what we thought we must do. We had to achieve a breakthrough, to pry open some heretofore unopened door, and discover the undiscovered. That is what we thought artists do or should do with their lives.

What we did accomplish was to drink excessively. Yvonne did like the occasional joint, but mostly we preferred to drink scotch, or vodka in the simplest mixtures. The result was that we'd get a pleasant high and could still work. So, we drank at night, and painted, and drank even more. It made us argue and usually about nothing. And we surrounded ourselves with other artists and collectors who did the same.

In the summers we would escape to a small town Upstate. Woodstock was a two-hour drive outside of the city. It was hidden in the Catskills, and friendly to artists. The famous concert had put it on the map for musicians worldwide, though it had always been a town of painters, going as far back as Frederic Church and the Hudson River School.

Ten years after the Woodstock concert, the town had fallen out of favor with the rock musician constellation. The promoters who had followed Bob Dylan and the Band quietly departed. Mostly, it was an ordinary rural town of artists who had been here years before the big concert and a few musicians drawn by the

20

initial spectacle who had simply stayed mostly out of boredom and few prospects.

We'd also tried Provincetown on the Cape a couple of times, but it had a flat feeling. Provincetown seemed so much like the New York world we sought to escape that we couldn't go back anymore. In fact, I spent most of my time there sailing. Yvonne didn't like the open sea or the tourists, so she sketched or painted small canvases.

Since Yvonne and I had been married for a while, we figured we needed a regular getaway. During our second summer in Woodstock, we bought a house on Wylie Lane nestled in a clump of old growth trees on the way up to Mount Guardian and the turn-of-the century Byrdcliffe artist colony. When we bought the frame house, it had been closed for almost two years. The various family members of the deceased owner had wrestled with what to do with it before they eventually turned it over to a local realtor to sell the property. I found out about the Wylie Lane house from Leah who owned the Garden Café, asking her over lunch about interesting places for sale.

The house had a rich history. It had been a well-regarded dance academy in the 1960's and a summer boarding destination for girls who wanted to make careers in the Broadway musical theatre, and for ballet.

The school was created by a cranky old-time choreographer. Inside the house was a cavernous room and a wall of windows overlooking a large spacious lawn. That large space was the dance rehearsal hall. There also was a colorful tiled swimming pool across the street which needed considerable repair, and beyond it, you could see the mountains. A small rectangular building you might call a pool house was adorned with torn couches that smelled of decades of wet bathing suits, and Hawaiian tanning lotion.

On the second floor above the Great Room there were small bedrooms which surrounded it in a horseshoe shape. There was one larger room that we decided was the master bedroom. There were plenty of bedrooms and we thought friends might visit for weekends. Yvonne and I were an affable and approachable couple and we liked being around a lot of people. Other artists were never competitors. They were friends and colleagues. We learned from each other, and gave something back in return.

Maybe we should have thought about children. Yvonne never brought it up, though it must have been on her mind. She was of the age when most women considered the prospect of motherhood and heard the so-called ticking of the proverbial biological clock.

Nonetheless, we were secretive about our own emotions. We never told each other our deepest thoughts or discussed anxieties that troubled us. We saved it for the canvases and disappeared into that expanse.

Yvonne had grown up in Brooklyn, one of three children. She was the only girl raised by a single mother and by all measurement a happy child. She'd gone to Pratt on an art scholarship and the rest was history. Her family were working class Puerto Rican and they were not particularly close.

Her father had left them to go to St Louis for some mysterious reason when his youngest child was four. And he subsequently fathered another three offspring there. Yvonne hadn't spoken to him in ten years or longer. He never sent her as much as a birthday card. I did meet her mother, Conchita, of course. Even though I didn't enjoy being around her, we did see her on occasion. She had come over for Christmas brunch twice, and the perfunctory exchange of gifts at the Chelsea loft.

During Conchita's visits, it soon became evident that she didn't like me for some unknown reason. Her most common tactic was to only speak Spanish for the entire day she spent with us, even while sitting across from me as we exchanged Christmas gifts.

I feared that Yvonne might feel guilty and invite her mother to the Woodstock house more frequently. I would have been satisfied with just a few or even no visits, but I kept my own counsel about her mother. In the end, she never visited.

Yvonne's eldest brother had made a career in the military and was out of the picture as he was usually overseas on assignment. Her youngest brother was a slacker who sometimes worked as a garage mechanic for his uncle in Queens, though mostly he stayed high with his friends in some overcrowded back apartment bedroom. Yvonne often lent him money but in amounts that I'd never miss from our joint bank account. It had gone on for years, usually harmless.

Something slowly started to happen with Yvonne. She became more distant with me. She didn't want to paint with the same intensity that we both had for years. That stopped. Although I noticed it happen, I ignored the change. In the recesses of my own troubled mind, I figured it would pass. As an artist, Yvonne had changed from one medium to another which is always significant. She went from paint to charcoal to assemblage, and then to fabric though nothing captured her fancy.

The house was a monumental undertaking and we had hired a contractor who did all the heavy work to get the interior livable. The Great Room and kitchen were renovated; the roof leaks were fixed.

The first year, we spent our free time there. We both went up before Memorial Day and moved our belongings in two painful prolonged trips from the city. A third trip would be needed to transport art supplies for the studio.

May is a cool month in the Catskills so I arranged for a half cord of firewood to be delivered and we made fires on most mornings for warmth. With a room that large downstairs, it takes a blazing fire a few hours each day to heat enough space, but it was cozy by mid-afternoon. We were comfortable there.

Yvonne had arranged a gallery visit in the city and she planned to spend the weekend at the Chelsea loft while I stayed in Woodstock alone. That was fine with me. Getting comfortable with the old house, I could continue to be useful in some fashion. As a craftsman not unfamiliar with saws and hammers, I've learned to work successfully with my own hands.

One afternoon, I walked the few minutes into town for lunch. I ate a ham sandwich at a café across from the Village Green and the hundred-year-old white Dutch Reformed Church. There were people strolling past the café window along Tinker Street going about their weekend business in small town fashion.

Once in a while someone might appear in eyeshot dressed in tie-dye hippie garb. Woodstock was pleasant in the way I remembered from those Illinois prairie settlements. People usually said hello as you passed them on the street, made eye contact, although it still had an undercurrent of big city seriousness. It was the eyes; they told all you needed to know.

The cafe waitress had grown up here, her parents were local merchants. She thought the whole area incredibly dull, except for the out-of-towners much like myself.

It was flattering to hear although her digs were meaningless. After all, she still lived at home. My feeling was that she needed to taste more independence wherever she happened to settle, Woodstock, New York City or even Cleveland.

Chapter 2

Back in the Woodstock house, I busied myself with touch ups on door jambs. It was after sunset before I finished. I made myself a drink and sat down in front of a fire as the sun disappeared over the mountain peak. The first drink was followed by a second. The lunchtime ham sandwich had been enough to assuage my hunger, so I sat there silently enveloped within my own thoughts of the past, and of what I hoped to do with my art.

I thought about Yvonne too. How could I fix what was troubling her? If she'd only confess to me. Did she even know what it might be? Was it as simple as the need for children? Maybe, I reasoned. That can be fixed, right? We'll talk about it, I convinced myself. I would take the initiative and broach the subject.

Cleaning up the paint supplies for the day, I brought everything out to the garage. Staggering over through the coming darkness I turned on the overhead bulb. The walls inside were painted with girls names who had been at the dance school mostly in the middle Sixties. There were approximately thirty names and the dates they had attended painted in white, red or blue. I put the brushes and paint cans down on a wooden workbench, when I noticed that there was a small hard covered book next to it. Curious, I picked it up. Standing in the light, I looked at the dark bluish colored cover, turning it over in my hands. Embossed on the front cover were the words *Dance Notes*. I took it with me back into the house.

Written clearly in schoolgirl cursive, was the name, Lizzie Connelly. I assumed it was her textbook, or a notebook that dancers used to prepare for numbers on stage. It noted what steps you needed to remember, and when you moved from left to right, that sort of thing.

Markings were printed that looked like hieroglyphics employing these bent stick figures. It was all a foreign language to me, though I could determine when you moved your body to left or right, and maybe raised your hands in the air. That much was evident. Looking through the book, I could see the girl's notes on half the pages before they stopped. I assumed she had completed the course, or just quit writing.

I held it up looking at the cover more closely and a lock of dark hair fell out of the center onto my lap. It was wrapped in a hair tie though flattened so it would fit into the book. The hair was black and shiny, and I put it up to my nose. It had a perfumed smell to it, almost like rose petals.

Who was this Lizzie Connelly who snipped locks of her raven hair, and put it in this dance book? Why? Did she have one of those short haircuts girls sometimes get, after wearing her hair shoulder length for years? I looked around the spacious half empty living room which had been used for the rehearsals. I could almost hear the girls dance those staccato footsteps, and the dance mistress calling out the movement changes.

I flipped through the dance book for a minute. I thought about how this had belonged to one of those dancers who was determined to make it big on Broadway, so full of ambition and talent, bubbling with infectious excitement. They believed the world was theirs for the taking. It made me smile to think about that. That's how I thought about art when I was starting. About eleven o'clock, the fire had died down to a few embers. I put the screen on the hearth and climbed the stairs for bed. We had halfway furnished the main bedroom with a double bed and night tables. I slipped into the cool sheets and pulled up the comforter. Soon, I was fast asleep.

In what seemed like a dream, I abruptly sat up. I thought someone had called me, not by name, but through some kind of summons. I could see at the foot of the bed a standing figure which looked like a young woman encased in white gossamer. I called out, "Yvonne, is that you?" But there was only silence, and I think the figure had shaken her head, no.

Looking closely, I could see that it wasn't Yvonne. This was a much younger woman, a girl really, and probably no more than sixteen or seventeen. She was dressed in a white smock, something you might dance in. She was swinging slightly from side to side, moving her head, her hair flowed through the nighttime air. I could see her facial features very clearly.

Frightened, I called out, "Who are you? What are you doing here?"

She turned in a sort of dance movement, putting her hands together above her head as I'd seen ballerinas do, then twirled around in a circle, and then again. By this time, my feet were on the floor, and I was trying to reach out in her direction to touch her though she backed away ever so slightly. She then darted into the corner by the window, and spoke softly, "I'm here for you."

"Please tell me who you are," I uttered. I was convinced that someone had found their way into the house and was tormenting me with some ridiculous game. It was a prank or joke, something the locals did to scare new people.

"You know you love me," she answered and, in an instant, was in front of the window.

"Goddammit, stop this," I shouted out in the darkness, but she only giggled like the young girl she obviously was.

She didn't move from the window. I could clearly see her outline in the moonlight. It was as if I could completely see through her. She had no solid form.

"OK," I told her, "I'll play your game. Let's start with your name."

"My name," she whispered, and her face seemed to glow.

"Your name," I insisted.

"Lizzie," she said, very softly.

"You're Lizzie. That's your name."

"Yes."

I was standing next to the bed, and she stood directly in front of the window. I raised my voice, asking,

27

"Lizzie, do your parents know you're here?" I wanted to scold her.

"I must go."

I lunged toward the window but she, or whatever it was, had vanished. Only the moonlight shone, coming in through the window panes on my bare legs.

"Jesus Christ," I said to myself, "the scotch's got to stop." I got back into bed undaunted, and fell right back to sleep, only rising with the breaking dawn light on my face from the window.

The next day, I had pretty much forgotten the dream until I'd gone back into the garage for a tarpaulin. I noticed fresh painting on the wall. I looked at the words that were newly painted and wet. It said, 'Lizzie loves John' and it was done with almost a professional artist's touch, the letters and the sensibility of stroke. 'Lizzie,' I thought aloud, and a guy named John. I thought about how strange it was that we shared the same name. I touched the paint and it was tacky as if this paint had been applied to the wooden wall a few hours earlier.

Looking around the walls at the other names painted, they all looked rather childlike, probably painted by adolescent girls. This one, however, looked so much different, although the paint seemed to be a regular house paint that you'd buy at any hardware store.

For a moment, I thought that I had a hangover. I must have dreamed what went on in that upstairs bedroom. That's a wakeup call for too much drinking. It's time to cut down on the liquor consumption, or you'll be seeing visions, I thought to myself with a shiver.

Curious, I went back into the house and up to the master bedroom. I walked over to the window and glanced around for any proof that someone had been there. I was looking for evidence of a ridiculous visit from the town teenagers to scare the newer people though I found nothing. As I leaned on the window ledge to look up at the crest of Mount Guardian, I shrugged my shoulders as I considered these absurd thoughts.

In the light of day, I was reassured that there was no power in the previous night's dream. Smiling, I rubbed my hands together and started toward the bedroom door when I noticed something sticky on my hands from the window sill. It was white paint, almost the same consistency as what I'd seen on the wall in the garage, and that frightened me. It was scary because I didn't know where it came from. As I looked around the small bedroom, I figured there had to be some reasonable explanation of why it was there. Maybe it was the contractors?

Downstairs I drank a glass of water and calmed my nerves. Calling the contractor, I asked him if his people had done any work in the bedrooms. They had painted all the bedroom walls an off-white color, except for the master. Yvonne had wanted that color to be coral. All the sills were white, the same as the frames. That was the obvious explanation. On the phone with the contractor, he had apologized, saying the master bedroom was the one room that his people had missed in the touch-up painting. No one had done any painting in there except for the coral walls Yvonne wanted.

Was it possible that one of his workers had started but then quit before the job was finished on the sill? He reckoned anything was possible. They were laborers from El Salvador who worked cheaply, though the contractor said that he checked that room himself and planned to be back the next week to finish it.

Painting the window frames and the sill in the master bedroom was the last thing on his list. There was little more to say to the man, so I thanked him, hanging up. I was still uncertain of all that had happened, or that I imagined had happened last night.

Going out to the garage, I looked at the workbench surprised to see another book: *The 1966 Broadway Dance Workshop of Woodstock*. How had I missed it? Glancing through it, I saw pictures and biographies of the girls who had attended the camp. It

29

was dedicated at the front of the book to Elizabeth "Lizzie" Connelly who had disappeared that Christmas.

I took it into the house, dusted the cover off with a wet kitchen towel and put it on a table next to the fireplace where I could examine it later.

That night after dinner I thumbed through the book. The girls were listed alphabetically. I turned immediately to the C's where in the middle of the page I found the picture of Lizzie Connelly.

When I saw the picture, the hair on my neck stood up stiff and I felt a tightness embrace my skull. I had only experienced this feeling with the worst kind of fear. The black and white photograph of the young girl looked exactly like the person in my dream. It was the same girl I imagined was standing in the bedroom last night and had spoken to me. She had answered my questions, as I had asked them.

Lizzie Connelly was sixteen years old and lived in Riverdale, next to the Fordham campus. She was the oldest of two sisters both of whom were interested in the theatre. Her father was a pediatrician and her mother had been a school teacher who also taught dance and had been on Broadway for several years in minor roles before she married. They were a gifted and theatrical family as the biography suggested.

Lizzie was dressed in all white in the picture, which was the dance costume she had chosen for her final musical theatre number. She looked just like the young girl I had seen last night. I became convinced they were one and the same. It could have been her sister who wasn't shown in the yearbook that night, but why would that be? Do sisters come here from Riverdale, and haunt Upstate dancing schools? Do they invade this house every summer because of something that occurred here? What could have happened?

I read and reread the yearbook dedication, and it provided little concrete information. It stated that they were all sorry about the loss of their 'dear dancer' friend, far too young to have that this tragedy befall her. What exactly? I repeated under my breath and poured myself a glass of wine from the nearby bottle.

I made it a point to investigate this thing. I locked the Woodstock house on Wylie Lane and headed back to the city. I was determined to check further on Elizabeth Connelly, but I let life get in my way with a busy week.

Yvonne had an important group exhibition and needed to stay in the city for the weekend, so I went back to supervise the last of the contractor's work on the house.

When I drove into our driveway on Friday night, I noticed the contractor had taped one of his business envelopes to the side door. He enumerated the work done that past week, and it said they were all finished. It was the end of our agreement for the renovation, and his crew had completed the rest of the inside painting including window frames and sills.

I had stopped at the supermarket in Hurley Ridge and picked up some prepared foods for the weekend and another bottle of wine. In the kitchen I heated a turkey meatloaf in the oven and then prepared a simple salad. When it was ready, I wolfed it down at the blond wood Ikea table we bought for the kitchen and cleaned up the few dirty dishes before going into the living room. By now, the fire that I had started when I'd come in the door was roaring. It was a comfort to sit in front of it watching the flames dance in the darkness. We had no stereo or radios in the house yet, so I quietly listened to the mountain wind rattle the windowpanes. Before long, my eyes were heavy from an exhausting week in the city, and I climbed the stairs for bed.

It had been rainy, so the bedroom was cool for June. With the comforter on top of me, I soon fell asleep. The foolishness of the earlier weekend had escaped me and the night started out peacefully.

Then in the middle of the night, I was startled awake and saw a bright light in front of the window. It moved nearer to the bed as it seemed to notice I was awake. It stopped at the foot of the bed and quickly

31

changed into the young woman dressed in a gossamer white dance smock that I'd seen the week before.

This time I didn't speak out, instead I silently watched the image. She moved from side to side in what I'd interpreted as a dance routine. The movement was slight, true, yet it couldn't be confused with anything but dance.

Suddenly, the whitish apparition spoke, pointing her index finger at me in the bed, "I've waited for you." With that telling remark, I started to shake uncontrollably. Out of some bizarre survival instinct, I slapped my own face hard twice, back and forth. I tried to bring back some sort of reality, or consciousness, anything, that I had now abandoned. Nothing changed except for the painful sting on my face. She remained there.

The young woman moved away from the window and before long she danced in a circle, humming an unfamiliar melody. Within an instant, she was on the side of the bed. Propped up in a seated position, I was trembling, and her hand touched mine which was tightly gripping the mattress. Her touch was warm, almost hot. She was so close I could see her features clearly. I stared at her wide liquid eyes.

I said, "Why me?"

"We're meant to be together."

The apparition instantaneously disappeared from my sight, and I sat there shaking. It took a moment before I could compose myself enough to switch on the bedside lamp. The room was unchanged from the time I entered it earlier preparing for bed. Suddenly I found the courage to get out of bed to walk over to the wooden window sill, and with a trembling hand, I reached down to touch it. There was wet white paint on it that stuck to my fingertips.

I hurried downstairs into the pantry, then grabbed a flashlight and ran out to the garage. I threw open the door waving the light beam around and saw nothing unusual. Quickly I flicked on the overhead electric light. The earlier damp white paint I'd noticed before that said, 'Lizzie Loves John' had dried, but my heart almost stopped as I looked below it. Painted in the same cursive style were the words, 'Very much.' I touched the letter 'V' and wet paint stuck to my finger. Confused and frightened, I thought I was losing my mind.

Closing the garage door but leaving the light on, I ran back into the house. Breathing heavily, I rebuilt the fire, adding new logs, and sat down with a kitchen knife as protection. I was afraid to return to the bedroom. At some point, I drifted into a sound sleep in the stuffed chair and in a few hours awoke with the knife still in my lap.

Undone, I made myself a coffee, still in my bathrobe, and quickly went back to the garage where I had left the light on all night. Someone, or something, had turned it out, and when I flicked the switch on again, I saw the painted words, *Very Much* were painted under Lizzie's name. The ghost of Elizabeth Connelly, and the thought of her somehow loving me terrified me. Would she harm me in some otherworldly fashion?

I called Yvonne and told her I wanted her to come here next weekend. I said I couldn't spend another weekend apart from her. She laughed at me through the telephone. It troubled me to hear it.

"This from you, it doesn't sound like the man I know," she said almost too sweetly into the receiver. "I promise I'll be in Woodstock next weekend, OK?"

We made small talk about our lives, art and the people we knew in the city, but nothing of any consequence really. I had a show in London at the end of the month at White Chapel Gallery and planned to be there for the opening. Yvonne would stay at the Woodstock house alone for at least one weekend. I would be able to see what her experience was.

The London gallery had a good crowd assembled for the opening. They were attentive even if they didn't seem to be buying. Abstract art had some cache on this side of the water. For more comfort during the short visit,

I stayed in a small private residential club in Sloan Square arranged by the gallery owner. The three days in London were productive. On the second day in town, I visited the Tate and a few other smaller museums who were in the acquisition mode for new and exciting art. They were all complimentary about the non-objective painting I was doing and two of them seemed to have a real interest in acquiring something, the Tate being one.

Back in New York at the Chelsea loft, we had dinner out the night I returned. Over the meal I inquired how her weekend was passed in Woodstock.

"It's a quiet place," Yvonne said, matter-of-factly and didn't add anything else to the description.

"And the house, were you comfortable there?"

Grabbing a roll on the table and taking a big bite before answering, she said with a half full mouth, "Why wouldn't I be?"

I didn't want to say anything just yet of my earlier experiences, so I continued to troll her in our rather inane dinner conversation.

"You slept soundly in the bedroom, right?"

"Of course."

I poured another glass of wine before I was ready to continue, asking her, "The country noises and the wind didn't keep you awake?"

"What are you driving at? There were no bats trying to get inside the window, or damn ghosts, c'mon."

"Well, I hoped you'd be comfortable at the country house, because I want to spend a lot more time there. That's all."

"I was comfortable. Slept like a newborn and had coffee next morning on the terrace with the birds singing. No, they were trilling, because birds don't sing, people do."

"Good," I answered behind a rather false smile.

The mystery of what I had experienced those nights on Wylie Lane was something I'd have to figure out for myself. Maybe I was finally paying for the LSD and magic mushroom trips I'd taken through my twenties.

Could you have delayed reactions to those hallucinogens? It was possible.

I asked her if she liked the coral color in the bedroom, saying I believed we'd hired the right local contractor for the work. She smilingly said that the house was 'absolutely wonderful' and would be an important part of our lives from now on. The addition of this second home seemed to please her. The despondency she'd shown over the past six months seemed to lessen, or mostly disappear.

The excitement of the Woodstock house seemed to serve as a buoyancy in our lives, enriching it, and at the same time, maybe smoothing the rough places out. The next weekend, Yvonne was with me, and we slept in the coral bedroom without incident for two nights and drove back to the city.

We spent all of July and most of August living on Wylie Lane. Everything was normal, and pleasant with the warm summer days. We both worked in the garden, planting flowers and ornamental bushes to enhance the house with our own special signature. It wasn't until the third week of August that Yvonne had reason to go into the city alone. I asked her if I should join her, and she said no. She'd only be gone for two or three days at the most. She'd take the bus back to Woodstock on Sunday night, and I could pick her up at the Village Green.

That Friday night came, and I had trepidations. I couldn't get to sleep for half the night, which was particularly hot with a late summer heat wave. Since we didn't have air conditioning, I had opened the bedroom window for the breeze. The night appeared to be too quiet for me. It was about four in the morning when I woke and looked furtively around the darkened bedroom. I didn't see anything shocking, so I tried to close my eyes again.

A gentle voice whispered to me. I sat up startled. I could see that same white apparition. This time, she was over by the small dresser we had in the room. She was

35

sitting in the rocking chair we'd bought at an antique store.

"My grandmother had one like this, only painted forest green," the ghost said to me.

I hoped she was a teenage girl who would then tell me that this was prank, and apologize for frightening me. She didn't say that at all. Instead she called out my name clearly and in an endearing tone.

Surprisingly after a few moments, I found that I could slow my heartbeats and a calmness came over me. I even attempted a wan smile in her direction. My hands had not obeyed whatever calmness had stilled my mind. I moved them nervously from side to side, until at last they rested on my lap in some kind of uncomfortable repose.

The white apparition that was Lizzie Connelly moved and sat on my bed. The moonlight made a golden aura around her lovely young head. She had long straight hair that hung down to her shoulders, but it had a few tangles.

She somehow sensed that I was staring at her hair, and very softly said, "Oh, I must do something with it," then reached up with her slender arms and hands to touch the strands.

"It's quite lovely," I managed to utter. I don't know why because I knew what I was experiencing couldn't be real. I was sure I was in some type of self-induced hypnotic trance. Yet, I couldn't stop myself from mumbling.

"Oh, you're just saying that to make me feel good," she responded. She put her face close to mine where I could feel the warmth of her breath. It felt as real as if Yvonne were there next to me in this bed, though of course she wasn't.

Lizzie's ghost reached up with her slim hand and gently touched my cheek. It felt quite human. It had the same texture as a woman's soft skin, the same as Yvonne's. I'm an artist and I have an acute sense of the tactile from clay and wood and paint. It was the touch of a human being. I gulped with unnatural anxiety. I reached

36

out across the bedspread frightened and yet excited and touched her arm with my fingers. I finally managed to speak.

"Who, and what are you?"

"Silly, I'm Lizzie. You know that," she said, and the whiteness stood up and walked toward the window.

Within seconds she completely disappeared. I saw nothing but the moonlight outside reflected on the trees, and the asphalt of Wylie Lane. I didn't turn on the bedside lamp though continued to sit mute in the room's bright moonlight. I was convinced that I had been chosen for this unnatural experience. I couldn't comprehend why. Surely it had to do with this house, and what had happened here as that seemed to be the only explanation for this visitation of spirit.

The next morning, I called the New York Times and arranged for copies of any articles they might have run on Elizabeth 'Lizzie' Connelly aged sixteen or seventeen in the last twenty years. They would do a search of the newspaper microfiche in their so-called morgue of past issues and print out copies of the articles for twenty dollars a search.

The Times clerk took down my information. They would send whatever articles they found, along with an invoice. It was straight forward. The man on the other end of the telephone told me such a search was done the day after a request was made. It was a procedure they had done countless times.

There was really nothing much happening in the Manhattan art scene for the month of August. New York was sweltering. Yvonne and I planned to remain in bucolic Woodstock. Why wouldn't we? The weekenders from the city were arriving by the carloads to stay at local inns to escape the heat and the noise.

It must have been a week after I called the Times that the postman delivered a manila envelope to me with the newspaper logo printed on the front. Yvonne was in town shopping. She'd found an art supply store called Catskill Arts where she could buy drawing paper,

37

charcoal, and chalk pastels. That had kept her busy. I sat down at the kitchen table with the envelope, tearing it open with trembling hands to see what the contents might be.

There were two newspaper article reprints inside. One was about a young woman who had gone missing after a dance performance at the Riverdale Yacht Club on the Hudson where her parents were members. She, and four other girls, had choreographed and danced in a modern dance number scheduled for the pleasure of the club membership. It had been attended by twenty-five people, a combination of parents and friends and others on an early Saturday evening.

The yacht club was in walking distance of the parents' home, a large five-bedroom Tudor on a well-lit street. Lizzie and her teenage girlfriends often walked home after an event at the club. There was an ex-boyfriend present at the recital. The couple had stopped dating but, the boy had remained a close friend of Lizzie and her circle. His parents were also members of the yacht club, and well known in the Riverdale community.

According to the article, Lizzie had wanted to stay at the club. She loved the water and was active with the girls' competitive sailboat racing team. Her parents had agreed. Her father, a pediatrician, had said for her to call him, and he would drive the four blocks to the club to pick her up. He had picked her up before when the club had sponsored teen nighttime events. The area was considered very safe. There was no recent history of any violence in that section of Riverdale, according to the village police. She was never found.

The second article from the Times was an interview with the parents eight months after Lizzie Connelly's disappearance. It traced the broad investigation of state and municipal area police agencies to locate the missing girl. The parents offered a one hundred-thousand-dollar reward to anyone who had information which would lead to Lizzie's return. No one had ever come forward to claim the reward money, nor were there any strong leads which pointed to kidnapping or even murder. The suburban New York City teenage girl had apparently vanished into thin air. There was no trace of where she'd gone.

The article chronicled her history for the two years before her disappearance. It reported a one-month residence in Woodstock at the Broadway Dance Workshop on Wylie Lane. The workshop was a comprehensive summer dance program that was conducted by former Broadway musical theatre performers for promising teenage female dancers.

Elizabeth Connelly had been a student at the Wylie Lane studio. She shared a room with another girl on the east side of the building which was the second largest room on that bedroom floor.

She had excelled at the residential dance camp. According to its director and her other instructors, she was popular with both the faculty and her fellow students. Renee Glickman, a Broadway choreographer who taught at the summer dance program had claimed that Lizzie was easily the best dancer among her class. Renee said to the Times reporter that Lizzie appeared rather mature for such a young age. She was poised, and kind to all she dealt with at the workshop.

"It breaks my heart that this has happened," Glickman was reported as saying, clearly saddened by the unfortunate event.

The first article concerning Lizzie Connelly's disappearance consisted of stringing together interviews with friends who had been with her during, and right after, the dance performance, yacht club staff and parents of her friends. The last fourth of the article consisted of interviews with the police detectives who had investigated the case.

The law had come up with a big zero as to her whereabouts, and never found a body. Unfortunately, this was still the New York City area where murders had, and did, happen on a daily basis. Not far from the quiet leafy suburban Riverdale neighborhoods and near the Jesuit university Fordham, there were pockets of crime. Men and women who commit these murders could walk six or seven blocks to the Hudson River and the yacht club and kidnap this young girl at knife point at the water's edge.

After the dance performance, the yacht club had laid out a light buffet dinner for the participants and the audience. It was part of the ticket price. Several of the dancers had congregated at the dessert table. They talked to Lizzie at leisure. She was reported as eating a chocolate éclair and some of the custard had squirted onto her chin, which caused teenage laughter from her friends.

Where she'd gone afterward was uncertain. Someone had thought they remembered her walking onto the outside wooden deck facing the broad river. She may have taken the stairs down to the dock which protruded into the water where two power boats were moored.

Two fathers who were at the performance said they had seen her leaning on the rail looking at the water alone. Then she had either gone back inside or walked to the lower level while they remained outside. Lizzie was a regular at the yacht club so she knew if she took the side stairs, they would take her to the riverfront where the small racing sailboats were kept. She might have done that.

From there, she could've easily walked down the concrete sidewalk which led to the Hudson River, and out on the boat docks which would give her a panorama of the wide river vista back toward Manhattan. It was night and from the docks, she could see the New York skyline lit against the black sky. All this was strictly conjecture. No one saw her standing on the docks. She was last noticed on the outside deck visible by the two fathers interviewed by the NYPD detectives, and later the Times reporter.

Her former boyfriend had attended the performance. He had spoken to her afterward, hugging and congratulating her. They were both seen laughing.

Her teenage circle considered them friends since their romantic relationship had cooled. Girls and boys of this age were often caught up in the infatuation of first love and it quickly and predictably ends.

The young man left the yacht club almost immediately after congratulating Lizzie. He had been seen walking through the club parking lot by several parents who knew him. He had greeted one of the familiar couples. They last remembered him on the road which would eventually lead him to the Riverdale residential neighborhoods.

For safety's sake, the yacht club parking lot was well lit with overhead halogen lamps. The neighborhood had a string of bright street lamps lighting the entire well-marked two-lane street all the way to its intersection with busy Broadway.

The police had questioned her ex-boyfriend several times, once at his home and several times at police headquarters, where experienced interrogators were involved. The teenage boy had no criminal record, and was an athlete on the St. Ignatius Academy football team. However, he had been involved in a fight with another young man in a restaurant and the local police had been called. He had been given a stern warning by a magistrate as was the other young man involved, but it had been dismissed.

He had also served as an altar boy for three years at Christ the King Catholic Church. He was active in a boy scout troop where he had been working on achieving the Eagle Scout rank. In fact, his record was squeaky clean, almost too clean, as one of the detectives said in a much later interview.

On the football team he had excelled as a tough competitor. Although, he had a reputation in the Catholic School athletic league as a late-hitter on the gridiron. It had been reported twice by opposing teams. But nothing had been done about it by the referees. His own father had played football at Fordham University where he'd been a standout, and was still a trim six foot and two hundred pounds. Jack Donovan was the youngest of three sons, two of whom had followed each other to Notre Dame. One had played football, the other hadn't.

The Donovan name was the only name to surface. But they mutually ended the relationship, according to the testimony of both the boy and her girlfriends.

I reread the second news article of the interview with her parents that was written almost a year after Lizzie vanished. I could find no trail to pursue. The only thing left to do was to forget about it. I should get on with my life, though I somehow couldn't.

The next step would be to see if I could get access to the Riverdale and New York City police files on the case under the Freedom of Information Act. A few phone calls later, I had made the official request. I would be provided these files within two to three weeks.

In the meantime, I said nothing to Yvonne about what I was doing. We carried on our life as we had before. We devoted ourselves to beautifying the Wylie Lane house as only two committed artists could. She wanted to return to the city after Labor Day, but I pleaded that I needed to finish the work on the house as the Fall weather was really mild. I wanted to do stonework on the crumbling garden walls. Yvonne muttered, "Be my guest." It was a reason to spend one or two weekends at the house alone. I wanted to see if there would be any more nighttime manifestations from the apparition.

I drove up to Woodstock from the city on the weekend of September 15. I pulled into the driveway at sunset which was glorious. I made myself a quick whiskey. I sat on the side deck as the sun slowly dipped over the Catskills, shading the pale blue sky with an orange tint, and finally magenta.

I relaxed listening to some jazz tapes that we had brought with us from the city and fell asleep for a short time in the chair. When I woke, I slowly made my way up the stairs to the second floor and the master bedroom. I found a thicker comforter for the cooler fall mountain temperatures in the closet.

After settling in the bed, I was asleep in a matter of minutes. Then during the night, I heard a loud sound and felt prickles of awareness. Opening my eyes, I saw the same image of the girl-child smiling at me. The gauzy whiteness called out, "Johnny." At first, I feared the ghostly phenomenon might possibly hurt me. I sought to understand its behavior through the rational mind. I spoke to her, or it, in return, softly saying, "Lizzie."

Now emboldened, I asked, "I read newspaper articles about you disappearing from the yacht club that night. What happened?" I don't know why I expected her to answer me, though I believed she would.

She began the adagio dance she had done the last time she appeared.

"Do you like my dancing?"

Uncertain about what else to say I replied, "You're such a great dancer, Lizzie. You'd be on Broadway for sure if you hadn't disappeared."

The image of translucent whiteness continued its dance. She hummed a tune in accompaniment, starting to move faster and faster, and in the end, jumped into the air with her legs spread wide. I saw she wore ballerina slippers. Immediately I started to clap my hands together hard and continued for a few seconds.

Lizzie stopped, stood up straight and took a bow. She moved forward, and extended her hand, "Come dance with me."

I can't explain why but I kicked the bedclothes off my legs, and with some new found courage, walked toward what I believed didn't exist. Standing next to her, she seemed to take on a more defined human look, and the body of a real person was there unabashedly right in front of me. I felt her warm hand that I took into my own, and I put my arm around what seemed to be a waist. She felt real. She put her dainty head on my chest as she was much shorter. It rested there with the same weight as if

Yvonne were with me. I smelled women's bath salts, even her scent was real.

We danced very measuredly in a series of circles around the room. At the conclusion of the dance, I looked directly into her face. She was beautiful with that first blush of youth, a cream colored and flawless complexion. I said, "I'm falling in love with you, Lizzie Connelly."

To that she laughed a fawn-like laugh, whispering, "I know."

In the next moment, I stood at the bedroom window alone looking out into the night. My trembling hands and the front of my pajama tops smelled sweet. Not an overpowering perfume that was so frequently worn by the women I knew in New York. No, something much purer and innocent. I began to think that I was losing my mind. This madness couldn't be happening to me, though it was.

I thought about how it felt to hold Lizzie Connelly in my arms as we danced in the bedroom, only a few circles that took perhaps ten or twenty seconds. Her head rested comfortably on my chest. I remember the pressure of her face. I can clearly recall how her hair smelled like a pine forest. It was so inexplicable. Where had this vision come from? How could I begin to fathom the humanness of that apparition, whatever it might be?

There was no doubt in my mind that for some few seconds she was in human form. She was the same young woman from that dance camp yearbook photograph, Lizzie Connelly. She was dancing with me in this very bedroom, of that I was certain. Now she had vanished.

The moonlight was particularly bright that night, and looking out the window I could see the moon was at its fullest in the darkness. The light on my hands from the window panes had a color of which I'd never encountered. It was white, yet it had a phosphorescence and unique glow. The trees outside were couched in complete darkness and from the sky a path of light to the bedroom window almost appeared to be some path into the heavens.

I said aloud to myself in a raspy whisper, "Elizabeth, Lizzie. Why have you come in this way to me? I don't know what it means."

Wanting a drink, I walked downstairs into the pantry and found a scotch bottle and a nearby glass. I poured myself two fingers and sat down in the living room chair by the fireplace.

Within my troubled mind, I painted a self-portrait of a seated man. The figure in my cerebral brush strokes was in total darkness except for a blinding light that came directly to him from the heavens. I thought perhaps it could be Jacob's Ladder, that biblical path which led directly to God.

I was sorely confused, but in that uneasiness, I began to pray for a sign or guidance of what had happened, and what I must do. I half expected an answer, though there was only the howl of the night wind, and my own feverish thoughts.

Tilting the glass to finish the whiskey, it tasted harsh. Its burning continued from the inside of my mouth slowly down my throat. A frightening thought had come to me in that burning. Was what happened an act of God almighty, or what I believed this higher power to be, or rather of Satan? Had Lizzie Connelly returned to torment and torture me with my own insanity? Would she lead me to some horrible end? The thought of this eventuality sobered me up as the liquor made me more somnolent. I straightened up in the chair disoriented.

"No, no," I cried out. I wondered was I being punished for something I'd done, or not done? Was I sought out by the universe for a reason of which I had no knowledge?

I thought only of saving myself in that frightful moment. In a near panic, I remembered that Catholic priests had long experience in thwarting demonic adventures on earth. It occurred to me that I must see a priest.

What twenty minutes earlier had been this euphoria following my moonlight dance with the apparition, suddenly terrified me. I now feared that I'd become the target of the Devil's revenge on this earth. Lucifer had chosen me to suffer his terrible evil, his practiced inquisition that was over two thousand years old, or as enduring as original sin.

The light of dawn gradually removed the darkness as I sat there. I thought that perhaps my own fear had created this mirage. It was little more than some self-induced hallucination I'd developed. Perhaps everything was the direct result of a neurosis which had been hidden before yet was now quite real.

Over the years I had known artists who suffered nervous collapses. Men and women who had broken down as the world around them became too much to suffer. Some had been institutionalized for a few months, or longer. Then it had somehow cleared for them, at least partially to where they could function, though often not as before. Was this what I had to look forward to in my own life, an attack of runaway psychosis followed by demise? It chilled me to consider that.

Chapter Three

The next morning, I drove back to New York. When I saw the surprised Yvonne, I told her I needed to be back in the city to organize a new art exhibition. The show was finally in the works after the barrier of gallery inertia appeared to be broken. She stared at me following my convoluted explanation for the early departure from Woodstock, and said, "Are you alright?"

"Sure," I answered. "It's time to move a few things forward. You know how we waste time up there." I followed that disingenuous remark with an empty laugh.

In truth, I hoped this was the end of Lizzie Connelly in any form. I threw myself into painting for the next week, putting in ten-hour days at the studio. I was creating at least a basic structure for a new series of work, and possibly a new direction.

The work started as pure abstraction without any shape. Then I added geometry to the paintings with hard edge lines. At the conclusion, I inserted female figures inside the picture plane itself. Of the six canvases I had been working on, four of them had a wispy white-clad woman in them. These females all resembled the anatomy of young girls in their body language. Disturbed with this result, I started to make the women more voluptuous and mature. But, one by one I brought the various canvases back to their original figure, this post adolescent girl.

On the opposing wall, I put up thick large paper and began to paint faces. I painted womanly portraits of wanton desire. Within two days I'd obliterated all that and started again with the adolescent innocence I sought to portray. I don't think I'd ever worked so feverishly in a studio since I started painting as a kid. When Yvonne came to see the progress, she was astounded.

"These are marvelous," she said, standing in the doorway. She moved around the studio, and kept shaking her head from side to side. She wasn't smiling and her lips were pressed tight together as she stared at the canvases and the few drawings.

"This is so unlike you, all this figure stuff," she finally said, letting out a long sigh. "What's the motivation to do this, after years and years?"

"I don't know."

She looked closely at the paper and turned to me, "Is this someone you know? This model, the woman?"

Shrugging my shoulders, I told her it came out of my imagination. It was nothing else, maybe from magazines or books, nothing specific.

She touched one of the dry portraits, and said, "It seems like a real person, someone who you know very well. It's all Freudian maybe. You're not having an affair, are you? Please don't tell me that." Then she gasped and put her hand to her forehead.

"It's something I've thought about. Just some imaginative person."

"Oh really," Yvonne added.

I walked over to where she was sitting on one of the chairs in the studio, and said to her, "But do you think they're good?"

Again, she sighed but longer this time, "Yes, they're great, and when you're finished, this will make a fantastic show. Take them to London."

Yvonne asked me why they were so austere. I had only used tones of blue in the paintings, and white with black highlights.

"They're midnight blue," I told her.

She said, "As long as I've known you, you've never used these colors. This isn't you. Where did it come from?"

"I don't know. It's a color that makes me feel I can step through a portal to the other side."

"What?" She shook her head in disbelief.

After a few minutes, I cleaned up. We had an early dinner at an Italian place on Tenth Street where we've eaten many times before and knew the owners. She

48

sipped her wine and kept looking quizzically at me without saying a word. At last, I asked her what it was.

"There's no other woman in your life?" she asked, not really expecting an answer and added, "Because if there is, I'll shoot you, dammit."

In reassurance, I put down my wineglass and reached across the table. I took her narrow artist's hand into my own, and shook my head no.

"Yvonne, you know as well as I do, you take whatever comes to you. In the daytime on the subway, or a dream in the middle of the night. And we use it, because we've got nothing else, nothing. We're painters."

With that, she smiled her lovely toothy smile, and held up her glass to toast our togetherness. We intertwined our arms to drink, laughing raucously all the time as the restaurant owner's wife smiled. She held up a small glass of red wine she had placed behind her near the cash register and held it in the air, toasting us.

The following week in the studio the paintings came to life. It pleased me to see the fruits of my labor. This was art, and I had gone beyond imagination and observation, and found the place of creation to occupy. The work had meaning and that meaning had gravitas. It contained awe and pain and wonderment. It offered up some statement on humanity, something relevant to the lives of people. The paintings were successful. I could see that, and I was pleased, and so was Yvonne when she saw the finished work.

"This is some of your best, or maybe the best," she said as we left the studio at the end of the following week.

There were heavy rains in New York all week, and the weather had been worse Upstate. I felt compelled to return to the house to see if everything was fine, or if we had suffered flooding. I drove up Friday night.

Yvonne had begged off because of early dinners or something she planned. I told her I'd spend two nights and come back Sunday afternoon to the city. In truth, there was a spot in the side yard where we had set up the barbecue that tended to collect runoff water. It was close to the old warped cellar window which hadn't been replaced in years.

Was it the macabre which drove me on? Or was it some sort of curiosity to determine if I was getting psychotic before turning fifty? I had carefully planned to find a reason to be at the Woodstock house by myself. It was easy to conjure a reason since a second home did require attention, particularly if you lived two hours away.

As before, I timed my arrival before sunset. I stopped at the Sun Frost grocery to get some ground beef, a bag of greens, and corn on the cob. They had local produce that was particularly fresh. The old hippies who ran the place seemed pleasant. I bought some fragrant goat cheese from a guy who had once been a roadie for Janis Joplin. It was made from his herd of eight goats only a few miles outside of town. A beer and a thick hamburger really hit the spot. I watched the sun descend in the sky seated at the picnic table, we set up next to the barbecue. The rain had stopped and I nestled comfort-ably under a flashy red Campari umbrella we found in Chelsea enjoying the countryside's fresh smells from the mountains.

Art always summoned me. I set up a small studio in the room off the foyer and worked on drawings on an easel that I'd brought from the city. I must have worked for two or three hours while drinking several cans of beer in the process, and found a bag of pretzels to munch on. The work was abstract. The motif was to work with the vertical images of trees without branches, against a vague hillside. It eventually became an idea for a color field painting where you couldn't recognize anything from the natural world.

Exhausted, and bracing myself for the unknown, I walked up the stairs to the bedroom right before midnight. Undaunted I slid under the cool sheets pulling up the comforter.

Within fifteen minutes I was fast asleep. The quiet was a feature of living in a country setting. The noise from the street outside the Chelsea loft always remained unabated for half the night and contributed to tossing and turning.

At three in the morning, I felt something on my face. I thought it might be a fly or a spider because the woods were filled with them. It was neither one. It was the soft touch of Lizzie Connelly I felt on my cheek. She had gently rubbed the back of her small hand against my face to wake me, to bring me into whatever world she occupied. She had awakened me.

"I knew you'd come back," she whispered and then sat on the foot of the bed. Her legs were young and strong and looked so well formed to me, as did her face and mouth as she spoke. How can any hallucination have such dimension, I mused?

"Where do you go when you don't see me?" I asked her, uncertain if we could carry on any kind of normal conversation, and braced myself for silence.

"There's a place," she admitted, and gave me a teenage giggle putting her hands through her thick hair as young girls do. "It's quite special."

"Lizzie," I said, and coughed still trying to form the thoughts and words I wanted to express to her.

I uttered with this sheer nervousness: "Where did you go after that dance performance? You remember at the Riverdale Yacht Club? What really happened to you? Did someone harm you?"

"No," she said, "it was time for me to leave all that, I had to."

"But I don't understand," I continued. "Your parents never saw you again."

The vision that was Lizzie Connelly leaned over the bed and kissed me gently on the lips. In a single bound only a ballerina could accomplish, she was on the floor in front of the bed. Slowly, she continued her dance steps turning feverishly in ever tighter circles, and corkscrewed to the floor in a single movement.

51

"I want to sleep in the bed tonight."

"Oh no, you're too young, you can't."

"I'm much older now, I've become a woman," she said to me.

"No, that can't be," I insisted. She only laughed and continued to dance.

I beseeched her to tell me where she went when she didn't appear to me, but she said nothing about it.

"Why have you chosen me?" I haltingly inquired, hoping for the smallest clarity in this impossible hallucination which consumed me.

"It had to be. There was no one else. Only you."

"Will you take me somewhere that I know nothing about?" I asked.

"It will be a journey together," she answered.

"Where will we go?" I managed to finally spit out. I thought that I'd already lost my conscious mind. I had somehow stepped into a mysterious Jungian world where we have no will, where we must follow what's laid out before us.

"Have I been there before?" I asked her, frightened that something awful, and therefore Satanic, might occur to me in the darkened bedroom.

"I will take you with me, and you'll come because you want to," Lizzie said, this time in an older voice that was womanlier.

I started to get up from the bed and put my bare feet on the floor. But as I looked in front of me to where she had been standing, there was only the empty moonlight.

The next day, I walked around the town and ate a nice vegetarian dish lunch at the Garden Café on the Village Green. I made friends with the tall gaunt woman owner who had been a painter in Manhattan for a decade. She told me she gave it up because the city became too much. Her life Upstate wasn't perhaps easier, yet different in a better way. She and her young daughter lived simply after her divorce from a failing gallery owner. Her small restaurant had thrived.

Nothing happened that night. In the morning I made myself some toast and coffee then sat on the side terrace and watched the mountains come alive with birds. Hawks flew in circles searching, forever graceful in their flight.

I'm not sure quite why, but I got it into my head to go back into the garage again mostly out of morbid curiosity. I pushed open the warped door with some force. flicking on the overhead light bulb, I looked around the narrow-planked space for some kind of clue to what I was experiencing.

Painted freshly on a blank wall, in the same white paint, was an unfamiliar message. I walked closer and touched the paint with my fingers. It was still tacky suggesting that it had been painted recently, maybe last night or the night before. What is it with this paint?

It said, *French Quarter*. Why on earth was this painted now at this exact moment, like this, and what could it possibly mean? I was totally confused at what I read. Was I supposed to go to New Orleans, and randomly walk around the French Quarter? What might happen if I did? I shook my head with dismay noticing on the back of the door to the garage in the same white paint, the word, *Monteleone*. Was this someone's name? Maybe they could shed some light on what was happening to me? It was all uncanny.

Inside the house I called New Orleans information, and asked for Monteleone. In a few more seconds, I was automatically routed to a female voice which answered, "Monteleone, how may I help you?"

"What or who is this?" I asked the woman speaking.

"The Monteleone Hotel," the female voice said politely.

"A hotel in the French Quarter?"

The voice answered yes, and then asked if I wanted to book a room.

53

"First," I said, "can you tell me if you have a guest staying there by the name of Lizzie Connelly or Elizabeth Connelly?

"Please wait a moment while I check the guest register," the woman at reception told me with a sweetened politeness.

I heard what sounded like a book being opened, and pages turned. Then she spoke to another clerk in a lowered voice.

Once on the telephone again, she said, "Yes, Miss Connelly is a guest at the hotel, and made reservations for John Howard. Would that be you, Mr. Howard? With the telephone receiver in my shaking hand, I answered that it was me, I was John Howard.

"From Woodstock, New York, where the concert was, right?" this woman asked with a lightheartedness in her manner. "That's so interesting."

"Your friend booked you for this coming Friday. Is that correct?" the woman continued and repeated to me what had been requested. There would be adjoining rooms, separated by a door with access to the other room. "A Queen size bed, I believe was what had been requested," she uttered into the phone.

"Fine, and it has been paid for already," she said. "For two nights, Friday and Saturday, correct?"

"What? Already paid?"

"That's correct." she added, returning to officiousness.

"Right," I answered without thinking since the process had become so convoluted in my head.

"Well, if there's not anything else I can help you with I'll say goodbye until then." the woman said into the telephone.

"Yeah, goodbye."

Immediately I went into the dining room and grabbed a bottle of Johnnie Walker scotch and poured myself a half glass and walked into my alcove studio. Inside on the chair in front of the easel, I drank the whiskey in a single gulp. My life had ceased to be my own any longer.

Would I go to New Orleans for the weekend, and meet an apparition? I couldn't take Yvonne. Instead, I would have to make up some lie about art exhibits, or some teaching opportunity at one of their universities.

Was I a foolish, sick man who let this imaginary voice and some paint scribbling on garage walls determine the direction of his entire life? I should say, the hell with it and go about my business in New York. I should paint my canvases, sleep with my wife, and talk to gallery owners at cocktail parties. That's what I'd do, dammit.

What business did I have meeting a dead girl in some New Orleans hotel? Was I completely insane? How did she get a credit card? She was dead, perhaps murdered, all those years ago. What was this I'd become involved in? The occult?

I went back to New York. On Sunday night Yvonne and I met some friends for dinner in Chinatown. It was one of those evenings full of witty banter and lots of laughing. At home, we both fell asleep in each other's arms. The next day we went about doing those things we always did. It wasn't enough. No. As I worked in the studio, I kept pacing back and forth in front of a wall of canvases. The only thing I could think about was meeting Lizzie Connelly in New Orleans.

I made the plane reservation from La Guardia to New Orleans for early Friday morning. I booked an eight o'clock direct flight, slowly creating the lie that I'd tell Yvonne this evening. I played the blatant lie over and over in my mind until I was convinced it would work. If it didn't, I would revert to righteous indignation and claim she was jealous of my success and sought to inhibit me. I needed to be free to pursue an international market for my art. It was imperative.

Elizabeth Connelly disappeared from the Riverdale Yacht Club eight years ago. She would be twenty-five years old now. I wondered if one aged in this other worldly dimension where time has no meaning? Was she this same young woman? The one who purposely came back to the dance camp and for what reason? Could it be that my presence in the Woodstock bedroom, without Yvonne or anyone else, might free her from some horrible Purgatory she inhabited? Would I become a willing tool for a purpose I clearly didn't know, or even vaguely understand?

Why did I buy that airline ticket to New Orleans? And who expected me to stay at that French Quarter hotel, and exactly why? How could a ghost pay a hotel bill, use a credit card?

There were psychics in New York. I called a painter friend who was in her late seventies that I knew who believed in this kind of thing. I took the subway uptown to her live-in studio twenty blocks past Columbia well into Harlem. She was a Haitian woman by birth and parentage. To me this association might have brought this obvious Voodoo connotation, though her work was never about that. It was solely about the psychic power of color in the universe.

When I arrived at her studio she was at work. She stopped to brew an espresso for us. Cordial, we sat in the paint-spattered chairs lit by the sun coming through the taller Harlem buildings. For the first few minutes, we made small talk about art, and the people we had in common, and those New York things natives discuss.

Finally, she asked me why I came. She was certainly glad for my company though she expressed the intuitive belief that there was a more pressing reason for my presence. She knew these things. Breathless, I asked her in general terms about her beliefs concerning the spirits. She was forthcoming on what she knew, or felt. She explained several things she had experienced with visitations over the course of many years.

She confessed: "When I used to travel to Haiti to see my mother who lived in the country it seemed that the night air was forever full of beings I couldn't see. They were human apparitions that spoke to me,

56

sometimes in tongues, or in the creole patois of my childhood."

"What did you feel from those encounters?" I asked her, reluctant to explain my own dilemma, and having trouble putting it into words.

"Encounters!" she repeated and got up to pour the remaining coffee into our two half full cups.

She sipped her coffee and sat down, saying, "Yes, they were encounters, truly. The people who came to me were quite real. I touched their black flesh and it was solid like mine. You see they were in human form, though perhaps for only a short time, and then they would be gone."

"Did anything ever happen to you here, in New York?"

"Only once or twice," she stated, telling me the circumstances which started with dreams, and continued later into a presence.

"They were troubled souls. They sought to attach themselves to someone as sensitive as I am, and for that reason, I feared them, pushing them away. With that rejection, they disappeared."

Slowly I began to tell her of my experience and what I had learned in the research I'd conducted with the newspaper articles. I recounted the police reports of Lizzie Connelly's disappearance that had I poured over for several nights.

The New York police are a very thorough and dedicated bunch of public servants. Resources were expended to interview possible suspects. They were unable to find any suspects, additional friends or informants. There was no one who might provide them with the smallest thread to follow in the girl's disappearance.

One of the older busboys at the yacht club fancied Lizzie Connelly. He had mentioned this in passing to one or two of the other workers. This fact propelled him into the police investigation, though after three or four interrogations with the principal detectives on the case it became apparent that he'd only spoken to Lizzie once as he served her from a luncheon buffet. It was a harmless crush.

I told my artist friend what had happened to me in the Woodstock bedroom. I also told her that I had touched and talked with this apparition. I mentioned the dance camp yearbook, and the whole newspaper account of the girl's disappearance.

"You've told Yvonne none of this?" she asked, and let out this prolonged sigh. "You were afraid to tell her?"

"Yvonne would think I'm losing my mind," I offered, "and I'm not sure that hasn't happened."

The woman shook her head vigorously discounting that possibility. She sipped her coffee again before speaking.

"I believe that there are spirits in this world, celestial energies that can take human form, and then leave it at will. I believe that, and I've seen it in my life."

I told her about the French Quarter hotel, and the mystery surrounding the reservations in the name of Elizabeth Connelly and me.

"How could that happen?" I begged her to answer. She could only reach across to pat my hand in a calming motion.

"You must go to that hotel, you've been summoned," she summarized. 'If you choose not to go, Lizzie Connelly's spirit will still search you out wherever you are. It could be here in this studio. Anywhere."

I uttered a loud painful sigh walking across her studio nervously.

She added: "That young girl has been directed to you by a force I know nothing, or little about, but something more powerful that we can imagine. This was not an accident, and it's not somebody's trick. It's deadly serious. You really must go, John."

With that dire pronouncement, I moved with her to the studio door and left Harlem for Chelsea. I felt only the smallest relief that I'd actually found someone who believed me. She didn't blame mental illness. She warned me not to share this with Yvonne. Yvonne would think that I had entered a horrible drug induced state, or full-blown madness. She'd observed these issues with other artists we had known over the years. Any explanations involving rationale would be futile.

With a barrage of lies about how a prestigious gallery in New Orleans had assembled a cadre of several wealthy collectors who intended to buy my paintings, I prepared myself for the weekend trip. Yvonne had been skeptical from the beginning about the prospects, though after several long-winded rambling and impassioned arguments she conceded; telling me to go.

Through artist friends, I found a prestigious French Quarter gallery. I had several telephone conversations with the longtime owner who welcomed a visit if I was in the city. Furtively, I had done this to protect myself from any further scrutiny and to cover my tracks. Now I was totally free to find out what this phenomenon of Lizzie Connelly might become. The prospect was daunting.

I couldn't not do it. I had to go there and see this for myself. A small voice inside me reminded me constantly that this was a journey I must undertake. It demanded I do this. There was no choice. Forces inside me simply refused to compromise and let go. I was duty bound to finish what had been clearly set before me. In fact, I was commanded.

In lucid moments, I did think that this awful obsession had taken over my entire life. It had become an illness. Maybe it was nothing more than a dream, or even a nightmare, or an evil vision of a troubled and sick mind. For several days before my departure for New Orleans, I thumbed through the telephone yellow pages under the headings of therapy or psychiatry. I was searching for a name which somehow might call out to me, but none did.

I thought about going to a Jungian master that other painters I knew had consulted to break through their periods of inertia. He had worked successfully with them using hypnosis to erase the creative blockages.

Finally, I broke down and called the doctor. By invoking the names of my painter friends, he agreed to see me for a few minutes on short notice.

On Wednesday afternoon, I went over to his Lexington Avenue office around midtown. I was ushered into a brightly painted inner sanctum he called his medical office. His office looked as if the Pop artist Peter Max had personally added the wild fluorescent brush strokes covering the walls. We chatted for a minute about my painter friends. Then, he asked me to tell him what was on my mind and why I need his help. It was awkward to tell him the story of the psychic journey that I'd experienced thus far. I attempted to be truthful in explaining all that had occurred. He listened quietly sometimes rubbing his face.

At one point, he interrupted me, holding up his hand, saying, "John, let me interrupt you for a moment." His manner was professional, caring, and wasn't threatening.

"In fifteen years of practice, I've never heard anything like what you've told me.

I hardly know what to say. This is so unbelievable to me, though I believe that what happened to you did occur."

"I don't know what to make of it all," I told him honestly. "But I feel that it's something that I must do."

"Let's go back to the beginning of what you said, alright," he commanded. "Tell me about those very first moments you saw this, this...We'll call it an apparition, this girl."

"Do you think I'm going insane?"

"No, that's not what I believe from what you've told me," he counseled in a hushed voice. "I think that you've experienced this unique occurrence of a force that escapes most human consciousness. There are certain things in this physical world which defy those descriptions we have for them. So, we deny that they exist."

I went on to tell him about the trip to New Orleans, and what I had planned for myself in that city.

He got up from the chair. He slowly walked to the office window which looked out on Lexington Avenue. He was silent. In a moment, the doctor turned to me with a blank face, "What you intend to do has left me speechless."

He came back and sat down in the same leather chair across from me. He reassuringly reached out and patted my hand the way you might calm a child.

"I think you must complete what you've set out to do in that New Orleans hotel. I don't say this from a doctor's perspective, because it seems dangerous and even wrong to suggest. But, I believe you've have made contact with the other side. In my years of study and much self-examination, I'm convinced that it exists."

At the door of his office, he didn't tell me to call him from New Orleans, or to plan to see him again when I returned to New York, nothing. Instead, he shook my hand and pointed me to the reception area and the door to the building elevator.

It was an uncanny few minutes that I had spent with him. I felt as if I'd learned nothing from the visit, nor did I believe I'd entered into some psychotic state. On the busy street walking toward the subway entrance for the downtown train, I knew that what I had talked about in this psychiatrist's office had only encouraged me to go further.

Why didn't this so-called psychiatrist do something? Instead, he agreed that whatever was happening to me was not only unusual, but unprecedented in his many years of treating patients with issues. He agreed that the trip was something that I should follow through with. I began to have doubts about him. Did he honestly believe all he claimed? Maybe he did, I don't know. Maybe I'd be invited to stroll through a portal into the spirit world, for a time, for a day, for a month, forever, who knew? Lizzie Connelly had summoned me to join her, and go where? To hell to mingle with the tortured souls of the past ten thousand or half million years? It was frightening to me. Yet, I had every intention of stepping onto the American Airlines flight to New Orleans on Friday morning.

When I walked out of the mid-rise building, I looked up to where the psychiatrist's office was and saw him at the window on the fifth floor looking down at me. He had a smile on his face, but with the reflection from the sunlight it was difficult to determine. He had raised his hand in what seemed a pontifical manner of a blessing. It was all unnerving, so I hurried on without looking back.

On Friday morning I got up without waking Yvonne. As I moved toward the door with my small suitcase, she came out of the bedroom to say goodbye. Yvonne gave me a gentle kiss on the mouth and a wave as she trudged back sleepily to the bed.

The taxi dropped me at the LaGuardia departure gate almost three hours before my flight. I wanted to be early because the anticipation of this memorable trip had become so overwhelming within my life, and fraught with so many dangerous shoals.

There was a café open. I was able to get a hot coffee and collect my scattered thoughts once I had been ticketed and went through security. By habit, I'd brought a sketchbook and a small case of pencils. I sat at the airport departure gate, sipping the coffee and making random abstract markings on the blank page. At one point, I started to draw a woman's face. After I spent time detailing the eyes and mouth, I realized I'd been drawing a portrait of Lizzie Connelly.

Perhaps I had remembered the photographs that I'd seen in the Woodstock summer dance workshop yearbook. Maybe I recalled the one that had been in the newspaper. The Woodstock picture of Lizzie was far more natural, a candid view of her dressed in her dance costume. The picture was a medium close-up of her with a wide smile. She had brown eyes, though they were dark in the black and white photograph, and her hair was raven-colored that hung long to her shoulders.

A middle-aged woman was two seats away and looked over at the imagined image of Lizzie, and said, "That's wonderful. You must be an artist to do that," and beamed with approval.

I didn't want to encourage conversation, so I politely answered, "Yes, quite right. I'm a painter."

With that, I closed the sketchbook, deciding to take my bag and walk down the concourse, first to escape further scrutiny and also to refill my empty coffee cup.

The concourse café had a few tables. I sat there and waited for the New Orleans flight gate area to fill with passengers.

When the flight was finally called to board, I walked on the airplane without incident and took my seat over one of the wings at the window. For some reason, it was only half filled with passengers and my row remained empty when they closed the door for departure.

Chapter Four

Landing in New Orleans at the small but crowded airport, I easily found a taxi outside. I arrived at the door of the Monteleone Hotel in about twenty minutes, however, the ride somehow seemed longer. The driver tried to engage me in inane touristy banter, but I discouraged him. Looking out the back window I remained silent for most of the route into the city to the French Quarter.

At the hotel reception desk, all was in order. They had no problem with an early check in. Since I had little need for a bellman for my small bag, I pocketed the room key. I took a quick look around the spacious lobby and stuck my head into the Carousel Bar. This room featured a moving bar and circus calliope music I found vaguely amusing. Being a popular tourist town, the bar was filled with men and women talking loudly and laughing as the carousel turned slowly in its inexorable circle.

I asked the front desk attendant if she remembered the woman who made the reservations. She replied that she didn't, but thought to ask another receptionist who was on duty. She had finished her shift and was behind the front desk inside an anteroom. She would call her. In a moment, a tall young woman came to hotel reception, and greeted me. She asked how she might help.

It felt awkward explaining that the reservations were made by a female colleague that I hadn't met. Did she remember her by chance? That way I would recognize her later in the lobby as she might be in a crowd of strangers. It all sounded ridiculous to me, though I fabricated the unlikely tale anyway.

"Oh yes," she said. "A graceful young woman in her twenties, with white, white skin and a lovely face. She seemed slender, and I thought she might be a dancer the way she moved across the lobby toward the desk."

"A dancer. Exactly, she's a dancer in New York, that's her."

"That's what I thought," the smiling hotel clerk added, "I recognized that fluidity in her body because I danced myself for some years, before this. But I was never good enough."

Laughing uncomfortably, I thanked her, and as she walked back toward the anteroom, she asked, "Where does she dance in New York?"

I answered, speaking perhaps too loudly, "Oh, on Broadway in A Chorus Line."

"My goodness," the young woman shrieked, "how wonderful," and she disappeared into the back reception office while laughing.

I walked to the elevators. I thought to myself with trepidation, she's already appeared in human form. It's now real. She can go back and forth from the dead. My hands started to shake uncontrollably as I stepped into the empty elevator, pushing the button for the twelfth floor.

I opened the room door expecting to see her, but she wasn't there as the bright New Orleans sunlight enveloped the hotel room. Putting my bag on a chair, I marched into the bathroom and threw water on my face. It was a pathetic effort to stay alert. Now, I felt myself ready to call her. I walked to the door separating the two rooms and found it locked on the other side.

Slowly knocking on the connecting door, I called out, "Lizzie, are you in there?" I called out to her several times in a normal voice. I heard no response.

I put my ear to the door connecting the rooms and listened for some small sound which would tell me she was there. Nothing. I grabbed the room telephone and dialed the hotel operator asking him to connect me with Lizzie Connelly's room. I could hear the telephone in the next room ringing, though no one made any attempt to answer. Determined to find something out, I planned to try again a little later. If I still didn't get a response, then I'd simply wait until she came to me.

With no real purpose in mind, I thought I'd go somewhere in the French Quarter for coffee. I stopped at the front desk again. I asked the clerk if Lizzie Connelly had left a message. She said Miss Connelly had left earlier this morning, having arrived a few days ago.

When I heard her say this, my heart started to race. I didn't want to show her that I was visibly excited, so I quickly nodded and uttered a thank you before heading for the door to the street.

Unfamiliar with the area, I asked the bellman where there was a good place for coffee and a donut. He directed me to The French Market, which was a ten-minute walk from the Royale Street hotel.

It was a sunny day and the temperature was rather warm, certainly compared to New York. I started to walk toward Esplanade Avenue at the end of the Quarter where the café was located. In two or three blocks I was at the Mississippi and followed its meander for an invigorating late morning stroll.

Before I realized it, I was at the French Market café. I sat outside under a covered terrace out of the sun drinking an espresso with a beignet, a local creole donut. As I watched tourists file by on the narrow sidewalk in groups, I detected German, French, and Spanish spoken as well as the harsh American accent from Queens. In truth, I've always sort of loathed New York accents. They seem to change from borough to borough of the city, but I still smiled at its familiarity.

I've always carried my pocket sketching pad and a pencil. I lounged at the café drawing until one in the afternoon before I returned to the hotel. It was enough time for two detailed drawings of the Quarter Street.

This time I didn't inquire if Lizzie Connelly had returned. Instead, I went quietly to my own room and stretched out on the bed for a nap. I had slept very little the night before and I fell asleep in minutes. I slept soundly until the sun had disappeared from the sky and twilight was overtaking the city.

Rising, I took a shower and changed my clothes into a casual outfit. I called room service and ordered dinner for two to be served at eight. Then, I sat in a chair in front of the window on the street and waited.

At eight, there was a knock on the door as room service had arrived. The hotel waiter pushed in a covered table and quickly set up a dinner service for two people before he excused himself, perhaps a tad skeptical because he only saw me. Perhaps he figured my wife or girlfriend, or whomever, could be absent inside the bathroom, or perhaps late to arrive. I had ordered a fresh fish creole dish, and cheesy scalloped potatoes with mixed greens. I also asked for a white wine to be brought with the dinner. It was all laid out elegantly and two silver candlesticks were lit on the table alongside a vase of flowers.

Returning to the chair, I impatiently waited. There was no movement. I had no appetite to touch the food myself because of my heightened state. I did pour myself several drinks of whiskey from the hotel mini-bar during the long ordeal.

By eleven, I determined that nothing would happen, with me sitting in wait for a ghostly apparition or another human being of which I wasn't certain. So, I removed my linen sport coat and sat on the bed. Nervous and fidgeting, I decided to call Yvonne. Uncomfortable in my false report of the day, I told her about the glorious day at the French Quarter gallery and the busy day tomorrow which will be followed by meeting the wealthy collectors. It was all a blatant lie, of course. We ended with marital small talk before hanging up.

At midnight, I blew out the candles and covered the table. I was determined to dump some of the food in the toilet tomorrow morning. I didn't want piqued interest from the housekeeping staff regarding the meal. It seemed the prudent thing to do.

In the early morning before dawn, the scent of candles burning awoke me. As I sat up in the bed, there was a woman sitting at the far end of the table.

I saw in that New Orleans hotel room, an attractive young woman in a flowing gown of powder blue with a pale complexion. I blinked once or twice defensively, but nothing changed the vision. She remained there in front of me. It was a real-life countenance of the girl Lizzie Connelly, the same as when she appeared and spoke with me in the Woodstock bedroom, although somehow older looking. She had been almost eighteen when she had disappeared from the Riverdale Yacht Club eight years ago. Now, she would be twenty-six if she had aged naturally.

She had planned to study modern dance at New York University. She had been enrolled in their freshman class as an arts student. Lizzie would have begun classes during the third week of that following September. Her first choice of study had been the Julliard School, but that was strictly a professional conservatory for the arts, and her doctor father convinced her to follow a more traditional degree regime.

I got up and moved toward the dinner table. It was still set near the window overlooking the French Quarter Street.

"Pour yourself some wine, I've filled mine already."

I did as she suggested, barely taking my eyes from her. When I had filled my glass, she held hers across the table to meet mine in a clink of wineglasses.

She took her shining sterling silver fork and cut a tiny piece of the flounder on her plate putting that morsel into her mouth, chewing it thoroughly. "Quite tasty," she exclaimed, "Good choice for the dinner."

"Will you tell me where you come from?" I asked her in a plea from across the table. I waited for her to answer, though she didn't. She kept on eating and said to me, "Pass me the rolls, please. I love them."

She proceeded to take one of the rolls from the basket, and put butter on it before placing into her mouth. She washed it down with another sip from her wine, and looked directly at me, smiling.

She stood up from the table and walked toward me. She was next to me in the flesh, a perfect form of a young woman. I ventured to touch her arm. It felt real, as if Yvonne were next to me. Lizzie Connelly slowly bowed her head and kissed my forehead gently. I would swear it was a human kiss. She said right next to my ear in a faint whisper, "I will come to you tomorrow night."

When I raised my eyes to look at her again, she wasn't in the room. I could see the candles had burned down completely in the silver hotel candelabra. There was only a weakened flame lighting the room. I rose from my chair and moved to where she had been sitting. There was a fork on the plate and perhaps three bites had been taken from the piece of broiled flounder. A butter knife sat next to the flaked fish. She had taken two sips from this half full wine glass. It looked as if there was a lipstick mark on the rim.

I slowly rubbed my finger against what appeared to be a red smear. It came off easily on my fingers with a scent of jasmine. Indeed, it was lipstick. The whole room had a faint jasmine scent. I walked to the adjoining door between the two hotel rooms. It was cracked open. I took one small step inside the other room. I could see by the faint moonlight that it was empty. The bed was still made.

What was the purpose of all this? I wondered. I crawled back into my own bed to calm myself. I drifted off, sleeping soundly until eight. After showering and dressing, I went downstairs to find a place to eat. I asked the woman sitting at the concierge desk if she had any suggestions.

Without missing a beat, she directed me to the *Court of Two Sisters* that had a marvelous brunch in their courtyard garden off the street. While I enjoyed spicy creole eggs from the gourmet buffet, I noticed I was surrounded by ten rollicking people from Munich to my dismay. Like in New York, people traveled the world, so why not come to New Orleans? I thought of the unique smallness of this planet, and then, I thought of those other unseen places that I might now visit.

To occupy myself during the day, I visited several of the better art galleries I'd known about. I found that the paintings I observed inside were pedestrian. There wasn't anything that would invite a second glance in New York. The local scene was strictly second rate within the big-time international art society which I frequented and with a glance, I easily dismissed them.

Night couldn't come soon enough for me. I called Yvonne in the early evening telling her that the trip proved to be disappointing. The art galleries and collectors here weren't prepared to spend the money New York commanded for contemporary painting. It was that simple.

In postmodern art so much time is wasted in the dance between painters and galleries. I'm sure Yvonne felt it was a similar scenario that we had both heard two dozen times before. Yet you went on making the gallery calls anyway.

She said cheerfully, "See you soon, babe," and hung up the telephone.

I began my evening with a drink in the Carousel Bar as it turned around and around. I happened to sit next to a couple from nearby Mobile with a mild interest in contemporary art. They were mostly interested in watercolors of the Gulf Coast. The coiffured woman talked incessantly about its physical beauty until I could finally extricate myself from her company, and left.

Sitting in my room, I heard some revelers return to the hotel from a festive night in the Quarter. A woman was singing loudly off key while the husband, I assumed by the tone of his gruff voice, asked her to quiet down. In response, she had let out shrill hyena laughter. She taunted him with some ridiculous name calling until they'd finally left the hallway for their room, and hopefully to sleep it off.

I still smoked cigarettes, though not much anymore. Nervous, I smoked one after the other, and

70

finished three small bottles of bourbon which were left in the hotel room bar. It seemed that I developed an absurd obsession with Lizzie, if it could be called that, though I didn't care what anyone thought. It didn't matter to me.

For three, then four hours, I sat in the same chair and waited while looking out at the flashing lights of the French Quarter. I continued to listen to the sounds of music and conversation from the street below. Half groggy with the liquor since I was never a successful drinker, my head began to drop to my chest. As I glanced at the floor to the side of the chair, I noticed two feet in women's shoes.

Quickly I glanced upward, and saw Lizzie standing next to me. She put out her hand touching my face and gave me her familiar smile. What occurred was almost inexplicable. She sat on the broad arm of the stuffed chair, stretching her long legs out over mine. I could feel the pressure of them on my own flesh. I took in a very deep breath, and she leaned her head next to mine. This was a human being, she was real. I could feel the warmth of her breath on my own face, and was terrified.

"We don't have to talk," she said to me, "just sit here and listen to the Quarter below."

"If you want," but fear kept me rigid in the chair. Though there was so much I wanted to ask her, I couldn't. Lizzie Connelly was no longer a vague apparition. I stole a glance at the pretty face of a young woman which she would've been had she lived, and maybe she did.

I thought that she had perhaps created this whole disappearance. Maybe she left with a lover her parents or friends knew nothing about. Maybe they had been living here in New Orleans. But that didn't explain the Wylie Lane appearance at night, and how could she simply vanish into thin air? What phenomenon would allow her to accomplish that feat? It was all too impossible. Afraid to confront my inner thoughts, I let her lean on me. I put my palm on the warm small hand she offered to me.

71

The whole experience may have been little more than Satan playing with a weak mortal. He was playing with someone whom he had determined was vulnerable, and therefore could be manipulated. Would he have Lizzie Connelly escort me to Hell one night? Would I be bound to him forever? Had he seen I was a venal man, and perhaps enough of a fool to seduce me with his evil magic?

"Lizzie, what place did you come from?" I asked at that moment when I thought she might answer me, "Where?"

She moved her head ever so slightly, answering softly, "Far away."

With that, she rose from the chair arm, and whispered, "I must leave."

I said, "Wait! What did you bring me here for?"

"I wanted you to see where I lived."

She walked toward the door adjoining the two rooms, and within a second or two I could no longer see her. Had she rushed through that narrow door? No, I would have heard some movement. Yet there had been none. There was only the noise from the late-night crowd below and their music which continued unabated.

At noon the next day I left New Orleans, none the wiser for the experience. My obsession with this now ruled my life. It was the only thing that I could think about, or wanted to think about. Yvonne had become some kind of background noise and I sought to shut her out.

That weekend, in the solitude of my studio, I re-read the police reports from Lizzie's disappearance. Three miles of the Hudson River had been dragged afterward. Police boats had gone up river as well checking the banks for bodies. They found nothing. The cops had interviewed her ex-boyfriend several times.

Now I thought that the only connection might lie with him. I found their private secondary school which was forthcoming with his college information after a few lies and small encouragement. He had finished law school at St. John's and started work at a law firm in Manhattan.

I managed to reach him. I convinced him with the friendliness in my voice and manner, that I was working on a book about missing persons in New York. I had one or two fairly innocuous questions about the disappearance of Elizabeth Connelly, whom I believed he had known.

He agreed to meet me for coffee near his Bryant Park office. He had an All-American look. He was a young lawyer who played lacrosse at Georgetown with a healthy Irish Catholic manner which attracted people to him.

We met at a faux Belgian café called Pain de Quotidien on 46th street. We were able to find a table in the back, which gave us some privacy. Sipping coffee, I asked him about Lizzie. What kind of young woman was she? Had she done drugs in high school as was the case with many upper-class kids in the city?

"Oh no," he explained, "Lizzie was a good girl, around me anyway."

I tried to prod him to talk about the time and the local dating scene and the sex his contemporaries might've indulged in. He quickly thwarted me with lawyerly discretion, and said nothing on the subject.

"Were there other boyfriends you knew about after you two dated?" I asked him pointedly. To look official, I had brought along a pair of horn rim glasses that I'd worn for lecture classes in art school that I still had in a dresser drawer.

"Not to my knowledge," he said, quite matter-of-factly. "It was a very macabre thing, her disappearance, and I'm at a loss for words on what exactly to say about it."

"You knew her parents?" I pressed.

"Oh sure, the doctor and my father were both on the staff at St. Luke's, him in pediatrics and my father in child psychiatry. They were friends, I think, and both were members at Riverdale. I know they did the sailboat races together for a few years."

"What do you think happened to Lizzie?" I finally asked him, and he just shook his head.

"Honestly, I cringe to think about what occurred."

I coughed and reached out for the most obtuse question I could ask him and asked it anyway. "Do you think she might have run away with someone she met, some guy somewhere in the city? And didn't care if she ever saw her parents again? That does happen sometimes."

"Lizzie?" he stated, surprised at the question, "Impossible. They were a model family. At least the times I was over at her house, say on holidays or for dinner during the regattas. Everybody was loving and kind."

"No friction?"

He laughed. "Now if you came to my house, there's a good chance my father might be half drunk, or maybe even my mother, or both. They'd be yelling at each other. Sometimes it got pretty ugly, so I stopped bringing friends home by the end of high school."

"I see," I noted, and wanted him to give me more. "Her parents?"

"The whole time I knew Lizzie, and that's maybe three years off and on, I never heard her say a mean thing about her parents. Nothing."

I motioned to a waitress with a coffee pot. She refilled my cup and looked toward the young lawyer. He shook his head as she showed him the pot.

I told him I didn't want to ask this, but I felt I had no choice, and said, "Do you think someone might have hurt her?"

"This is New York, and the streets are filled with...you know what I mean," he uttered, the Irish smile gone from his chiseled face.

With that, he looked at his wristwatch for a second, and said, "I'm sorry but I simply have to go. There's too much work back at the office."

He left me sitting alone at the table and didn't bother to wave, or even acknowledge the conversation.

That gap of knowledge in what had really happened to Lizzie Connelly in this life continued to trouble me. I wondered what New Orleans had meant to her and why had she summoned me to meet her there?

There was a painter from New Orleans who lived in New York, who had always called himself a Cajun. I recalled that at some opening he told me his older brother had been on the New Orleans police force for years. He mentioned he was a homicide detective. I thought, perhaps, he might know about the case, if something had happened to her in New Orleans. Maybe her parents had found out that she ran away and the story had never appeared in the New York press. What I didn't know about Lizzie, was everything.

I found his number and we connected. I met him at his studio which was in Yorktown on the Upper East Side. He lived in a vintage building that had once been a clothing factory. He was a decent painter, and a pleasant fellow, and he showed me all his recent work. We talked for fifteen minutes about collectors, other painters, and this upside-down world we occupied called art.

When I mentioned his brother, he told me he had passed the thirty-year mark in the New Orleans police department and was retiring within a month. I asked him if he would talk to his brother as a favor. I wanted to know if his brother could find any information regarding a missing person. She may have been in New Orleans eight years ago. I wanted to know if his brother could check police reports to see if she was found or possibly killed. He then gave me his brother's name and phone number. He said he'd call him first and tell him to expect my call and what it was about.

By the end of the week, I figured the painter had called, so one afternoon I dialed up his cop brother, and we spoke. I explained to him that I was curious to know if eight years ago there had been a report of a seventeen-year-old girl there who might have been a runaway from

75

New York. I wanted to know if there was any record that she had been murdered, or found dead under those circumstances.

He asked for the name and description of the girl. I told him all I knew about Lizzie Connelly. I could hear him mumble over the telephone as he took notes on the case. He said young girls, particularly from the rural south, poured into New Orleans for the excitement of a romantic French Quarter life as a singer or dancer, or to meet a rich man. Most of those dreams ended in disappointment and some of them in tragedy. Over the years, he'd investigated the deaths of maybe a half dozen young women. He had managed to find the killer in all but one case. He said the job took a heavy toll on your heart to see the worst of humanity on the streets.

After that sobering conversation, I tried to dedicate myself to giving Yvonne some attention and finding solace in my own studio. I failed at both miserably. It took a week for the homicide lieutenant to get back to me. I had him call me on the studio phone to keep Yvonne from overhearing the conversation. He told me that he had gone into their central criminal files, and checked all the related deaths and missing person reports for young women of that age range for a two-year period starting eight years ago.

There were forty reports of missing girls. Thirty of them had eventually been located. Of the ten remaining, one had been found dead, by apparent suicide. She had jumped from a fleabag hotel window to the street in the French Quarter. The jumper, as he called her, had been identified as someone from a small Texas town around Galveston on the Gulf. The other girls, in order as he read off the cases, included two deaths from beatings or stabbings by men they knew, or had recently met. These men had been eventually caught, and both were serving life sentences in Angola.

"Those sons-of-bitches think about me every day they look out of the bars," the detective said proudly, with a western sheriff brand of justice in his voice.

Of the remaining unsolved cases, only one girl fit Lizzie Connelly's description. She had worked briefly as a dancer at several of the better clubs but had also been beaten. She had been found in an alley behind a Quarter residence two blocks away from the club where she had danced. The nightclubs paid their dancers, who usually came and went after several weeks, in cash in those days. The young women often used phony names to hide from parents who might have remembered the girls saying they were going to New Orleans.

This particular girl had been well liked at the club where she worked. As he investigated the murder case, he remembered the owner saying that the girl had auditioned for the New Orleans ballet. Surprisingly, she had been accepted in their ballet school. She had told him she could work for him for three months before the school session started. His dancers came and went, so that was fine with him, and he told her as much. There would be someone to replace her within a week or two.

In this case, the detective reported the girl was still alive when they found her. The medics on the scene rushed her to one of the hospitals where she stayed in a coma for three more days before she finally died of trauma from the beatings. She had no identification on her, and her face bones had been all but obliterated. Though the description of this girl had gone into the national law enforcement missing persons data base, which the New York Metropolitan department had access to, nothing ever came of it.

I asked him if they took dental images to use for identification. The detective said yes, but there was no record of that in the file he had in front of him. As a well-placed officer of the police department, the clerks had allowed him to remove the files, or they had simply turned their backs. I didn't inquire which.

Before the New Orleans detective finished, he said there was one other thing mentioned in the death report. The victim had been wearing a gold charm bracelet with one charm on it, a replica of the Eiffel

Tower. That had been noted, and put away in the evidence morgue for safekeeping along with the case papers.

"A gold chain with a charm," I repeated into the phone, and he said, "Yeah, a bracelet." He'd seen it in a plastic bag. The whole box was given to him to examine by department colleagues.

The next morning, I called Lizzie's high school boyfriend's law office, and managed to get him on the telephone. He sounded harried but took the call anyway, answering by saying, "How can I help you?"

I said this would take only a minute, and appreciated his patience with me, and so I asked him about the bracelet.

"Do you possibly remember if Lizzie had a gold charm bracelet she wore in high school? One with a charm of the Eiffel Tower on it?"

He answered, "Oh my God, yes. She was so proud of it. Her parents had gone to Paris for their anniversary and brought it back for her sixteenth birthday. I saw it on her wrist every day we were together."

"Thank you for telling me," I said, and then he told me to wait as he felt I was ready to hang up the telephone.

"What have you found out about Lizzie?"

I told him what I'd learned from the detective because I figured he deserved to hear it, and he kept saying into the phone, "Good God." Finally, I ended the conversation. I told him I didn't know what to think, but the worst. There was a slim chance that this bracelet could have been lost or stolen from Lizzie and found its way into someone else's hands. I told him that I'd tell him whatever I found out, and thanked him for his help. I didn't know if he would take this info, share it with her parents, maybe they would re-open the case. But I wasn't going to wait.

The next day I couldn't let it go, and called the New Orleans detective. He hadn't returned the file yet, so he was able to look at it again. I asked him if there was anything in the interviews from her employer or were there any observations I might follow up on.

"Yeah," he said, and I could hear him thumbing through the pages over the telephone. "OK, here it is," he continued. "The guy who managed the place and hired the dancers told the cops that this girl said her name was De Loris, two words, which seemed to be a stage name like the other girls. She had a boyfriend who sometimes came by the club to watch her dance. He had told the owner that he was a musician, a horn player. One night this guy had a loud argument with the girl and stormed out the door knocking some glasses on the floor, causing a commotion. This happened sometimes with the girls, the owner said, because the dancers were transients, you know. They'd meet a guy in the Quarter and then they broke it off in two weeks."

"Did he say what club the guy worked at, that the cops might have followed up on?" I asked.

"Wait a minute," the detective mumbled, and I heard more pages turned.

"Okay, one of the investigating officers went to Blue Jasmine, a French Quarter jazz club, and they talked to the manager. He said this horn guy played for a couple nights one week, and then he was gone. They paid him in cash, and he gave them some name like Nashville Eddie for the act billing. That was all they learned. There was no other contact, no address, and hardly any conversation passed between the performer and the club management. It was an itinerant business."

"There was another thing in the report," the detective went on. "Let's see. The Blue Jasmine manager remembered the girl. She was tall and had dark hair tied back in a tight bun. She wore a white gown, and it trailed behind her, very theatrically. He remarked on it when she told him that Nashville Eddie was her soul mate. He later told the cops that she had specifically called this guy, her soul mate. So, they figured that there was some kind of romantic relationship between the two and marked him as a suspect in her disappearance."

"Didn't they try to track down this Nashville Eddie by name somewhere, at some other gig, or through the music business? Something?" I added, getting almost frenetic.

"Yeah, they tried," the New Orleans cop said. "It was good police work, don't get me wrong. But this is a big town and resources are pretty strung out, so something like this can linger without much manpower to close the gaps. They didn't find the killer. That's all I can tell you."

I thanked him, and told him his brother was a good friend and a great painter. He laughed, saying, "Now, if he could only make a living doing it!" We both chuckled at that.

As Yvonne slept soundly on my arm, I looked out the loft windows at the New York skyline. I couldn't stop thinking about Lizzie. Maybe Lizzie had known this man in the city? Maybe she had met an older man, this musician, and followed him to New Orleans. She wouldn't be the first seventeen-year-old girl to do that.

This whole thing had taken over my life. It had become a maddening fascination which was beginning to rule me. Maybe it did rule me. I felt I had little choice but to continue on, and wait for whatever I learned next from Lizzie. I had to maintain this secrecy.

At this point, the bloom was off the rose with Woodstock and Yvonne. She was a city girl, and she didn't want to spend each weekend at our second home in the country. Too much was going on in our lives in New York for her to sit in front of the fireplace each Friday and Saturday night, so we neatly divided our time apart. It worked for both of us, and without any resentment. I had a long list of necessary repairs and additions that the older house required. She knew it was something which needed to be done with some haste before the onset of usually harsh winter months.

Oddly, during the same week I had returned from New Orleans, I had a call at the studio from the psychiatrist whom I talked with briefly. He said, "I wanted to call you and say this again. I believe what you told me." The doctor went on tell me that quantum physicists have said for years now that energy can change form.

"I don't want to insult your intelligence, but you know what I mean when I tell you this, right? It's important you know that this 'unexplainable' thing happening in your life can be reality. You have seen this woman, and she can be real to touch and hear and have human form. She can think and feel."

"Yes, I believe she's real. But I don't know how to interpret it. I'm at a loss. Where does she go when she leaves me? All that is a mystery."

It sounded like he lit a cigarette as he spoke and soon there was a pause as he took a drag and exhaled.

"I can't tell you where this spirit, and I'll call it a spirit, goes. It's far beyond what the medical degree on my wall, and twenty years of patients can teach."

Frustration overtook me, I blurted out, "What do I do?"

"I don't know. I have no answers," he stated, and warned me: "Be careful, the human mind is fragile. We can be broken beyond repair, certainly for this life. Move with caution. That's all I can tell you."

The call itself seemed otherworldly and it appeared strange that he bothered to call at all. I took it as a warning, which was how he had meant it.

On Friday afternoon I drove to Woodstock, and occupied myself around the village in various stores. By seven or eight that evening, I placed myself in front of a roaring fire. There was a chill in the air, and the warmth from the fire was welcome in the spacious house. It did have a furnace though the house was built with a cathedral ceiling with large windows. This made it difficult, or impossible, I'd soon learn, to heat properly.

Yvonne hadn't asked many questions concerning the New Orleans trip, although it seemed wise to bring it up periodically to air the frustration. That sounded more like truth to me somehow. I told her of my irritation with

81

those galleries. I vowed to concentrate on people in New York and London where the market in contemporary art existed. I'd stay away from unnecessary forays into the hinterlands. What I said sounded convincing to me, at least, and I'd assumed to her as well.

Making a fire had always been a path to serenity even as a young boy. I would camp with school friends in the Wisconsin and Michigan woods. With the fire crackling, I sat back closing my eyes and tried to think about new paintings, though that was futile. The only thing important to me now was to see Lizzie Connelly again.

What if New Orleans was the last of it? What if she had remained there? Then I wouldn't see her tonight or ever again maybe. Would I have to return there? Was it over with her, and nothing more would come of the visions and dreams? How would I cope with that? What would I do?

These were troubling thoughts, though I managed to calm myself fortified with whiskey. I reasoned that if it was over and I wouldn't see her again, that life would return to what it had been; I'd paint in my studio, live serenely or not with my wife, and we'd go about our Manhattan life. There was nothing more to add, end of story. With that last thought, I finished the whiskey and started up the stairs to bed.

Sleep wasn't long in coming since I was physically and mentally exhausted, quickly drifting off to what was a sound slumber. I wasn't sure of the time, yet the room was dark when I woke. I felt a pressure on my toes, a squeezing sensation that was gentle, though constant.

When I looked up, Lizzie was sitting at the foot of the bed. She wasn't wearing the powder blue dress from New Orleans, but her favorite white frock. It was heavier, it seemed for the fall season, perhaps made of wool. She wore a cream-colored sweater with several blue stripes down the front, which struck me as rather stylish for an apparition. Was this some conjured vision of the mind, though who was to decide, certainly not me?

82

"New Orleans was wonderful, wasn't it?" she said in her familiar voice which I had come to recognize. She had a girl's prep school sort of intonation that you'd hear on the Upper West Side. Seemingly, her parents had spared no expense and had sent her to perhaps the most exclusive and expensive school in the suburbs.

"It was, Lizzie," I said. "How old are you? I'm curious." came out of my mouth which surprised me, yet there it was.

"You already know," she said, "twenty-six this past November."

"You're a Scorpio."

"I'm too soft to sting. I'm a dancer," she literally sang out to me. She smiled as she ran her fingers through the thick dark hair she had down to her slim shoulders.

I felt emboldened now, and ready to find out more about this person, or this vision, whatever it was sitting on the bed in front of me. Feeling comfortable when no one in this lunacy should be, I sat up straight against the headboard, and for the first time in her presence, I became relaxed.

"I think I found the gold charm bracelet you lost," I offered, and waited patiently for her reaction.

"It wasn't lost," she said to me, "I never took it off my wrist ever. See?" and she held up her thin wrist. I could see a gold charm bracelet in the waning moonlight from the window.

I nervously examined the bracelet as she laid her hand on the light green comforter. I could clearly see that it had one charm connected to it. It was of the Eiffel Tower. Taking in perhaps the deepest breath that I've ever inhaled in my entire time on this planet, I fought for the courage to speak again.

"You had a lovely dinner for me," Lizzie whispered, "with the candlelight. That was so beautiful, against your blond hair. You wear it long."

My hand instinctively went up to my head. I touched my temple where grey had started to mix with

83

the blond. The flowing hair covered half my ears, and I smiled at her in response.

It was time to broach this thing which had constricted my throat, and I fought to summon whatever courage I could muster in my soul to do it, to ask the horrible questions, and so I did.

"Lizzie, did some man hurt you all those years ago. Hurt you badly?" I uttered with the words rushing forth like cascading water off a precipice.

After I had uttered the words, I thought I saw a moment of pain on her alabaster face. She rose from the bed and walked toward the window without answering me. A few moments later, she began to dance, whirling around the room in a tarantella movement. She finally stopped to bow her head as if to invite audience applause.

Feeling that I must, I clapped my hands loudly, and said, "You're such a marvelous dancer. I can watch you forever."

"We'll be together. You'll come with me when that time comes."

Frantic, I asked, the anxiety raising the pitch in my voice. "Is it a place I know nothing of?"

Lizzie now started to hum. Her precise dance steps resumed, and the moves became formal ballet steps, and she did a pas de deux. Her long slender arms sliced the mountain moonlight. I watched the gold bracelet slide down her wrist, and my heart stuck in my throat.

I called out, "Lizzie," as she swung in a half circle, then jumped across the room in a ballet movement, and her feet hit the bedroom wood floor with the softness of a feather.

In that instant, I realized what was happening to me had gone past all understanding. I had become a slavish prisoner to this comely apparition, and whatever dimension it occupied in this world, or any other. There was nothing I could do but obey this obsession that now ruled my very breath. A cosmic force from infinity had chosen me to fulfill a purpose I could only imagine. There was no other path to trod but the one laid out in front of me in that Woodstock bedroom on Wylie Lane.

"I must go," Lizzie Connelly whispered to me, even as I stared at her seemingly real flesh and bone standing in front of me as a dancer at rest. She vanished as rapidly as she had appeared.

I had learned so little this night, but I saw that same gold bracelet. It was as the New Orleans detective and her high school boyfriend had described to me. It existed, though I hadn't touched it. I shook my head in total amazement, and in confusion as well. The reality of what I had entered was without explanation or rationale and was beyond any possible faculties I could bring to its understanding.

The next morning was a cool Catskill Mountain Saturday. I lolled around the house, fixing one or two, minor things. Then, I walked the brisk ten minutes to the Village Green for a coffee. I sat outside of the Garden Café as the only patron in their chilly outside dining area with my hands warm on the steaming mug, dressed in a heavy fleece and ski cap.

A man with a Van Dyke beard who looked to be in his early sixties stopped and introduced himself. He said he recognized me from Wylie Lane since he lived in the house across the road. Also a painter, he had moved from New York thirty years ago to escape the stink and crowding of the city. He still showed with a single gallery in the city, but said that with his absence from the so-called action other New York galleries had dropped him from their roles.

"I never had the cache of some of the bigger stars," he laughingly admitted and motioned to the side window of the cafe for a waitress to bring him a coffee outside with me.

"There are a few galleries in the Hudson Valley, but no one pays the prices they do in New York," he pointed out. "These are retired stockbrokers up here and the like who were never collectors in the first place."

"It's a good place to live, isn't it?" I asked, sipping the lukewarm coffee.

"Oh, sure," he confessed, "The people are nice, and with the city so close, it's a sophisticated town. You know, decent music, a little drama." Then he laughed loudly as the waitress came outside with a scarf around her neck.

"Tell me about the house I'm in," I implored him. "Did you know it when it was that dance camp?"

He looked over my head and glanced to his right and left for a second before answering which struck me as odd.

"Katrina, who ran it, not the original owner whose health was bad, and went to live with her daughter in Nyack, was a...." he stammered. "Let's see how can I describe her..."

"So, you knew her? This Katrina."

"We had her over for several dinners, and I liked her, my wife not so much. There was this faux sort of Czarist side to the woman, all the references to Moscow and the Bolshoi, and that. You see, my wife came of age with the rock crowd, though she was always a serious artist, with fabrics. Well, there's nothing pretentious about her as you'll see when you meet her."

"I'd like that," I volunteered, with a smile.

Someone walked by the table and crossed the street. My companion yelled out something to the man, who raised his arm in the air in acknowledgement.

"That's Jeremy. He's the present mayor. A really nice guy."

"About the dance camp...?" I asked perhaps seeming too anxious.

He motioned to the waitress again standing in the window, and pointed to his mouth, and she shook her head knowingly. He had ordered a croissant, which he usually had inside on a Saturday morning rarely changing his order.

The affable man finally spoke. "Well, Katrina was a professional, I'll give her that. She hired dancers from

86

Broadway who might come for a summer, and she put them in the house along with the girls. They had communal dinners, and so on. It all went well, except for one year."

"One year?" I asked. "What happened?"

"I don't know. I guess it's the luck of the draw," he stated pointedly. "That particular year, they got some girls who were getting their first taste of freedom and got a little too wild. They'd sneak out of the house, late at night and go to the clubs in town. Mostly to Joyous Lake which ran a bunch of rock bands on the way up, where everybody was half drunk. Maybe doing coke too."

I looked at him quizzically and he sensed he needed to add something in explanation to what he'd said.

"Hey it's New York. The city's two hours away."

"Sure," I agreed, and shrugged my shoulders in response to what he mentioned.

Finishing his pastry, he continued, "I think two of the girls in the dance workshop got involved with some musicians. The guys would bring them over to their place in town. That kind of thing."

"Was there some kind of scene with Katrina?" I ventured to inquire.

"Yeah, one of them, Lizzie somebody, had a loud argument with Katrina on the terrace. I think the two of them ceased speaking to one another for the rest of the time the two girls were at the workshop. That was it."

"Katrina didn't send them home for underage drinking?"

He summarized: "Well, probably if she hadn't been European, she would've. They see things differently."

As we were both going home, we walked together back to Wylie Lane, and took a detour into the cemetery.

"Since you're a painter, and live up here, you'll want to see this. You might not know this exists," he said as he walked determinedly on a path alongside the gravestones.

87

Halfway up a hillside, he pointed to a section of stones under a canopy of large trees, "That's the Artists Cemetery. It's been here since 1934, when the first artists were buried there."

I looked around and commented, "There's Milton Avery's grave. He is one of my favorite painters." He nodded, took a few steps to his left, and came to Bolton Brown's stone. "Brown's one of mine. He was one of the original founders of the art colony here."

I was thoughtful as we continued walking towards Wylie Lane. As I turned into my gate, I said I had one other question, and he stopped.

"Can you remember anything else about that summer and the girl that disappeared?" I asked him, my hand on the front gate.

He answered: "I remember I had a solo show that summer at the West End Gallery and sold two pieces for ten thousand each. It was nine years ago. My swan song. We had Katrina over for dinner when that was going on. She told us the whole story. Lizzie Connelly, that's the name I couldn't remember. Her father was a pediatrician, would you believe. She caused some trouble staying out a few nights while here at the camp, and then disappeared a few months later in the city."

Finished, he shrugged waving as he turned to walk up the road to his fine rustic cedar-faced home. Who had she met at Joyous Lake that summer? Who were the men she and her girlfriend were with? They might have played at the club. Was there somebody else? I needed to talk with Katrina if I could. Was she still alive? Did she live in New York, or Los Angeles or Moscow, or was she buried in the artists' cemetery?

Why didn't I just ask Lizzie herself what happened, and with whom? Did she follow a musician she met at Joyous Lake to New Orleans? Was it Nashville Eddie, and had he murdered her?

On the off chance that I'd learn something, the next day I stopped at the building which had been the Joyous Lake nightclub until last year. The new renovations to turn it into a restaurant were already underway. I stopped by the construction site in the middle of the afternoon. Carpenters were busy hammering and there was man in the back who appeared to be the foreman looking through architectural drawings. I introduced myself as a new homeowner in town. He was local and friendly about the interruption.

I lied telling him I was an author doing a book on old Woodstock after the concert. I asked him if he knew anything about the club in its heyday. He said he came up here then as a young man. When I inquired about the bands that played over the years, he told me that there were old booking records downstairs. They were written out in leather volumes marked by year in the basement. He suggested I go down and look at them. I thanked him and did just that.

The basement was lit as workmen used it to store tools and other building materials. I found the bookcase with the volumes, all marked by year as he had stated. Counting back eight years, I pulled the leather volume off the shelf and opened it. Everything was noted by individual month, and the specific information about the bands and personnel plus payment records was duly recorded.

In July of that year, eight bands had been booked. I went through the names of each and the members and the dates they played. There it was on the page under the band *Silver Tooth*. The horn player was Nashville Eddie Reece, and his home address was listed as 1118 Duval Street, New Orleans, LA, Unit 2. Now, I had him.

The club required the financial reporting information for the IRS and all the bands complied. They had played for two consecutive weekends, Friday, Saturday and Sunday nights. The band had been contracted to play two forty-minute sets. It was all there in black and white. Nashville Eddie did exist, and when I saw his name, I felt lightheaded.

Chapter Five

Walking back to Wylie Lane, I began to believe that I'd been called upon to find this man. Maybe I am supposed to avenge what he might have done. This could be a clear reason why Lizzie Connelly was now a part of my life. I was connected to her. Her soul may be corporeal, or in the spirit world, or perhaps both. All these events were driving me inexorably somewhere, some unfamiliar place and time, where perhaps they had no meaning.

Lizzie Connelly would have worn that gold charm bracelet as she danced the night away at Joyous Lake. Her lean dancer's body moving smoothly to the music in an almost perfect rhythm. I could imagine her wearing white summer shorts with a colored linen blouse and long dark hair. She glided across the dance floor as the other women moved aside because of her absolute grace. She had been a siren. But it wasn't her seductive voice, it had been her wondrous lithe body that Nashville Eddie had seen from the bandstand. She had captivated him, and forced him to act.

I had several musician friends in New York. When I got back to the loft, I called one of them and asked him if there was some musician's union, guild, or other organization with musicians listed. Maybe there was something like the Screen Actors Guild, which required producers to hire only qualified people and then pay them a guaranteed wage. Perhaps there was such a compendium for musicians.

He said there was. In fact, he said he was member. I asked him if he could check and see if a name showed up as a member. I also asked if there was information where the man might be located. I gave him Eddie Reece's name, and added the Nashville nickname. He took down the information, and said he'd get back to me.

He called me that night. He said that he happened to have been mailed a new union roster, and Eddie Reece appeared in it. He read me what was listed. It listed an address in New Orleans, and an email contact, and a telephone number.

I called the New Orleans detective and asked him if he would put this guy's name through the New Orleans criminal data base. He hesitated for a moment, and told me it was risky to play with the system protocols. But, since he had so many years of service, he could do most anything he wanted within the confines of the law itself. He agreed to do it.

The next day he called me at the New York studio in the afternoon. He said that the man did have a record. There was nothing from nine years ago when Lizzie disappeared, but more recently, Eddie Reece had been arrested on three different occasions in New Orleans.

Two of them were for aggravated assault, felony charges which had been pleaded down to misdemeanors. Reece had been confined for thirty days each time in the Orleans Parish jail. These were assaults on another man in some club or bar. The last arrest was where he had beaten a woman with whom he had been in a relationship. Reece had hurt her badly enough to require hospital treatment. The woman's nose was broken, and later it required reconstructive plastic surgery.

At that time, the District Attorney's office had been aggressive in prosecution of the assault as a new law-and-order team had recently taken command. It went rather rapidly to trial. Eddie Reece was convicted of aggravated assault, and sentenced to a three to five-year sentence in Louisiana's Angola Prison. He had been released from prison after serving three years.

Afterward, Reece was placed on probation for another three years. He had met regularly with a state appointed parole officer. The parole officer stated that Reece had not violated any of the terms of this probation. He had continued his livelihood as a musician in the city.

Since then, there had been no police record of the man. He was seemingly clean.

When the detective had finished his explanation, I asked him if there was any further info on the woman who he had beaten.

"Yeah, but I think this will be our last conversation on this," he advised, and his voice had taken on a new seriousness.

He added, "In that particular trial, the woman wanted to change her testimony because she loved this clown. But it was too late, he had already been charged. They ended up sending him to Angola where he probably became somebody's girlfriend."

I thanked him profusely. He was gracious about it all, and asked to be remembered to his painter brother who I hardly saw anymore.

Well, I had found Nashville Eddie. He had been in Woodstock playing at Joyous Lake nine years ago. The same July Lizzie Connelly lived up the road waiting for her opportunity to tip toe out the door. The two girls walked into town. It would take her no more than fifteen minutes to get to that nightclub on foot.

Was there anything else about that summer in the yearbook? I pulled it out and searched it carefully. Most of what was written was how wonderful Katrina was, or the other dance instructors. Then I noticed that there was a line written at the bottom of the page in memory of Lizzie Connelly.

A girl named Monica Shuster had written in a flowing hand, "I'll never forget that summer and Joyous Lake."

Of course, nobody had thought anything about what she wrote, why would they? Maybe Katrina had briefly noticed it, and grunted. This was all part of that awful coming of age, and the merrymaking that some girls passed through on the road to becoming women. They were far more subdued here than in her Russia, where affairs were notorious and often glorious.

Monica Shuster also appeared in pictures with the others at rehearsals, with Katrina, and the rest of the dance staff. It mentioned that she was a student at Barnard. Maybe she still lived in New York, or could be found. It excited me that I had come to know so much about this madness I'd entered.

I called the Barnard alumni office and told them I was an old friend of Monica Shuster. I asked them if they had a forwarding address for her since I'd lost touch. The cheerful young student assistant on the phone gushed that she was appearing in the latest Alvin Ailey production at Lincoln Center that very weekend.

Not one for dance, I somehow convinced Yvonne that it would be an interesting performance this weekend. I got tickets for us. We had dinner at a Greek place we both liked in Midtown, and walked over to the Lincoln Center dance gala.

It was held in one of the smaller Lincoln Center theatres. Sure enough, on stage as one of Ailey's principal dancers, appeared the wispy young woman named Monica Shuster. I couldn't take my eyes off her on the almost empty stage.

We watched as she moved effortlessly through the acts of an anti-war contemporary dance piece. She was poised and confident in her every movement. The printed dance program said the dancer also taught at the Ailey Conservatory in Harlem. I became determined to talk with her.

As we left the Lincoln Center complex, Yvonne turned to me while buttoning up her coat as the night wind blew, remarking, "You never cease to amaze me. Why do I think I know you?" and she started laughing. "Modern dance?"

On the subway home, she put her arm through mine and put her head on my shoulder as the car danced on the rails in its downtown journey.

The following morning, I called the Ailey Conservatory and learned that Monica Shuster taught classes on Monday and Thursday afternoons.

She had office hours Thursday afternoon at four o'clock. I represented myself as a potential parent whose daughter had questions about the Ailey dance company and mentioned that I'd seen Monica perform that last weekend. It all sounded quite legitimate, and they scheduled an appointment with her.

When I walked into the Harlem studio, the dance classes and rehearsals were in full swing. You could hear the music coming out of the larger studios, and the floors reverberated as bodies flew through the air.

Directed to a small office in the basement, I saw the young brown-haired dancer with a sweet smile working at her desk. She greeted me with cheerfulness, and asked how she might help me. Lying, I told her I was writing a book on missing persons. I wanted to ask her about the summer she spent in Woodstock those many years ago, and a girl she may have known named Lizzie Connelly.

Her reaction was to put both of her hands up to her face. She had this look of dismay, saying, "Oh my, I haven't thought about her for so long."

She wasn't hostile about answering my questions. She told me that she and Lizzie were high school friends, both dancers, and been at the Woodstock Dance Camp together.

"I was so broken up about her disappearance," she said to me, and finally had the courage to ask me, "Was she ever found? I never knew."

"She's still missing."

Monica started talking in a stream of consciousness and there was no need to question her.

She related: "That long ago summer in Woodstock at the Dance Workshop was absolutely wild. We were just two young kids."

She continued in her soft voice that Lizzie was so excited to be on her own. They were best friends and Lizzie had pressured her to join her some nights. They broke school rules by sneaking out of the Wylie Lane house when they went to one of the local nightclubs,

Joyous Lake. She told me they had managed to get inside the nightclub and passed through the front door by complicit bouncers. It had all been Lizzie's doing, though Monica went along with her a few times that July.

"Lizzie hooked up with a guy in one of the bands, and we went afterward to the house where they all lived, and drank more, and yes, did drugs too. I admit that."
I nodded, encouraging her to continue.

"I was there for that 'madness' one night, high on God knows what."

Smiling with compassion, I thanked Monica for her candor. I bid her to go on, sitting quietly listening to the tale she told.

"The guy called himself Nashville Eddie. He was Lizzie's so-called boyfriend of the moment. He was a horn player and did vocals for the band, a sort of Cajun rock fusion something."

"I remember I didn't like him. He had this mean side to him, that the other guys in the band didn't have. But she was crazy about him. Yeah, he was good-looking with his leather vest and jeans. He almost looked like a movie-star. And we stayed over one night; I admit it. Two prep schoolgirls, looking to grab ahold of life. What did we know?"

I asked her to describe Nashville Eddie, and she did the best she could. I asked her if Lizzie had seen him after that summer in Woodstock. Did she know if they continued with their relationship?

She remembered him telling them that he had plans for some gigs with other bands in New York. "The band we heard at Joyous Lake, this *Silver Tooth*, wasn't really a band at all. They were some musicians who just got together for a while."

I thanked her for her time. I told her that my wife and I loved her performance at Lincoln Center. She gave me a broad smile, and shook my hand.

As I walked to the doorway, she said, "If you ever find out anything about Lizzie, please tell me, alright?"

Shaking my head, I answered, "I will, I promise," and in the next minute I was gone.

So, Eddie Reece was definitely a part of Lizzie Connelly's young life. Few people in her New York existence knew anything about it. I reasoned that he may have found his way back to the city for a time after Woodstock. Perhaps he continued his liaison with the teenage Lizzie, as he worked or bummed around New York. Did he convince her to follow him to New Orleans? She was a teenage runaway and Ivy-league bound girl, so much in love with the handsome itinerant horn player. Did he murder her there?

I had remembered what Monica had said to me before we parted. She told me with a saddened look on her oval face that the guitar player she'd spent the night with in Woodstock was a nice person. He had told her that Eddie was a *sicko* whatever that meant at the time, and there had been talk of heroin abuse.

He said that Eddie Reece was far different than other rock musicians who were often sensitive and softhearted guys who did drugs and enjoyed the steady stream of impressionable young women. They wouldn't hurt a fly. Eddie was badly broken inside. His propensity for violence was beyond their understanding. The rock musicians might have liked him and respected his talents, but they were afraid of him. All the players in *Silver Tooth* knew Eddie would maul them in a bar fight if he wanted.

They saw him in action with loud drunks and were always careful around him. They were fearful to complain too much about him coming in too soon on a solo, or too late on the bridge for a musical number. The way they spoke to him belayed that hidden fear. They simply wanted to do Joyous Lake because Jimi Hendrix had played there. Maybe they'd do a few weeks in the city with Eddie, and part ways. He was too violent for their tastes. But, Eddie had a way with women and somehow, he seduced innocent Lizzie with his moody demeanor. She was too naïve to know the darkness that lurked inside him.

96

"We were two teenage girls, that's all," she finally admitted with shrugged shoulders trying to make some sense of that time.

As I walked to the subway entrance to head back downtown, I had only one thought and that was to find Eddie Reece. Once I found him, I would kill this animal, maybe with my bare hands. But I wasn't a murderer. How could I ever do such a thing?

Chapter Six

That week a storm struck New York, and the city was covered in so much ice, the buses and taxis stopped running. The entire Manhattan subway became unmanageable as the crowds burgeoned below ground.

Upstate, the winter weather had been worse. A large tree limb had fallen on the Woodstock house roof, damaging a metal gutter, or so my vigilant painter neighbor told me in a kindly call.

"You should see the damn thing," he warned on the telephone. "You may want to get up here and see if it damaged the house."

I thanked him for his watchfulness, and made plans to go Upstate. I waited for the roads to clear to drive up and see what the extent of the damage had been. It was a necessary journey.

Yvonne became convinced the second home idea, this 'marvelous' getaway from the city, was more trouble than it was worth. It was a drain both financially and with all the attendant headaches that came with the aging frame structure. She said she had no desire to freeze in Woodstock. Instead, she preferred the relative comfort of where she was. I drove there myself, content that I'd see Lizzie again.

The New York Thruway was icy, and navigating Route 28 into Woodstock wasn't much fun. I never exceeded twenty mph like all the other cars moving blindly in a jagged line down the two-lane highway. Turning left from the main highway into Woodstock, I literally skidded onto Tinker Street.

A quick assessment of the damage to the house showed it to be fairly minor. A large tree branch had fallen on the roof, but it had only rearranged a few shingles. It hadn't punctured through the interior wood surfaces. I dragged it off, did some stopgap repairs. When the weather changed, I'd have a roofer look it over.

The bent downspout that sagged toward the ground was easily fixed with some metal elbows. I bought them in town at the hardware store, which had been well-stocked for these winter catastrophes. It took me perhaps four or five hours to get everything out of danger for another storm.

An easy dinner and a few whiskeys in front of the fire mellowed me out. With Lizzie constantly in my thoughts, I moved up the bedroom stairs with a flush of excitement.

Hours ticked by, and by three am, I was still awake. Exhausted with the wait, I collapsed into a dead man's sleep. Lizzie did come to me, and the touch of her fingers on my lips brought me out of that deep slumber.

This time she sat on the bed right next to me. Then she took my hand into hers and held it for a moment. She didn't speak, though her look said something.

At last, I admitted to her, "I talked to your friend Monica Shuster, and she told me all about Joyous Lake and Eddie Reece."

"Oh, I know that. I was there too, but you didn't see me," she added.

The enormity of the circumstance in which I'd entered into of this world, or the next, became sorely evident. This ghostly woman might disappear as quickly as she had reappeared. Time and space had little to no meaning, or presented no barriers to her and others inhabiting her spirit society.

"Please tell me where you go when you leave me?" I beseeched her, though she only laughed, ignoring what I was asking her.

"We'll be together soon enough, and that's all that matters," she whispered and moved off the bed to begin her nighttime dance across the room. As she danced, there was something familiar in her very steps and soon I realized Lizzie was mimicking those same movements that Monica had performed on the Lincoln Center stage. She was exacting in the careful dance choreography.

What could this mean, except that Lizzie was able to see and know all that happened around me? She would point me to whatever role she and others of her spirit world wished me to play.

"Tell me about Eddie Reece. What did he do to you?" I asked, lowering my voice as if I were being overheard. I was anxious to know.

Without answering she looked at me softly.

"Did he hurt you? Did that man beat you?" I inquired. She said nothing to me, nor was there any change of her facial expressions. She remained serene, and lovely, a gossamer wisp in the bedroom.

It became clear to me, what I would be called upon to do. I was to find this man, and break him in two. I had been charged to make him pay for his acts, hunt him down like the trash he was, and crush him beneath my heel. I felt an anger slowly build in my heaving chest. This is why she comes to me in this Woodstock house. Out of all this and the next world, her spirit had found the right man to avenge her death.

Yet I was a simple artist, even a pacifist, a man with no real capacity for violence. Why would I be the one chosen for this vengeance? Though I had been selected.

Lizzie took my hand, murmuring softly, "Dance with me." She led me into the moonlight. We embraced as I slowly danced in a small circle, holding her body close to mine. There was a wonderful scent from her hair below me that I had never smelled before. It had a freshness and purity which transported me to fields and flowers where outside there was only snow and ice. There were no bare trees from the cold in this mythical kingdom of hers. Not in that moment when I looked, and whispered, "I love you."

She shook her head yes. She understood what I had said to her. Before I could speak again, only the emptiness of the room was there to hear me. Lizzie had vanished as quickly as she had appeared. I stood at the window as I had before when she was gone. An awful heaviness had come into my heart, a sadness that I couldn't explain. My eyes filled with tears as I glanced outside at the mountainous blackness.

The next night in Woodstock Lizzie didn't come to me. I slept an uneasy sleep and prepared for the trip back to New York. It was sunny though cold, and I stayed in the house making sketches for later paintings on large canvases. They were all of Lizzie. There was nothing else to do but try to paint myself into that paranormal experience. Nothing else had any meaning to me.

I'm certain Yvonne noticed the distance. Yet, I had always been distant with her compared to the yelling and touchy family and the Latin culture she'd grown up with. Her father would slap her at the kitchen table as a child and subsequently kiss and hug her, and then cry. That sort of extreme emotion was part of who she was. With me, she had stuffed it, or because of me, it was hard to determine which.

Before long, I disappeared into the studio for long hours. I drew and began to paint canvas after canvas with Lizzie's likeness. Sometimes I stayed up all night and painted feverishly. It didn't matter any longer.

After three weeks of this, Yvonne finally had enough. She screamed at me over dinner one night, "What are you doing? Living in the studio? Tell me."

I tried to calm her though to no avail. She was furious with the lame excuses that I conjured for these prolonged absences. I held her in my arms until she calmed down. We talked calmly and sweetly about how to make things better between us.

Within a day, she showed up at my studio, more than curious to see what had been consuming me. She wanted to see how I had dealt with it artistically. She took a quick turn around the studio moving slowly from wall to wall where the raw canvases were nailed up. After that first turn, she stared at me with her fiery black eyes, asking, "Who is she?"

Yvonne didn't let me answer. She came over to me inches from my face, her fists clenched at her sides.

101

"Are you fucking her? Tell me." she hissed loudly.

I shook my head, walking away from her toward the towering windows facing the street. "For God's sake, I'm a painter. We invent things, I take them off damn billboards, off the stupid television screen, from the stinking subway, everywhere. You know that."

She pointed to a nude canvas of Lizzie, announcing, "You know this woman. You know her body and you know her soul. Don't tell me you don't. Liar!"

Exhausted with the tirade, I simply sat down in the chair. She continued to go from one canvas to the other, examining the features and body of this mythical woman I'd been with, who was my muse, and mistress as well.

"You can't paint anyone that well, unless they're a part of you, mister," she ranted on, "Give me her fucking name."

"Yvonne, this woman doesn't exist," I told her. "Knock, knock, there's no one in there," I said, mimicking a knocking motion in the air as I walked from canvas to canvas.

She sat down across from me, and stared hard at me before speaking, "I don't believe you." She banged her hand on the table in a cadence of anger.

At last, I held up my hands in dismay, and she in turn shook her head emphasizing the disbelief.

"OK, I'll say this. End your goddamn midlife crisis tonight," she insisted in her Puerto Rican Street voice that she reserved for the worst of her tantrums. "Get rid of her, and we can talk."

"There's no one, please," I pleaded, and it seemed to work. I saw some reason come into her frightened eyes. Within a couple minutes, she came over and put her arms around me, and it was over. The storm had passed and was on its way out to sea. As I held her close, I knew that I was already lost in this whole insanity.

The next day I hired a private detective that the New Orleans cop had recommended. He was one of his retired friends who had worked homicide in the city for many years. He knew his way around all the shitholes and the scum on the street. This man would locate Eddie Reece for me. He would tail him, seeing what kind of life this character had. I gave him the musician union information and the address in the union roster. He took it from there.

A week later he called me. He gave me a rundown on what he had learned: Reece had once lived in the apartment listed in the union roster, but he had moved several times since. Now, he lived in a studio in the back of a French Quarter club where he had played, and knew the owner. Reece was also a heroin addict, though he could still find work around some of the jazz clubs. He might fill in for another horn player who left a group. It was always on short notice, last minute stuff. The investigator told me he talked to one club owner who gave him the names of three clubs where Reece played regularly.

"Come here and see him for yourself," the detective told me. "He's a big guy and acts tough with his broken nose, but he's a punk that somebody's going to knife in an alley for another fix."

How was I going to convince Yvonne again that I needed to go to New Orleans? I didn't know, so naturally I lied, telling her I was going to Houston instead. She knew a lot of wealthy contemporary collectors were there with that oil money. Two years ago, I'd sold some pieces there for top dollar. I'd start in Houston, and maybe make one more trip to New Orleans, I suggested to her. I told her that dealers kept pressuring me to get known among major art collectors in town. It sounded at least halfway plausible.

I bought a plane ticket to Houston. I stayed the night and flew to New Orleans the next day to look for Eddie Reece. This quest was my mania. I needed to determine if he killed Lizzie Connelly. How would I know exactly? I was already convinced he'd beaten her to death, dumping her dying body in an alley all those years ago.

103

The first thing I'd do in New Orleans would be to meet up with the private investigator who'd tracked him down. I'd listen to what he had to say. He arranged to meet me the next evening in a popular ice cream shop in the Quarter. We could talk uninterrupted in a back booth. He used it all the time for his clients which were mostly late middle-aged women on the verge of divorce. The place was always filled with out-of-town tourists, and you'd rarely recognize any locals at the counter. It was a safe haven for sensitive conversations.

The man looked like he sounded on the telephone. He was Italian, stocky with a ready smile and a handshake like a vise. He had handed me two handwritten sheets listing the significant parts of the surveillance, such as addresses, names and telephone numbers of the clubs.

He explained, "Reece is playing tonight at a small club on Esplanade. It's right there on the block where the Quarter ends. The blue-fronted place with a neon sign that says Jazz. The manager told me he plays two sets, starting at 9pm, so you can get a good look at your guy. Size him up."

I thanked him and gave him a hundred in cash as a tip. He smiled as he pocketed the money.

"What you do from now on is your thing, my friend," he added, and with that he stood up, touched the brim of the pork pie hat and walked out the side door into the warm night.

There were a few hours to kill before the music started. I strolled over to one of the art galleries I'd known in the Quarter simply to say hello and cover my tracks should Yvonne ever call them. I had at least visited someone at a gallery and talked about business for a couple of minutes. After that errand was over, I went back to the Monteleone to relax for a few hours. Maybe I'd have a quick bite in the restaurant.

At eight thirty, I was back on Royale Street slowly moving toward Esplanade and the nightclub. I got there a few minutes before nine. I paid the admission charge and

104

ordered a bourbon on ice at a table close to the bandstand as the musicians tuned up, readying themselves to start the nightly entertainment.

The bassist ran the group. He introduced the band, going round to each of the four other members, of which Eddie Reece was one. Since I had never seen Reece before. I didn't know what to expect. His size seemed to tell me right away who he was. He was a large man, easily six feet two, and probably weighed two hundred twenty. He looked as if he could have played first string football for LSU, or even the Saints. The broken nose marked him. It was flattened across his twisted face.

As the band started to play, I looked closely at him in the spotlight, calmly holding his trumpet. Reece looked much older than I'd thought he'd be. If Lizzie was supposedly twenty-five, this man looked as if he could have easily been forty-five. Maybe it was all the drugs, hard living and prison time, which would age anyone. If you were a junkie, you could look a hundred on a bad day.

They played one number and another. They were a decent jazz quintet, but after all, this was New Orleans and good musicians abounded in this city. They had for many years, particularly in the jazz music game.

The investigator told me that Reece at one time had played with the Neville Brothers. They were a big-time concert act, and they had a national following. But they parted ways for unknown reasons, probably drugs.

Did this man beat Lizzie Connelly to death? I kept asking myself that question. I looked at the other musicians too. Not to draw attention to myself, I went to the restroom, trying to behave like a typical Quarter jazz fan. I walked around the club.

When they finished the music set, I asked the bassist over for a drink. I motioned for him to bring Reece with him, and he did. I bought them both a drink. We talked about Jazz and New Orleans, the lousy crowds in most clubs these days, and how 1980s stadium rock had ruined music. The bandleader excused himself to talk business with the club manager. I motioned the waiter over with another drink for Reece.

He was friendly enough, and in this boozy conversation I mentioned that I was from New York. I asked him if he'd ever spent time in that town. He said he'd played the city alright and had liked it, but he hadn't stayed very long. I laughed and told him that I had just bought a house in Woodstock, up there with the hippies. I inquired if he'd ever been there. It was a good town.

Reece leaned his large body back in the fragile wooden chair, and laughed loudly, confessing, "Yeah, I've been there. Played for a couple of weeks with a band at a joint called Joyous something, Joyous Lake."

"It's still going," I lied, watching his reaction, and added, "There are a lot of sweet young things up there too. The hippie spirit hasn't died."

To that telling remark he nodded. He leaned over the table and told me that he had a fabulous time when he played there, but almost got busted. Then he laughed again, this time even louder.

"Yeah," I admitted. "They still get a little touchy with the drugs, even today."

"Nah," he said, and his voice became more intimate, "I'm talking about jailbait, man. There were so many young honeys there. They'd take off their panties in five seconds." I joined him with a false laugh of acknowledgement, and slapped my sweaty palm on the table for the hilarity of it all.

At that point the bassist returned to the bandstand, and motioned to the other musicians to come on back to start the next set.

"Hey, good talking with you guys," I quickly admitted, raising my hand to his bandmate.

So here he was, Nashville Eddie, the musician who played both rock and jazz. The man who had done hard time in the slammer for beating up his girlfriend, and sent to Angola for three years because of it. Yeah, it was him, the musician who preferred jailbait, hapless underage girls who followed musicians around the country.

Was he guilty of also beating to death a teenage dancer from leafy suburban Riverdale? Did he kill Lizzie, who fell madly in love with the mystique of a second-rate hard rock band? Had he seduced her in that Woodstock cottage while in the next bedroom Monica also lay naked? After that, did he convince the misguided Lizzie to follow him into the city and eventually on to New Orleans? Had he made her getaway easy for her, providing that horrid road map of her eventual ruin, and death? Did he introduce her to the pleasures of the needle, and would she come to know the heights from heroin?

I watched him, and the rest, all those gesticulating players, on that small stage going through their musical numbers. I saw that the man was evil, and needed this final punishment to be meted out to him. It had to be done.

Slowly I picked up my soggy bills on the table, walking over to the bandstand. With a half-smile, I dropped a twenty-dollar bill into the glass tip jar, and saluted the band. I nodded in the direction of Eddie Reece who was waiting for his horn cue to come in. He returned the gesture of recognition.

None of what I wanted to do, or even planned, had to be done immediately. If Reece lived one more week, or month, or year, it hardly mattered. An awful vengeance would inexorably come to this man. It had been foretold and I had become its humble messenger. Now I was ready for Lizzie. My task was to be her champion and do whatever she commanded. I was her knight errant, nothing less.

I slept soundly in the hotel room, and she didn't come to me that night. The next morning, I had an early breakfast at the hotel, and took a taxi to the airport for a ten AM flight back to New York.

Lizzie had asked little of me. It was almost as if some other force inside me, independent of my own rational mind, was propelling me to act. I had planned to do nothing about Eddie Reece, until I'd learned more from Lizzie. I waited. I took the bus into the city from LaGuardia airport and unpacked when I got home. Yvonne was out somewhere so I went to the studio for the remainder of the day.

I sat there looking at my hands for maybe an hour. I kept entertaining the thought that I needed to call Monica Shuster again, and I did. She was in her office when I called. She picked up the telephone but when she learned who it was, a distant manner came to her voice. She asked what I needed to know.

I asked her if she remembered this man with Lizzie, and she told me, "Of course, Eddie."

Then I ventured to dig a little deeper, and said, "What did he look like?"

"Well, he towered over the other guys in the band. They were tiny, and he was muscular and pushed them around if they questioned him on anything. They were all afraid of him, and once he punched the drummer who quit the band. They had to find another guy. He was violent, and I didn't like him."

She described the man I watched on the bandstand at the jazz club, except for the flattened nose, which I guessed had occurred during his stay at the Angola prison.

"In the two weeks we hung out with the band, this guy had slapped Lizzie at least once, but she kept going back. He was rough during sex, and it made me shiver even then when she talked about it."

I tried to continue the conversation, but she cut me short, saying, "I'm sorry, but I'm uncomfortable reliving all this. Let's make this the last time we talk about it, OK?" I agreed. What else could I do?

Before long, I called up the New Orleans private investigator again. He said with disbelief in his voice, "You want me to investigate the murder of an unidentified girl eight years ago, dig into that, see what I can uncover because the cops never caught the killer, right? That's insane."

"That's what I want you to do, and I'll wire you five thousand dollars tomorrow to get started. Will you do it?"

"It could cost you a lot more before I find out a damn thing, even if I'm lucky enough to, sweet Jesus," he added impatiently. "John, you're a friend of a friend, and I'm not interested in burning up your money."

I took a deep breath to remain calm, businesslike on the telephone, saying, "This is very important to me. I think that there's a killer walking around the French Quarter who should be gassed." Then I regretted what I said to him.

"Yeah, there are a couple of killers roaming the Quarter alright," he added, and told me he'd work with me. We could see where we were at each stage of his investigation. He'd keep a strict accounting of all the costs. He was doing this as a favor, otherwise there were too many headaches involved.

"The first thing I'll do is get the police report for the murdered girl who was never identified. We'll go from there. And I'll dive into Reece, and see what I can learn. Trust me, he won't spit on the street without me knowing about it. I'll question his damn second grade teacher."

I said, "I want you to talk to the club owner where the dead girl danced who was interviewed in the police report. That girl gave him a phony name. The owner didn't care because they paid all these girls in cash, and they came and went. But he remembered she was going to the New Orleans Ballet school in a couple months, the one they've run for dancers for years. It's part of the civic ballet. She must have auditioned for the school, probably given them her right name, and they'd have a record. People keep records."

I heard him guffaw into the receiver. "Yeah, I'll do that. This'll keep me busy because you have to keep going back to get answers. I know from twenty years as a homicide detective."

Figuring that the civic ballet had conducted auditions and kept records on those who they'd chosen for ballet school, I wanted to dig there. In order to keep a professional school running, they'd have to know how many students they enrolled each term, or even within a year. The faculty would be adjusted to fit that number. If it were larger, more people would need to be scheduled, or hired, and maybe additional rehearsal space was planned for.

All this took money and budgeting, and these sorts of things were carefully recorded. The Chicago Art Institute had a database of everyone who went through their doors for seventy years, whether they took two courses, or spent eight years there. It was all on paper, or accessible in somebody's file somewhere.

The excited resolve I'd demonstrated to the detective to find these answers had been clear to him. I felt that I'd found a man who would uncover what had been lost, or conveniently buried. He told me that what I asked might take a month, or possibly two to accomplish. It was hard to know, but it couldn't be done overnight.

I told him I wanted the truth. I wanted to know for certain if that murdered girl was Lizzie Connelly. I wanted to know who killed her. That was our arrangement.

Without Yvonne noticing, I stuffed the warped hardcover dance movement book that had been Lizzie's in Woodstock that July into my overnight bag, and had brought it to the studio to stow out of sight.

When I got off the telephone, I retrieved the dance book from my art supplies locker and I sat in the studio chair to peruse it once again. Still inside the slim booklet was that black lock of Lizzie's luxurious hair. I raised the hair with shaking hands underneath my nose for her familiar scent again.

I looked closely at the hair. Its color was so rich, that it made me move to one of the canvases of her

110

likeness that I had been painting. I began to mix my own black paint, using four or five different pigments to get the right tone, and the deepest richness of the black. The face of the woman I had painted was alabaster white, and now I began to add the black that I'd mixed. Then I added blue to the mixture. The girl in the picture came to life.

Looking at it in the bright light, I held the black hair against the color I had painted. It was perfect. It represented her hair so exactly with its shine as if she were in that painting looking out at me, and perhaps she was, I don't know.

Carefully I removed several strands of the hair, which could hardly be recognized in this light from the windows. I lovingly pressed them into the wet paint.

"Now, you're here," I said to the image on the wall in a whisper, though no one was in the studio but me to hear. I took the paintbrush with the black and added more paint until the strands disappeared into the opaque color.

I mixed an even whiter white, a porcelain color with a glaze, changing her cheeks and forehead to gloss. Taking my smallest brushes, I tinted the white around her eyes to show the true shadow of her beauty and innocence.

I stood in front of the drying canvas pleased. Then my mouth hardened as I thought of Reece and his shattered nose, though the magnificence of the canvas calmed me. With a smile, I took my seat in the chair facing it. With all the quiet, I needed music, so I chose the melancholy notes of Chet Baker's sad trumpet, the last music he had made before he threw himself off a Paris balcony into oblivion.

The distance continued to widen with Yvonne. I pushed myself to do something about it. I spent more time at home. I helped her with an exhibition I'd managed to steer her toward. It was two-person show with a Dutch sculptor friend. He had taken over the bottom floor of a stunning two-story new gallery built on the Hudson River. It was located in a renovated three block section of restaurants and boutiques in once seedy Newburgh, an hour outside New York.

The new gallery had been built for sculptors by the owner of a metal foundry. The gallery director had been convinced to dedicate the upstairs floor to painters. Yvonne would be the first painter they featured, and the sculptor, Van Koop, had an international following with museums all over Europe. The Dutchman had done it as a favor to me.

I believed this would build Yvonne's confidence. It could turn out to be an important exhibit, with some cache added by the Dutchman's presence.

For almost a year, Yvonne had worked on a series of small paintings of her childhood neighborhood. She painted vignettes of Spanish groceries, bodegas, cigar shops, and the people she'd known. It was her authentic Latin remembrance of boisterous people and their color, leaning heavily on purely abstract interpretation.

A few New York critics visited the show, and commented favorably on the Dutchman's work, but only one bothered to venture upstairs. He, in turn, called Yvonne's work challenging in its interpretation of color in a few sentences at the end of his review for the New York Post, which was at least something.

Like so many artists who suffered from obscurity in this art world's putative star system, Yvonne was elated about her show with Van Koop. She beamed with the kind words of the Post critic. I was pleased that I had played some small part in the venture through my friendship with the Dutchman. I loved her.

The Newburgh gallery was already halfway up to Woodstock, so we went to the house for the weekend. It would be Yvonne's first time at Wylie Lane in what seemed like months. For some enhanced romantic atmosphere, I insisted we make a fire and relax for a couple hours, though it was getting late. She found comfort on the couch with her wineglass, talking about how wonderful the exhibition had been.

Looking around the room, I could see her eyes take in those parts of the Great Room that I imagined she wanted to change. She had a Spanish sense of bright color, and the dance school occupants had neutralized everything, perhaps a direct result of Katrina's Russian background. The color grey abounded.

"It looks like Rasputin lived here," she burst out saying, followed by a painful sigh, "This dull greyness everywhere. You expect to see the Tsar walking around in his nightshirt in this dim light."

"Why don't you transform the room, as you want it. Make it Latin. Do whatever comes to you," I suggested, smiling.

"You and your Latin everything. I do have other tastes, you know," she let come out, shaking her head in slight irritation.

"Your color sense, I meant," I said, correcting myself.

She got up from the couch going slowly around the room looking at the blank walls we had yet to adorn. Across from the staircase she stopped and touched a wall that went up to the banister to the second floor.

"It needs some big canvases, and that's you," she recommended. "For me, I think I want my stuff in the bedrooms. It's more intimate. Yeah."

"The girls that danced around here, this was where they rehearsed, huh?" she said. "You know the history. That's right, isn't it?"

Slowly holding her wineglass, she danced around in this impromptu adagio, moving back and forth across the room. When she got to the fireplace she threw her head back, stamped her feet twice, and cried out, "Ole."

I clapped, and yelled out, "Bravo, bravo,' and held up my own glass to toast her triumph.

"What happened with this place? Did the Russian dancer die, wasn't that it, or she was too old to do the summer school?" she asked, "I forget."

"Too old, and it took too much effort. They had ten or fifteen young girls here dancing for a month," I

113

added. "You had to house them, and feed them. And they were all teenagers. My God, that too."

Yvonne laughed loudly at that as she continued to dance though slowly, now almost a walk across the room again.

"I was after sex at fourteen, alcohol, and the clubs," she spat out, finally sitting back on the couch.

"You were ahead of your generation."

Upon reflection, Yvonne answered, "They couldn't control me. My mother gave up. She had her own demons anyway. I did what I wanted. Then, someone said, Hey, go to art school, Pratt, it's cool. And I said, OK."

I shook my head in agreement with her history.

She continued: "My brother had fights at school every day. Juan was too macho even for the gangbangers. Finally, some lame-ass school principal told him if you wanna fight, buddy, join the Marines. And that's what he did, quit school, and shipped out."

We talked for another hour. As we climbed the stairs for bed she had a beatific smile on her face. It was the same one I remembered from the night I'd met her. Putting my hand on the small of her back she jumped the stairs literally two at a time on the way up.

Asleep in minutes from the long day, Yvonne's head rested on my arm. I heard her soft breathing sounds as sleep came to her. Soon I joined her in that slumber, but it wasn't as deep for me.

Dreams came one after the other, and in a panic, I sat up. Yvonne was still sound asleep next to me, but in the moon glow, I saw Lizzie standing at the foot of the bed. I gasped, afraid that her presence would be made known to Yvonne whose steady breathing continued next to me.

There was a wide smile on Lizzie's face. She held her index finger up to her lips to indicate the silence of the moment, not to awaken Yvonne. She could see this woman next to me in bed, my wife, and would she know the relationship? I imagined that in the dimension that

Lizzie inhabited, all was knowing, and there was little reason to tell her who this person was.

Now standing in the doorway by the bed, Lizzie whispered, "I saw her dance downstairs. She's very fiery," and she let out a girlish giggle.

It seemed that Lizzie was going out the door about to descend the stairs, and I whispered to her, "No, wait, let's talk awhile."

"Later," she whispered, and waved at me, disappearing from sight.

"Wait, Lizzie," I pleaded, perhaps too loud. Yvonne stirred in the bed, now awake.

"What is it?" she asked, now awake, "Is someone there?" Her head turned furtively, and she attempted to look beyond me down the stairs.

"I heard you talking to someone. "Who?"

"Nah," I told her, "just dreaming."

Yvonne rubbed her eyes, and ran her fingers through her hair, looking again down the steps from the bed.

"No, you were talking with someone. I heard you."

"Yvonne, I was dreaming, and probably talking to Moses," I related with sarcasm, and started laughing.

"Not Jesus?" she answered, now her turn to grin.

"Maybe next time," I assured her then and turned to lay my head next to hers. It wasn't long before we both fell back to sleep.

We had breakfast in the square room that we made into a studio. It had large windows that let in the North light. I had arranged a table with chairs next to an easel, and sipped coffee satisfied. The sunlight warmed the fall season chill.

"This is a wonderful house," Yvonne concluded, "I love it, really. The things I've said about it aren't true. There's too much New York in me that needs to be exorcised."

When I heard that word, 'exorcised', I stiffened. I wasn't frightened that she had discovered anything but rather more chastened. This was the world we knew nothing about. We were like the rest of mankind, products of our own ordinary lives. The two of us continued through the day-to-day motions of what we thought we knew. Completing obvious lessons of daily life that we thought we understood.

Would Yvonne's Brooklyn parish priest exorcise Lizzie from my life? Will he swing his smoking censer back-and-forth in our bedroom? I doubted his absolute power to exorcize anything, frankly. What evil did Lizzie bring with her anyway? Were these evil words she had spoken, and by whose definition?

I had been happy with Yvonne. It was something I never questioned. I loved and respected her. Together we represented a vibrant couple of like-minded creative forces. Everyone who met us agreed. When people we knew spoke of either of us, it was always in the plural, John and Yvonne, or you two, or both. "You and Yvonne must see his or her paintings at Gallagher's."

Finishing my coffee, I divided the remaining liquid in our French Press between her cup and mine, and asked, "Yvonne, do you believe in the devil?"

"What?" she answered, squinting her eyes with the absurdity of my conversation.

"Satan, the devil," I said, "Do you believe he, or it, exists?"

She shook her head in disbelief. "You're asking me at seven in the morning if I believe in the devil? You are flat out crazy."

"OK, maybe not this specific form, not like a man. Forget the horns."

She laughed out loud, "You are too strange, baby."

As we sat in the narrow room with the morning sun bathing us in the most marvelous yellow color, I continued to talk. I talked about the age-old concept of personified evil, and of its continued existence, even today.

Yvonne listened closely. She slowly sipped her coffee without interrupting me. At the end, she said, not

116

with exasperation but truthfully, "I can hardly deal with what's in front of me. That's more than enough."

I talked more about how the line between life and death is blurred. I talked about the fact that some people can move back and forth between them.

"Look," she at last interrupted, "That's nonsense in my book," trying to appear at least a little conciliatory without accusing me of being half psychotic.

"When I saw my father dead on the floor of his apartment, he had a look of horror on his face. That's the end, baby. You live and you die, out the door. There's nothing more to say. It's over."

I leaned closer to her, more intense with my words.

"But there must be more, and souls can move between death and life. It only makes sense. Our very existence allows for this to happen," I answered, trying to convince both her, and to a greater degree myself, that I believed this.

Yvonne had begun to despair of continuing with anything this existential. She wanted to end the conversation.

"Okay swami, in my limited grasp of things, we have to worry about selling enough paintings to pay for this pleasant little joint," she added. "I don't think Wells Fargo holds any interest in the afterlife beyond their monthly mortgage."

I knew we'd come to the end of the subject. It was pointless to prolong her disinterest in what I had to say about anything demonic, or within the spiritual realm. I dropped it with a halfhearted smile on my face.

Yvonne saw the neighbor Gayle outside walking her dog and she went to say hello. They arranged for us all to have brunch later, and it was very pleasant. Yvonne and Gayle struck up a nice friendship, although Yvonne didn't come up very often.

Chapter Seven

Eddie Reece wasn't always thuggish. He started life as a decent kid in the Nashville projects whose single mother tried to make it in the country music business. Alas, she was never more than a sometimes back-up singer for those bands that never went anywhere. After ten years in backwater joints and roadhouses, she only appeared twice on stage at the Grand Ole Opry. That came as a favor from a singer-songwriter who had been sleeping with her for half a year.

By the time Eddie was fifteen, he could play guitar. He was getting really good, but tough kids in the project attacked him on a Saturday afternoon. After beating him to the ground, they had stomped hard on his left hand breaking three fingers.

They healed alright, but there was permanent damage to his hand. He couldn't bend two of his fingers at the first digit. He couldn't play the guitar well anymore, so young Eddie switched to the trumpet. With that, he became more of a jazz musician, and a lot less country. After a year, he grew tall and strong and sought out the boys who beat him. He broke the nose and jaw of the boy who had ruined his future in country music.

The authorities gave his mother a choice. She could send him to a correctional facility for delinquent youth or put him in some mental hospital with the criminally insane. A week before his seventeenth birthday, they sent him to a Tennessee correctional facility for boys an hour north of Chattanooga, where he spent a year. It was a prison really.

What he learned to do was fight. At the end of his checkered tenure there, he walked out into society feared by every boy there. During his last battle for supremacy he cut off a boy's index finger with a dining hall knife. Abject fear prevented anyone from reporting the incident to the authorities. That was Nashville Eddie, mean and vengeful.

Eddie returned to Nashville, though there was nothing for him beyond a broken-down alcoholic mother, and a country music industry that didn't want him, so he left. Reece went to New Orleans because it was a good town for horn players. He left Nashville one evening without saying goodbye; mostly because his mother was passed out drunk on the couch.

New Orleans fit him well. He was tough enough for the French Quarter clubs and he was a talented trumpet player with a great range. He could play jazz, and he could crossover into rock. He had natural abilities as a musician. He toured and played in other cities, but he always returned to New Orleans.

Young women liked him because he was handsome and rugged with long dirty blond hair and a chiseled jaw. He treated them rough like most musicians did in those days. He always had a good-looking woman on his arm willing to take his abuse.

He got into fights with loud-mouthed customers in French Quarter clubs who thought they were tough. He beat the hell out of them. Bouncers had to stop him from half killing these obnoxious drunks because he didn't know when to stop. He wanted to finish them off. There was a part of Eddie Reece that was out of control.

Even when he wasn't playing music, he invited trouble. The slightest suggestion of an insult would send him across the bar or over a table. Once the cops arrested him for assault and he barely escaped jail time. Another time, they let him sit in the slammer for a week, before they released him for lack of evidence. Reece was on the police radar as a troublemaker.

A year after his week-long jail stay, Reece attacked a girlfriend he was living with. He threw her down the stairs of their apartment. Reece was so angry that he kept slapping her until she lost consciousness. He thought she was cheating on him. When the police officers arrived, they had to pull him off the bleeding girl. Reece fought the police too. It ended badly for him, as back up cops jumped into the bedlam with night sticks and pistol butts.

In court, the combination of the assault upon the girl, and the attack on the officers who had tried to intervene guaranteed that he would see a prison term. The judge saw him as a brute and sent him to Angola. It was a place that housed some of the most hardened criminals in the entire country. There had even been an ex-warden there sentenced to 50 years for murdering his wife.

It was an archaic, medieval dungeon. If a man wasn't a hardened case going in, he certainly was coming out. Angola had one of the highest suicide and murder rates of all American prisons. Even the guards and the administrators had reputations for extreme cruelty. It was also the single venue for carrying out the death penalty in Louisiana.

On a cloudy, humid Labor Day weekend, Eddie Reece was removed from protective custody in an Orleans Parish jail cell. He was driven north in the back of a police van to Angola State Prison on the banks of the Mississippi. As he approached Angola, Eddie could see a swampy tree-lined entrance on this narrow asphalt road. Expecting a concrete high-rise of jail cells, he saw what looked like row upon rows of warped Quonset huts.

These were the dormitories, or cell blocks, in which the prisoners were housed. Some of the prisoners had been here for thirty years or more, and would die in these bunks of disease and old age. The crimes that brought them there were often too heinous to imagine or mention, far beyond macabre. The inmates were serial killers, cannibals, child murderers, rapists, bank robbers, and the cruelest and twisted individuals from the Gulf Coast. It was the end of the road for any show of propriety or even humanity.

As they checked in Eddie Reece, there was a strange mirth among his jailers, who themselves were hardened men. Still, no one smiled. As he was escorted to his bleak prison dormitory hut, Eddie noticed armed guards on horseback.

They each carried a loaded shotgun across their leather saddles. They were poised to use them if the slightest misstep occurred. That was the hellish atmosphere of the prison, where any escape was deemed impossible. This old Civil War stockade was bordered by several deep Oxbow lakes and a mile of fetid and dangerous swamps. If that wasn't enough, you also had to fight the unforgiving harsh currents of the Mississippi River.

Angola would transform Eddie Reece into the most violent of men. Yet he would play his horn there too, entertaining the warden and prison guards. There were well-attended and festive jazz evenings with the Angola music quintet, but it was also the place where he slaughtered another man. It might have been in self-defense but he killed him just the same. That heinous act itself would be one of many unsolved crimes inside the horrid compound of misery.

That first night after the dormitory doors were locked Eddie Reece sat on a hard bunk in the middle of his hut dressed in his ill-fitting prison clothes. He slowly looked around, and instinctively knew that survival in this pestilential place would require whatever courage he had inside him. This was a hard labor gulag. Eddie was assigned to a prison crew that cut sugar cane in the fields around the prison. They worked six days each week from dawn until dusk with only water and a soggy sandwich for nourishment. The days were long and blistering under the hot Louisiana sun. The work crew cut and stacked the mature cane stalks on carts all day long that were transported to the mill for processing into powdered sugar.

Several of the armed guards on horseback were always in the vicinity. Sometimes they would dismount and walk through the fields to monitor the pace of the fieldwork. On occasion, they might even speak to the inmates they knew.

There were a few scheduled smoke breaks during the long day. Also, an inmate was assigned to push a water cart up and down the rows offering water to the workers.

At first, Eddie didn't notice any malice practiced by the guards. He quickly learned that the hierarchy of inmate life inside Angola was rigid and fraught with peril. He was approached by a black inmate on one of those workdays, who made obscene comments to him, and finally touched him. Eddie pounced on the man and punched him repeatedly in the face with his big fists. The mauling was stopped by a guard, though the other inmate was badly beaten, and required medical attention.

This act of self-defense that particular day won Reece loyalty among his fellow white inmates, mostly from the same dormitory. It also insured that he would have more trouble from the organized prison blacks and it came quickly. A few days later, as he returned from dinner, he received a bad beating from four black inmates. One of the guards looked the other way until it might be time to slowly intervene.

His eyes were almost swollen shut. It was difficult to work in the blazing sun, though Reece soldiered on, and didn't complain. He had three years to serve.

The months rolled on and the bruising work in the cane fields continued. Reece remained silent until one night after dinner in the exercise yard when he was provoked by a black inmate. They fought and Eddie knocked the man unconscious with a single blow. He had been carried away while other inmates continued to threaten Eddie.

The blow Eddie had leveled with his big fist caused a brain hemorrhage and the inmate had been helicoptered to New Orleans for surgery. The prison code had produced no witnesses to the fight, nor had there been any accusations made against Eddie himself. From that time on he remained in constant danger from the black prisoners that were organized into small gangs. After a week, the inmate had succumbed to his head wound. It was a fatal assault with no witnesses, or anyone accused. Eddie had killed him.

Wary of all around him, Eddie found his way into the prison jazz band. The band was a favorite of the present warden, his top administrators, and their families. Elevated to this position, he was moved into a special dormitory for musicians and other inmates who had been granted privileges within the prison: working in the medical clinic, the library, and even in prison office areas.

A month before the end of his third year, Eddie Reece was released from Angola and placed in a two-year probation program for ex-convicts. He would report to a parole office twice a month for that entire period. He would also seek legitimate employment, and for him that meant going back to the French Quarter clubs where he could play with various bands. Eddie spent these two years playing clubs in New Orleans. He avoided any appearance of trouble. He mostly kept his temper in check because the thought of returning to Angola terrified him.

Those three years in Angola left their mark on Eddie both physically with a nose smashed beyond surgical repair, and a battered psyche. He had been beaten and stabbed twice, once with a sharpened spoon near the kidneys that put him the prison hospital for a week. The thrust had only missed his kidney and spleen by a half inch and created horrible internal bleeding. It had taken him a year to recover from the stabbing and he had trouble urinating without pain. He had a long crescent-shaped red scar as a reminder. There wasn't a night later after he'd been released when he didn't put his fingers on it and remember the horrible attack.

Even with the strength of a big man, and enough courage, the bestial environment fed on his soul. It created a primal lashing out at anybody, mostly at the men who had been there for more than a month. Within that first month in Angola, you could easily be gang raped or beaten to death, as it had happened repeatedly to other inmates. The prison completely erased whatever decency Eddie Reece had left, and it turned him deep down inside into a violent animal.

For months afterward, he'd lie awake half the night thinking he was still trapped in Angola. Even though he could hear the raucous French Quarter noise below his bedroom window and see a naked young woman in his bed, he was forever in that hell on earth. Perhaps he could smell the same Mississippi River through his Royale Street bedroom doors, and that earthy aroma brought him back there. Who knew why? Yet it did, unmercifully, night after night.

Eddie was never a coward, even as a young boy in the Nashville projects, or in the reform school, or inside Angola itself. He carried an unnamed fear inside him and would strike out against men and women in this blind desperation.

He never turned into a hardened criminal. Angola didn't do that to him, instead it simply erased whatever humanity he had left in him. He became a beast hidden in human flesh, ready to tear anything or anybody apart with his misdirected pain.

Those first couple of arrests in the French Quarter for assault were considered mostly nothing. They were just fights with loud drunks in clubs. This territory was familiar for brawlers and known to the New Orleans police. He was put on a short leash by the local cops, particularly after the second assault.

Following that incident, they viewed this as habitually bad behavior. They'll put you away for a while, maybe six months or a year if you're lucky, and hopefully not ship you out to Angola. But if you mess up again, well, then there's no choice. That's what happened when Eddie punched his live-in girlfriend Dee Landers into a bloody pulp inside the apartment courtyard in front of the other building tenants. The local authorities had enough of this thuggish musician and decided they were going to teach him a very hard lesson called Angola.

If anyone crossed the otherwise affable horn player, he'd hurt them. He'd hurt them badly, maybe even beat them to death. That was what I was convinced he'd done to Lizzie Connelly, the innocent young dancer who became his teenage plaything and followed him to her very death.

I believe Eddie Reece went temporarily insane when he attacked people. I feel his fevered mind devolved into that of a rabid dog or hyena.

I thought about collecting all this unfound evidence for the police. I thought of presenting the facts that I could ferret out, the details, fingerprints and even eyewitnesses to his propensity for murder. I'd bring this maniac somehow to justice and get him sentenced him to eighty years in that hell he feared returning to. Let him slice his own filthy throat.

It wouldn't be my role to rehabilitate this man, never. Rather my mission in this crusade for vengeance was to end his miserable life. I'd murder Eddie Reece with my bare hands, I vowed that.

Chapter Eight

It was winter and with the chill in the air, Yvonne and I spent weeks at a time in the city. I had stopped working on the portraits of Lizzie. I decided to do canvases based on my interpretations of the lines and figures she had drawn of the dances she performed in Woodstock. They were carefully laid out in her schoolgirl hand in the dance movement book I had gotten from Wylie Lane.

It was slow work and it took me almost a week of drawing to find a language in her dance calligraphy which meant anything to me. I needed to understand or to recreate it, at least taken abstractly, on the canvas. The vision did come.

Yvonne wasn't a fan of winter sports or the mountains. The thought of hiking around the snowy Woodstock hills and returning to a hot toddy in front of a roaring fire seemed to have little appeal for her. So, with the responsibility as house caretaker, I drove up one Friday with snow blowing across the Thruway.

Inside the house, I moved in all the dry wood I could find for the weekend. I had made an enormous fire. Then, I checked the things that needed to be checked like the heating system that needed to be set at 56 degrees to keep the water pipes from freezing.

My artist neighbor saw me working in the yard, and I invited him inside for a glass of wine and some conversation. We talked mostly about the history of the town and its oddball residents many of whom congregated on the village green with protest signs for every imaginable cause. Then we discussed the art business and aesthetics, a worrisome subject for older painters.

At last, we came around to the years of the dance workshop that he knew about, Katrina, and the ebb and flow of instructors she hired from the city.

"Stanley, that year you had your big show about ten years ago," I started to say, and cleared my throat, about to ask my next question, but he interrupted me.

"You seem to be fixated on that particular time, why?" he inquired.

I told him, "Oh nothing much. You know, I found their dance camp yearbook from that time. They dedicated it to a student here who went missing, in the city."

"Oh that, yes," he said. "That was quite awful. I remember that Katrina was over for dinner, and she told us about it. The girl just disappeared into thin air. They never found her, did they?"

"I don't think so," I offered in response disingenuously.

"It was one of the girls who went into town to the nightclubs," he added. "Gayle saw them sneak out several times, ducking down past the level of the front lawn bushes until they could get into the road. She worked late in the studio in those days. I've never had the energy to paint at night. The light isn't what I want anyway. Gayle recognized them. She would see them together outside in the morning on the terrace with their coffee and donuts, in their dance leotards. The two were close friends."

He continued, "One day this huge guy with a beard on a motorcycle came to the house. One of those two girls jumped on the back, and was gone in flash. I think Katrina was in town on an errand, or she would have raised holy hell. They were supposed to do nothing but the work at the school. She always operated it as if it were a Russian ballet company, which in her mind I guess it was."

I bid him to continue, and he did.

"I was in the yard for some reason, and I saw it all. Actually, I had called out, and said as a warning, 'you'd better not let Katrina see you doing that'. The guy turned the bike around with the girl on it and he rode over to me, looking menacing."

128

Urging him on, I refilled Stanley's glass, and he thanked me.

"I remember, he parked the motorcycle, and got off it, coming right over to me while she still sat on the back of it," Stanley said.

"Did he speak to you?" I asked him, morbidly curious at the outcome.

"Oh, indeed he did," Stanley remembered. "He told me he'd rearrange my face with his fist if I didn't keep my mouth shut, and stay the hell out of his life. There were lots of 'fucks' as I recall, and I took him seriously. He looked like a criminal who might beat you senseless."

"You didn't want to involve the police?" I inquired further.

"No, no, I wanted the problem to go away," Stanley noted. "I lived peacefully in New York for over twenty years before I came here. I never pushed those half-crazy types you'd see on the subway or the street. I ignored them, maybe I suffered an insult, or two, but who cares, honestly?"

"You didn't mention this guy to Katrina, to have her do something about it?"

"As I said, I dropped the subject completely," Stanley concluded. "Katrina might come over for dinner twice during the whole summer. It wasn't something we needed to talk about."

"Did you ever see the guy on the bike again, picking up that girl?" I asked, almost unable to stop myself from asking more.

Stanley said, "No, I didn't. That was the only time."

When it was time for him to leave, I walked Stanley to the door and said we all should have dinner together when Yvonne was up and that I'd cook.

He said he and Gayle would love to, adding, "Imagine four artists sitting down to dinner, arguing about art. I'd love it." And then he was gone up the road in the darkness.

I called Yvonne to say goodnight. After one or two whiskeys, I was ready for bed. I climbed the stairs to the unknown and felt restless. I kept looking at the window for Lizzie but there was only snowfall. By midnight, it was almost six inches deep in a blanket over the town and the mountain. When I eventually drifted off, it felt like I'd climbed into the grave with everything so quiet and not even dreams came to me.

The touch that I'd grown to expect in the night did come. At 3:00 am, Lizzie was stretched out on the bed next to me. She was propped up with the throw pillows we had. She was dressed in ski pants, and a heavy sweater. On her feet were Après ski boots women wore at the Vermont resorts. I was speechless when I took it all in, and then Lizzie spoke.

"You shouldn't trouble Stanley about that thing years ago," she admonished, "it means so little, a few misguided words."

"You're in the room sometimes, and I don't see you?" I asked. She simply shook her head, yes, which was my answer.

I turned to her and pleaded, "Lizzie, please tell me where you go and come from when you're not here."

She would only smile, answering so few of my questions.

"You know I'm only trying to solve your disappearance?" I said excitedly and put my hand on her arm which had form under the sweater sleeve.

"Johnny, I know everything you do," Lizzie said to me, her voice not yet serious, flat but still with a sweetness to it.

"Why won't you tell me everything, so I know what to do?" I continued, but she shook her head twice in a negative swing.

"You'll go with me. That will never change, and that's the only important thing," she whispered. "That."

As she did each time, she began a dance. She moved around in her precise steps, and hummed music which seemed almost to come from some string instruments in the shadows.

When she had stopped dancing, bowing in a dancer's bow to the audience, I said to her, "I'm making paintings from your dance book. I've started two canvases, and the color is coming to me, I think."

"I always watch you paint. It's so wonderful how you frown and then smile sometimes, and get angry too like a small boy."

"My God," I uttered, "you even see that."

Lizzie walked over to the bed and sat on it. She took one of my hands in what I know was a young woman's hand of flesh, with its warmth and dimension, and form.

"Tell me, I'm not losing my mind, please," I said, "I'm not insane, am I?"

Lizzie got close to my face. I could see the white skin of her youthful beauty in the moonlight. She said, "No, there are only things you don't understand."

With that, she stood up and put her hand into the air and wiggled her fingers as if waving, and started down the stairs. I could hear her booted feet and the weight of her body on each step. I counted all six steps until she got to the landing.

In a single movement, I swung out of bed and ran to the bedroom doorway. I stood on the second-floor landing looking down over the Great Room below. I saw nothing, no movement, nor did I hear a sound that might have been Lizzie. She had departed in the same manner with which she had entered my life, and somehow vanished into the air in the otherwise empty house.

Relentlessly, I questioned my sanity. I only held out the barest of threads which connected me to the Jungian psychiatrist who believed me and hadn't called me a madman. I had to talk to someone. Back in the city, I went to see my Haitian artist friend again.

We sat on the couch together and she offered me a coffee. I sipped it as we talked about what had happened in New Orleans. She listened quietly without interrupting.

Kissing an unknown object that she picked up from the table that resembled a seed pod, she replied in her French creole accent, "It's hard to know if you have been summoned by the devil, or by God. Whichever one commands, you must obey."

She touched my hand. It was a gentle, reassuring touch, and continuing, "This was no accident. The apparition you saw, it is real and taking the human form. You have been called from the other side, and these wishes must be fulfilled."

"Have you ever heard of anything as strange as this?" I asked her.

The woman laughed before saying, "I have seen the dead rise and speak. I have seen much of which can never be explained in this world, this world of New York, or Haiti, or anywhere on earth."

She leaned closer to me, and her voice was lowered, "Lizzie Connelly knew you would appear. She had been waiting patiently for your arrival. What will now happen is what was always written."

"Sometimes I think I'm going crazy," I couldn't help but confess.

She stood up and walked to a table. The woman picked up a thin cigar and lit it, blowing smoke straight up into the air in a deep exhale.

"In the other world, madness doesn't exist," she insisted. "You have been chosen to go to a realm with no earthly boundaries, where time has no meaning. You've been shown timelessness. Savor it, my friend."

On the way home my head was spinning with what the woman had said. She seemed envious of my experience.

The word 'chosen' kept coming back to me. I repeated it aloud, almost inaudibly, to myself for perhaps a minute or two, until I gave myself over to the monotony of the long train ride home. It seemed to me that the connection with Lizzie was more than a random paranormal encounter. There was the feeling that some force beyond my reckoning had selected me out millions of people for this contact. My thoughts flew by like the subway train lights.

Was I a one-man vigilante force called upon to avenge that brutal murder of Elizabeth Connelly in a dirty French Quarter alley? Me, a painter who hadn't been involved in any act of violence for my entire life? Why would such an all-powerful celestial force want me for its vengeance? What didn't I see in this present world that the spirits knew, and why had I become this willing vassal? My thoughts buzzed in their confusion.

As the subway train rhythm continued to lull my weary brain, I fantasized about how I would kill Eddie Reece. I began to make plans for that moment.

The logical thing seemed to be to shoot him in some dark place with a handgun, up close, where I couldn't miss the target. Put the pistol inches away from his heart. I'd fire three consecutive bullets into his chest, obliterating his pumping heart. There were countless ways to secure a pistol. Since I had no criminal past, I could walk into any sporting goods store in New York or New Orleans and buy one. But there would be a record. Perhaps the police would be clever enough to trace the ballistics back to me.

I could buy it illegally in some alley and it would be untraceable. Isn't that what the Mafia did? No one had ever traced a gun in some killing back to them. It never happened. They ended up throwing the pistol in the East River after a hit.

Maybe I'd stay in New Orleans for a week. I could tell Yvonne I was in Houston for the time on gallery business. I'd call her every night on my cellphone. Why would she suspect I was in New Orleans instead planning Eddie Reece's killing?

For a few days I would follow him around until I knew his every move. Soon the location to commit the murder would present itself. It would be obvious. Maybe he'd take an alley on Royale or something to get in the side door of one of the clubs he played at. There would be something. Nighttime would be best. It's more difficult to identify murderers on the city streets and the victim is more unsuspecting. The darkness allows you no warning before your assailant is on top of you.

Another idea occurred to me. I learned from the private detective that Felix's oyster restaurant hired ex-convicts from Angola. It was part of the old owner's longstanding policy of his civic duty. Some of the older countermen had been with him for years, cleaning the oysters for customers. I went to Felix's a couple times and I saw those men, mostly black. I figured that someone had been at Angola with Eddie Reece. They might have been in an opposing prison gang.

I would go there a couple times and learn if somebody knew Eddie, and may have had a run in with him, a prison yard fight, that sort of thing. I'd earmark that guy, befriend him anonymously a couple times. Then, one day, I'd take a napkin and steal the oyster knife he had used to shuck the oysters.

Oh yeah, I'd use a clean napkin when his back was turned. The knife would be covered with his fingerprints. I could slip it in my pocket and later stick it in Eddie Reece's throat with a gloved hand. As Eddie lay dying on the cobblestones in some French Quarter alleyway, the murder weapon would be found. Later the cops would examine the knife, and the fingerprints would match an ex-con in the police database. Naturally, this particular oyster counterman had been imprisoned for a few years in Angola. He was a criminal. The patsy would no doubt have committed multiple felonies, probably the most violent kind, or he wouldn't have been sent to the worst of all prisons.

That would escape detection. Another man would be arrested and perhaps convicted for the murder of Eddie Reece, himself a notorious fellow convict known to the murderer at Angola. The evidence would point to the settling of scores between hardened criminal types. No one would ever know the truth, and the beating death of that innocent girl would be avenged.

Approaching my subway stop, it became evident to me that I'd found a way to escape prosecution for cold-blooded murder. I would get away with it. The solution itself was both simple, and brilliant at the same time.

The only problem was how to surprise and overpower a man much stronger than I am. He's a barroom brawler of long experience. It came to me as I walked through the train doors into the half-deserted subway station, that the same element of surprise would allow me to accomplish it. It was like the biblical David versus his giant Goliath. I had the same power within my very hand. I had the unconquerable force of the spirit world. It had summoned me to this task. They would give me the superhuman strength to prevail. Where these the thoughts of a rational mind? Many would argue they weren't.

Chapter Nine

Life in New York with Yvonne continued as before. I spent more time in the studio trying to make sense out of Lizzie's dance movement book. In two slow weeks, I painted four large canvases. I painted figures of a young woman in various dance steps. It felt artificial, contrived. I painted and repainted the woman in the center of these otherwise blank color fields. It became frustrating and eventually depressing.

Finally, as Yvonne had a rendezvous with girlfriends uptown, I stayed late in the studio, staring at the dancing women. I'd move periodically from the chair to add a brushstroke somewhere, and maybe paint over the same spot three times.

As I moved to the canvases again, to reconfigure an arm and the flow of hair, I felt a subtle pressure on my arm, pushing it downward with the brush in my hand. It was Lizzie in jeans and a cashmere sweater here in New York. She spoke softly, "That's all wrong."

I stiffened in surprise.

"You're an abstract painter, make the legs and arms lines, make it in motion, that's what dance is, a line in the universe," she said. Then she walked over to the table. She took a paintbrush, dipping into a blue paint and added white. She mixed the color on the glass palette until she was satisfied with the tone. She returned to the canvases, working feverishly with her arms moving in space. Lizzie reduced the figures to simple lines. It was exquisite. It took my breath away with its motion and the enormity of what these lines meant.

I called out to her at the canvas, "Oh my God, Lizzie, this is perfect. That's what was needed all the time, and I couldn't see a damn thing."

"You would find it, but it would take so long," she added. She put her hand on the small of my back and I felt the pressure of a woman's touch. It was real to me, this apparition that had now taken form.

"Make me a coffee," she suggested, and I went to the espresso maker and brewed us two steaming cups.

Lizzie held the cup in her slender fingers. I noticed she had blue paint on one of her white fingers. I laughingly pointing to the color. I handed her a rag I used to wipe my own hands. She slowly removed the paint, and smiled back at me, the demitasse cup held up almost in a toast.

We looked at the paintings for maybe a half hour, then I asked her what she thought about the direction I might take to finish. Lizzie answered me with detail and much insight. It seemed to me as though I was talking with a fellow artist. Her suggestions for improvements were aesthetically informed choices. I asked her if I might draw her, nothing more than a sketch, and she readily agreed.

Locating a large pad and some vine charcoal, I set about putting her likeness on paper. I started with her dark eyes, and the bridge of her aquiline nose. The face of a beautiful young woman began to appear on the blank paper in my hands. She would laugh and move her head with the laughter, though I pleaded for her to remain rigid. We talked about art, the masters and the hacks, and the journey of the artist in the world. Her opinions were those of a woman who profoundly understood art, certainly within this world, and perhaps within the next.

In the strong light of the studio, Lizzie Connelly looked like a normal and beautiful woman. My heart was in my mouth for most of the conversation. Sometimes it would be difficult to articulate what I wanted to say to her. She would only giggle and sip at the espresso.

I mentioned nothing about Eddie Reece, the past, or what I'd learned of her spirit world. We talked as friends, close friends, perhaps even lovers. There was nothing that I wouldn't do for this woman next to me. Emotional to a fault, I reached over and embraced her hand that she willingly put into mine.

Finally, she stood up, telling me she must go. She walked toward the studio door, not confessing to me where she was headed. She left the same way as any other visitor to the studio might, through the open door gently shutting it behind her.

I walked over to the canvases she and I both had painted. I knew at that moment this was the best art I'd ever done. The world would recognize that, and even if it didn't, I knew this to be masterful.

Yvonne was a woman given to mood swings. She had a constant anger just below the surface. Her anger was born of her mean upbringing and neglect. Her father had abandoned the family when she was nine and her mother had done the best she could: raising the three children, trying to keep them together with waitressing, or factory work if she could find it.

Considering the mean streets that surrounded Yvonne for most of her childhood, she had turned out well. She had gone to Pratt and managed to stay there long enough to get a degree. She found a small role among better painters trying desperately to make their mark in an otherwise unfriendly city.

If she loved me, she didn't much show it, not as I had wanted. She could be physical at the drop of a hat when we first lived together. After a while, sex became less important to her, and she readily admitted it.

"I don't care much about sex. I get it when I want it," was her attitude for lovemaking before, and mostly, after me. We found that we had relied more on the friendship we shared together.

She could be jealous. It came from her street beginnings. She had been an attractive teenage Latina having sex for the first time with some flashy dude in his late twenties. He had been useful, and then became transitory. She only wanted what was right there in front of her. Those things she could control.

Yet, she had a passion for art, but it wasn't as deep as mine. Art was mostly process to her, doing some piece that was quirky and without substance. Yvonne rode on what people thought of her or her art only for the moment. The moment was all that mattered to her. Perhaps she was simply shallow, and didn't care.

It took a week to finish the four abstract canvases Lizzie had started. When Yvonne had at last come to the studio, it was a short stop on the way to somewhere more important. I recall that as soon as she walked into the studio, she blurted out, "Her again! Shit. But, God, it's wonderful." She walked up to each canvas looking closely at those purposeful brush strokes. She peddled backward like a retreating basketball star waving her arms in wild enthusiasm.

"How did you get there?" she asked, more excited about my paintings than she ever had been, "Tell me, what did you find?"

I laughed, and shrugged my shoulders, nonchalantly. "They were originally dancers and their movements, and I made them lines."

"No, that's not the way you think," she insisted. She put her face an inch from the largest of the four paintings. "Somebody pointed the way for you, they did."

"What do you mean by that?" I answered, a bit taken aback by the remark.

"That woman, the one in the portraits you did, she's a dancer, isn't she?" Yvonne said in an accusing manner. "That's it."

"Yvonne, what nonsense," I offered. "You don't believe I can get to some symbol that has meaning, on my own? Please." I let out an overblown dramatic sigh that she recognized as false.

"You had those dancers up there last week. I saw a couple sketches. Now you've painted their legs as they dance into thin lines, and manipulated the arms. You're mixing ballet and modern dance. You don't know a damn thing about dance. It's that woman you painted, her. She's a professional dancer, there's no doubt in my mind."

I shook my head, and probably too defensively, "You're crazy. Jesus, this is stupid. I'm an abstract painter, it's what I do."

We talked more about the work. Gradually she calmed down, but when we left the studio to go home, she still suspected me of infidelity that birthed this art. I could see the evident mistrust in her brown eyes. They were hot and angry above her straight mouth.

On the subway, I tried to explain myself. I outlined whatever empty rationale I could figure out to explain the departure from the earlier portraits of Lizzie. She glanced at me in her penetrating look of disbelief. It was a vacuous look of distance from the present and willful projection of some other, very different place.

Yvonne shook her head from side to side as she ran her hand through her thick dark hair and moaned once or twice. I asked her what was wrong. She only smiled while looking at the subway windows mirroring her face and mine, or up at the garish advertising placards.

She spoke without really seeking anything from me: "I've used painting to get away too. I'd transport myself to a grassy meadow with its flowers and honeybees. From that shoddy holy roller storefront church behind Prospect Park with the broken plastic sign."

Yvonne looked back at me. "Even if you haven't done anything with that dancer, stop the obsession," she warned me, "I won't put up with that shit." After she said that, she held up her palm toward me, announcing, "End of this conversation."

As our subway station appeared in the electric light through the train windows, Yvonne rose to go through the open doors and said, "Last warning."

I followed her up the dirty steps. I thought of the irony in what she had said. I was involved with a woman who had been dead for years. She existed in the world that only I could enter, and then only when Lizzie Connelly summoned me to it.

If any psychiatrist asked me point blank, was I seeing people who weren't really there? How would I answer them? Logically, I might offer: "Well doctor, of

140

course I can see a young woman who's with me. You might call me insane, clinically, and you'd be quite right. If you're speaking of that dimension we're occupying in this instant, that is." But I didn't think I was crazy. I felt quite the opposite; I felt enlightened.

How would a doctor respond? He would probably say: Take a deep breath. You're absolutely wrong. Look around. There's only what you see in my well-appointed high-rise office with these leather chairs we're sitting in. Those are my medical diplomas on the wall over there, earned at concrete buildings in New York and Boston.

I followed Yvonne a half step behind her on that block from the subway to our loft apartment. I continued to replay the upsetting scenario in my clouded mind. I dwelled on these thoughts repeatedly without any resolution. How could there be one?

While Yvonne went into the bathroom to refresh herself, I made us both quick drinks at the tall mahogany bar I had built. Quietly, I accepted this inevitable fate. Now I'd somehow exist in these two opposing planes which would never ever intersect, chasing a parallel life.

She went with me to Woodstock, and the weekend was without incident. For perhaps the first time, I think Yvonne began to enjoy the mountains and the snowfall. She made several sketches of the peaks in the distance, and drank mulled wine I'd made while she drew. At last, the wonder of a place beside Manhattan had managed to creep into her consciousness.

The studio in the city was where Lizzie started to appear more often. It was where we collaborated and talked about art without fear or interference. It was where I created the best paintings I had ever done.

There were eleven large paintings in the series. Two seven-foot canvases anchored the abstract dance theme. Lizzie would paint right alongside me many nights. When we were finished, she was elated.

Gallery owner Paula Kantor made the trip to my studio. She heard from word-of-mouth that I'd really changed. I wasn't sure what that meant.

141

In her crimson Italian leather jacket with matching boots, she marched from canvas to canvas saying nothing for maybe five minutes. Slowly she walked over to where I was sitting, her once pretty face blank. Finally, she managed to force a wry half smile, demanding, "I want a solo show of these after New Year's. You show only with me. You'll make a lot, I promise. These, these, they're exquisite."

She inquired further: "Where did you get the idea for the iconography with these dancers? Is your wife a dancer, or maybe you have a chorus line girlfriend?"

"What?" I uttered in surprise, a little irritated.

The high-powered woman quickly added, "No, she's not on Broadway. This belongs to a ballerina, this precision, and the beauty. Classical."

"From my imagination," I stated, a little smug in the tone of voice.

"You're lying. I know men, and this came from some woman you're involved with."

"Well, you're wrong, Paula," I answered, getting defensive in the conversation.

She strolled over to where I had stacked the first portraits I did of Lizzie. Paula pulled one out and propped it up against the only wall space I had left in the studio, and made a cooing sound. She crossed her arms over the crimson leather jacket and turned around to face me.

"This isn't your wife. I know Yvonne, not well, maybe, but I know her. These are paintings of a woman you're intimate with. This isn't some twenty-something model you hired for a couple days. Nope."

"Now wait a minute," I said, and felt the temper rise in me.

"Johnny, I don't care who you sleep with, or who your muse might be. That's fine with me, OK," she explained, comfortable that she could say whatever she wanted to any artist in New York. After all, she was Paula Kantor and everybody in the art game let her get away with it.

"Hey, no critics, either," she mentioned with seriousness, "Nobody leaks anything before they're on my wall. That's a deal breaker."

"Those guys don't speak to me anymore. I don't bother with the art magazines either."

"Good," she said, "we're on the same page," and that was the end of her visit. She glanced at her cell phone, and muttered something under her breath I couldn't understand.

At the door, she said tersely, "Someone will bring you a contract on Friday."

"You want to discuss the terms?" I volunteered, knowing from others that this woman could be a little thorny with negotiations.

"No need. You'll like them," she added, and closed the studio door without making an attempt to say goodbye.

I waited for two days before Lizzie came to me. I told her all that was said to Paula Kantor, and she only smiled, "I know, I was there the whole time." Suddenly, a girlish giggle came out of her mouth. "Poor Paula, she knows so little. Nothing that matters."

We sat in the studio chairs facing the dance movement paintings. I made myself a drink, and for some reason thinking that she was human, I asked Lizzie if she'd like a drink too. She piped up immediately saying, "Make me the same Johnnie Walker you usually have. It's bitter, but I'll drink it anyway." When I handed the glass to her, the elusive spirit graciously accepted, thanking me.

She sipped it, then spoke about the colors that I had chosen in the series. She asked me how I arrived at the individual colors, although she had painted alongside me. Sometimes, she would apply wet paint independently on a canvas next to mine.

I turned to her in the chair, "I want to ask you a question, and you must answer me, alright? You'll answer?"

Lizzie responded quietly, "I'll answer."

143

"Will I have to die to go with you, wherever you'll take me? I must know."

"Yes," she answered. "But it will be alright. Don't worry."

"Were you sent to find me, Lizzie?"

She didn't answer. She skipped over to the table with the brushes and paints, dipping a palette knife into the Midnight Blue and quickly added Titanium White to the glass plate then hesitated, "No, Lead White is better, isn't it?"

"For what you want to do, yes," I counseled her in mentor fashion.

Making the faintest strokes to one of the more defined dancer legs, she agreed, "I think you're right. I'll mix some more blue." and she did with the tube of Lead White which lay on a far table among the other paints.

She sat down next to me while examining her changes and shook her head in agreement. She reached for my hand which she held in her warm slender palm. For a long time, we both said nothing, but sat staring at the large colorful paintings in front of us. Eventually, she rose and walked to the studio door and then opened it with a gesture before disappearing into the New York night.

At length when I got back to the loft, Yvonne had returned home only a minute prior to me and was taking off her raccoon fur coat of which she was rather proud. She had bought it with cash from her first big commission for a regional museum in the Finger Lakes counties. "Politically incorrect for everyone in this damn town," she would say.

My hands were still spattered with blue and white paint. She grabbed one of them and examined it closely: "Hardworking man. Soon you'll be sleeping at the Goddamn studio. But a show with Paula Kantor, that's major." I offered a pained smile. I walked to the sink, cleaning the paint off my hands.

With a woman such as Yvonne, there was always an uncomfortable edge to her. Sometimes you wearied of it, though it was also balanced with a fierce passion. It was a life force that had its own energy and trajectory. It was what had attracted me. At the same time, it repelled me.

During the first year Yvonne and I were married, I think we made love every night, and often during the day. It was uncontrollable for me, certainly. It gradually lessened, though, as long as we had been together as a couple. Nevertheless, it was a driving force and inexplicable to me.

In the half-forgotten manner of Yvonne's, daily lovemaking was almost archetypal. It may have been inherited from the barbaric rites Yvonne claimed her grandmother on the island continued to practice. Maybe Yvonne could bite the head off a live chicken, and easily climb into bed with me the very next minute. Her lips stained with fresh spilled blood.

"I'm the spawn of Santeria," she once claimed, though at the time, the meaning had escaped me. Some crippled woman in her Brooklyn neighborhood had sold strange smelling herbs, and bottled chicken blood for a variety of ailments, and occasionally her mother bought something from her.

Maybe I harbored the same fantasies because I had gone from the present realm into the next. I had willingly set foot into the next dimension and embraced this spirit who donned human form. She pretended that moving through a portal was no more difficult than walking through an ordinary door. I had talked with and touched Lizzie Connelly, the missing young girl that was murdered.

I did hear more about the murder. Two days earlier I received an update from the private investigator. He had assembled copies of all the New Orleans police reports on the unidentified girl found dead with a gold charm bracelet on her wrist and her face mangled beyond recognition.

There were photographs of the young woman taken by police forensic workers. The investigator had

145

them all, courtesy of compliant friends in the blue brotherhood. I told him to mail them to the studio in a well-concealed, and tightly bound, package as this was not something that anyone but me needed to look at. I would be forced to lock them somewhere from Yvonne's prying eyes, and I did once they arrived. I had a metal file cabinet with a lock where I could safely store them.

The investigator had found a dancer who had worked with Lizzie in New Orleans and paid her a visit. She and Lizzie had been casual friends, but they did a few things together outside the club, like an ice cream or a lunch on Canal Street.

The woman said Lizzie confessed to her once. She told her about her boyfriend, Eddie Reece. Lizzie said he had hit her and had left bruises though it was hardly noticeable after she covered it with pancake makeup. The woman didn't like Eddie because the man had a mean streak. She had also heard stories about an ex-girlfriend before Lizzie who suffered from broken bones. In truth, the French Quarter is a rather small, incestuous society.

Even now, Reece was still playing the clubs. He rented a studio apartment off Esplanade. There was nothing hidden about the man, honestly, even if he were a murderer. All these details would be in the investigator's report that would be sent by mail. I said that I'd send him a check the following day for the balance of the work.

"If I were you, I wouldn't confront this guy alone. He could kill you," he cautioned me over the telephone. "Don't shoot him from across the street either, because the cops will get you. Look, his life's over even if you don't kill him. Hire a criminal lawyer to camp on the DA's doorstep and get them to reopen the case. I'll help you get more on Reece. We'll send him back to Angola. Just wait, he'll hang himself with his own bed sheet in a year, guaranteed."

It was time to confront Lizzie about Eddie Reece when she next appeared. I hoped to learn something but wasn't sure what.

Two nights later, she came. I was at the studio every night to work on the Paula Kantor show. Yvonne knew an exhibition of this magnitude with the top gallery in New York would cement my name among the more important artists. This gallery had cache in New York, LA and even London. When she sold your paintings, you had arrived at the top of the food chain in contemporary art circles. The wealthiest collectors, and well-endowed museums, would start paying top dollar for your paintings. Yvonne said nothing about the continuous nights in the studio.

I was almost finished working on the dance series canvases, and only needed to do some very minor touch-ups. As I was crouched straightening a line with a ruler and painting with a tiny sable brush, I heard Lizzie's voice.

There she was sitting in one of the studio chairs wearing jeans and cowboy boots. She slung one leg over the fat chair arm.

"Now, you're famous," she said, sighing loudly. "The best museums will be standing in line."

Putting the brush in a can of water, I slipped quickly into the other chair and kissed her on the cheek. She giggled.

"Lizzie, talk to me about some things you ignore, please," I pleaded.

She claimed she'd answer all the questions I had, but she wanted one of my espressos first. I set to the machine and made two cups.

I held my coffee cup up after I handed one to her and took a quick sip. "Well, is it good?" I asked her.

Lizzie drank a sip and raved about it.

For a minute or two, I carefully stared at Lizzie's human face. I looked for some evidence of that beating all the years ago, though Lizzie was a spirit so why should she abide by the rules of this flawed existence?

It took some courage though I eventually let it out, "Tell me about what Eddie Reece did to you. I want to know because I love you."

Lizzie didn't answer me right away, and I didn't want to make her uncomfortable, so I remained silent, continuing to sip my bitter coffee.

"He did an awful thing to me," she said. She used a voice I never heard her use before. "He beat me to death."

"Oh my God," I exclaimed, and I cried once the truth came from her mouth. I had to cry; I couldn't hold it inside any longer. I held her tightly in my arms while the tears began to run down my face.

It was at that instant when my heart nearly exploded inside my chest. I saw myself killing that vile creature. I saw me over his writhing body, his filthy blood all over my hands. I would bend down, and tell him, "I'm going to watch you die, slowly and miserably." I would spit into his pathetic face and tell him I would be with Lizzie in the next world, and we would experience everlasting bliss.

In a minute the weeping subsided. Lizzie held my weary head and gently stroked my wet face, before whispering softly, "It will be alright. We will be together, don't worry."

I rose to wash my face, the cool water refreshing me, but as I turned, she disappeared. Our conversation had ended for tonight.

I found another whiskey bottle since I'd finished the last one. I poured myself two neat drinks and drank them down rapidly. The raw liquor burned my throat. I savored that feeling, almost like some small penance for what had been validated this night. Though I remained near paralyzed mentally I knew the truth, having her admit it to me affected me more than simply reading it in the police report.

The heavens had named me to hear her confession and now I must grasp all that was expected of me. I must learn how I should act to fulfill this role. I poured myself a third drink and walked to the large studio windows. At the floor to ceiling windows, the crowded New York darkness became punctuated by a constellation of millions of lights surrounding me.

Since I had learned the truth that Eddie Reece was the man who had killed Elizabeth Connelly, it became my mission to track him down, and strike the deathblow. I must tell Lizzie that. I wanted so much more of her, yet I was forced to wait, and learn more of what this future would become.

I came to accept the inevitability of events thrust upon me. I began to plan. I started to think of the life I had been given compared to what Lizzie Connelly wanted of me. Would she ask me for vengeance? I was certain she would. I already had imagined the ghastly death of Eddie Reece. Without reservation, I prepared myself to accomplish that loathsome task however murderous it would become.

When the Paula Kantor paintings were completed, I retreated to Woodstock. Yvonne wanted to remain in New York because she'd found her own way into several important group exhibitions. It was fine with her that I get away. She would take the bus up to Woodstock if things loosened in her schedule. We left it at that.

The painful truth was that we were moving apart much faster than we both had envisioned. There seemed to be a mutual acceptance with that outcome.

Inside the Wylie Lane house, I left all thoughts of art and the Paula Kantor show at the door. I read novels and explored more about the town than I had done in the previous year. Rekindling the friendship, I had established with Stanley, I invited him and his wife over for a pasta dinner one night.

It was the Christmas season, and I made a small attempt to decorate the house. I bought a holiday tree, and several boxes of ornaments at the local hardware store. Hurriedly I filled the larder with cheese, wine, and pastries.

Stanley and Gayle came over bearing holiday gifts. We sat in front of a roaring fire with the decorated tree lit and talked of many things, but very little about art. Gayle told me that she had recently seen Katrina in Woodstock. They went for lunch and had a nice chat.

Gayle had mentioned that we'd bought the Wylie house. She told Katrina that I was curious about its history and had mentioned the disappearance of Elizabeth Connelly. Katrina said that she, too, had a run in with the awful musician that had escalated to a violent argument at Wylie Lane house. She had demanded that he stay away. He pushed her against the doorframe, and she hurt her arm with the force of his aggression. To be safe, Katrina decided not to involve the Woodstock police as she felt it would be a black mark for the school. News travels fast in such a small town.

She had spoken to Lizzie about the whole unfortunate affair. This girl who was normally cooperative on the rehearsal floor and friendly in most everything else became unglued. She had said abusive things to Katrina, but the dance world itself was a small cloistered one as well, and Katrina had kept silent.

Foolishly perhaps, she'd chalked it up to the usual teenage rebellion, however, Katrina became more vigilant about the musician. She checked more often on the two girls at bedtime, sometimes several times, during the night. She double locked the doors to make it difficult for anyone to noiselessly escape the house.

She explained that her precautions seemed to work, and they had come to the end of the dance workshop term. All the girls were ready to leave Woodstock anyway. Most had not even left the property for the entire dance course.

What surprised Katrina was that Lizzie Connelly had come to her before leaving and apologized for her earlier behavior. Lizzie admitted that it happened because she was madly in love with the handsome musician.

Katrina looked off outside the restaurant when she said that her eyes welling with tears. and Gayle had reported that she said, "I'm the same kind of passionate woman. I felt this young girl's agony. You see, I myself had an affair at seventeen with a married impresario at the Bolshoi that ended badly."

"It's difficult being a woman," Katrina told her, and moved her hand through the air with a dramatic Russian flourish, ending the lunch and the story.

I listened carefully and thanked Gayle.

Stanley started talking about the unorthodox town. He spoke of its rather odd citizenry, some of whom were left over from the rock music festival, and how it had continued to embrace artists of all stripes and beliefs.

As I sat there shaking my head in concurrence with Stanley's tales about eccentric Woodstock, my mind drifted elsewhere. The only thoughts I could safely harbor as the wood fire and its forest scents filled the living room, was that I must see Lizzie. I wanted the blood of her murderer on my hands, and soon.

There was little, really, that anyone could add about Lizzie here, certainly to what I knew already and the special connection we both shared. It was out of the realm of the known. The fact was that this young woman had been brutally murdered by a man who had escaped punishment for the unspeakable and barbaric act. Her youthful loveliness became the greatest gift I had ever been given.

Stanley and Gayle took their leave as it started to get late, and I bade them goodnight. Closing the house down for the night I headed to bed where I quietly waited. Lizzie knew I was anxious to see her, and came to me that night. Sitting next to me with her slim back flush against the footboard and her legs extended, we remained silent for the longest time before either of us spoke.

She was barefooted and her toenails were painted a deep ruby red. With a confidence that grew from our continuous interactions, I gently began to rub her warm foot. Her smooth skin was soft and pliable in my strong painter's hands. She laid back with a smile closing her eyes. We must have stayed that way for a half hour or more, when she said, "I love to have my feet massaged. I always have. But do you know what I like more?"

"I have no idea," I answered then listened intently for her answer.

"Well, I like to have my back rubbed, but only the tips of the fingers up and down the spine," Lizzie instructed me.

"Ah, I'm your humble servant. That's my specialty."

"Oh good," she squealed like a teenager offering her back to me.

"Where do you go when you leave me?" I asked with the familiar reticence that I wouldn't receive a straight answer.

"It's a catacomb of paths. There are no borders, and it goes on and on beyond the sun, the moon, and the stars," she said.

My heart started beating furiously. They were the most words I'd ever heard that described her infinity. Before that, it was only a mythical place perhaps as abstract as my own paintings, without form, or any true dimension.

"Can you come to me any time, and anywhere, when you want to?" I asked her excitedly.

She laughed, saying, "Rub my back some more."

I nodded, starting to move my fingers gently up and down her slim back.

"Where you go to, is it like where we are now?" I inquired further, thinking we now were close enough to share the secrets of immortality.

"It is, and isn't," she told me, her voice almost hushed. She ran her hand through her thick raven hair.

"If I went there with you this minute, could we live in a house like this, or an apartment?" I ventured with heated excitement.

Lizzie almost guffawed, shaking her head without giving me a hint of what that meant. "It becomes everything, the immensity, that's the word, I think. Or nothing. It's there, for you and me too."

"Beyond my understanding?"

Lizzie moved her legs and was soon standing next to the bed. She answered me with a terse, "Yes." As she stood in the bedroom doorway, Lizzie offered nothing more of this other kingdom she inhabited, and vanished.

The next day I called the private investigator in New Orleans asking that he continue to trail Eddie Reece, though not necessarily closely. He needed only to note anything untoward in the musician's life. Make certain he didn't suddenly disappear some night unobserved on a Greyhound bus.

"Eddie's acquired a new lady friend," he told me over the phone. "Some kid from backwater Mississippi who came to New Orleans for fame and fortune. The girl looks like she's maybe sixteen, for Christ's sake. She moved into his Royale Street rat trap within a week, hah."

He went on: "She's a dancer at one of the clubs he plays at. It was 'lust' at first sight for him," which was punctuated by a couple snorts.

The detective started to embellish his comments, adding, "I saw them at a late-night diner on Canal. His girlfriend was eating a plate of eggs and grits like a truck driver. She probably had maybe ten cents in her pocket after her bus fare."

I asked him what she looked like, and when he described her, the girl sounded a lot like Lizzie. She was tall and slender and looked like you'd expect a dancer to look with small breasts and boyish in body shape.

He added, "They were holding hands walking back to the Quarter until he got a little horny and then romance left him. Eddie pushed her up against some brick wall, humping her before they continued on to his place. He's a real class act." The investigator then regaled me with viler details over the telephone that I didn't really care to hear.

"At first, she tried to push Eddie away, but he wasn't having it that night. She just gave up until he finished."

More gratuitous laughing came over the telephone. The ex-cop ended by saying, "Honestly, when he was humping her, I would've gladly hit him with the blackjack just for the amusement."

I could feel my own hand around that leather covered metal. I could hear it hit home as his skull began to cave in, scattering his brains all over the filthy sidewalk, but I kept my own counsel with the ex-cop and said nothing.

"Watch that fucker closely," I ordered him, and said I'd transfer more money to his account so he could continue with the surveillance.

"You could always pay a couple guys to throw him in the river," he laughingly suggested to me. I made no response to it, and hung up the phone since we were finished anyway.

That night, I made up my mind to travel to New Orleans and murder Eddie Reece. When I said those words out loud, they somehow stuck in my mouth. Whether this was a brand of street justice or not, it remained taking someone's life. It was wrong but violating the Ten Commandments didn't deter me. I planned to move ahead. It was so unlike me. I was an artist, a lover. But the injustice of what had happened to Lizzie pushed me to a place beyond my control.

Chapter Ten

My relationship with Yvonne sunk to its lowest level. We stopped any intimacy. It had ended by itself, since both of us were uninterested. There was a seething anger that had taken over her every word and my distance from her further doomed our marriage.

After six months of this, she told me she wanted a divorce. We had only the charade after all, and so we went about those painful first steps. I found a lawyer who was unknown to either of us. New York State had recently passed a law where couples could now mediate a divorce without a trial. Once both parties were in agreement as to the settlement, the divorce was granted by a Judge without either party present. There was no need for shouting expletives, or mud-slinging or incriminating photos. Both Yvonne and I saw no future with these earlier regrets. It was over.

We agreed on dividing our joint assets. She would get the New York loft apartment we had purchased under a cooperative contract. I would take the Woodstock house. The values of the two properties were about the same. It suited both our purposes. I had tired of New York City anyway, though Yvonne would never abandon the metropolis. It was too important a part of her being.

After the Paula Kantor show, there was no reason for me to be in New York on a regular basis. I had already made my mark as a successful painter. My reputation as an important contemporary artist had been established. There was no need to attend those ridiculous gallery openings any longer and drink the cheap wine.

To get started with a new life, I planned on hiring a local contractor and turning the Wylie Lane garage into an atelier with skylights and high ceilings. I could afford to do that now. New York had no further cache, and like others before me, I figured I'd simply decamp elsewhere.

Yvonne moved quickly too. I suspected she had a man hidden somewhere, and would sail smoothly into that safe harbor soon enough.

Our friends were indifferent as to whether or not we continued as a couple or not. This was typical of most artists and bohemians. We wouldn't be dropped from anyone's invitation list. We'd probably be invited to the same parties. No one cared. Consequently, our social lives within this New York artsy bubble would remain unchanged. Honestly, I didn't care either way.

The divorce mediation went quickly. We met twice with our respective lawyers in a give-and-take atmosphere with no harsh words uttered

Within two weeks I'd emptied out my New York studio. I put some paintings in Paula's downstairs storage space and had my art supplies trucked Upstate.

As Yvonne was leaving on the sidewalk outside the law office building, she said goodbye. She hesitated before turning toward the subway, adding with a hard mouth, "Someday I'll find out who that fucking dancer was. I promise. It's just a matter of time."

"You're wrong," was all I could say to her in response.

I did wave at Yvonne once as she descended the nearby subway steps, but she didn't turn around to look back at me.

After that, we ended our halfway amiable conversations. Without children, or a deeper connection that we never had, there was no need to speak with one another again.

With whatever life I had transplanted to Woodstock, I gradually made the house more comfortable. I bought a few more pieces of furniture and hung some of my abstracts to fill the blank walls.

Stanley and I became closer friends. I came to like his wife Gayle as well. She was a sweet and accommodating neighbor and knew my situation as a single displaced man. Inviting me to a handful of dinners, they sometimes found an available woman dinner companion to round out the foursome. It was pleasant, and I enjoyed their company.

Alone in the house in Woodstock, Lizzie appeared to me more often. Within a few short weeks, I even mustered up the courage to ask her to be around me more, as if she were my permanent companion, or even a partner. But we never went very deep into these discussions. She mentioned only once that she knew all about Yvonne, and was sorry. No, our conversations weren't normal, everyday language. How could they be?

On another occasion, I inquired about us being together all the time. She said that we would always be together. I remained uncertain about what exactly she meant, but not long after that happened, I kissed her passionately. It was the only time. Lizzie had responded to me as any woman might and returned the kiss. When she kissed me back, the world changed for me.

Was I mad to think these thoughts? In my limited world, Lizzie Connelly existed to me alone and only when she sought it or was possibly sent by someone else: an all-powerful force within this illusion who might influence these outcomes. I had no idea what might occur between us.

There was nothing over which I had much control, nor could I make Lizzie truly human. Would she live permanently with me at the Wylie Lane house? Would she drive twice a week to the local grocery store? What sort of future might we enjoy together, if any at all? I knew nothing about it all really, not then, nor even now.

Several nights passed and Lizzie hadn't appeared to me. Undaunted, I made plans for New Orleans to end my thankless task of murderous vengeance. I wanted to be certain of Eddie Reece, and his movements, so I spoke with the private investigator again.

He said that for the present, Eddie was consumed with the teenage dancer from some Mississippi trailer park. His behavior had been the same for some time. There was no evidence that he'd break and run for cover anytime soon.

I made plans to fly out of Albany with a plane change in Charlotte. I would get to New Orleans the next Tuesday and then I'd plan the murder.

It never occurred to me that Lizzie might object to this plan; after all, she wasn't human anyway. Lizzie was the force sent to direct me on this very unknown path.

Now it became time to break ties with the investigator. I wired him the last payment, thanking him for all he'd done. It was over between us. I made that clear to him, and he didn't know I was coming to New Orleans. It was better that he not be involved. He wouldn't want to be brought into this as an accessory to murder.

Once I arrived in New Orleans, I found a single room in the French Quarter where I could pay in cash. I picked a place where names were unimportant. It was little more than a flophouse, though it served my purpose. I was two streets and four short blocks from where Eddie Reece and his Mississippi dancer lived. That suited me fine.

The first few nights in the Quarter I watched them move about from the shadows. His girlfriend danced at a different club from where Eddie played horn. They'd meet back at the apartment nights after their work finished. When he walked back from playing, he went through a single alley a block from the jazz club on Esplanade. It was maybe a quarter of a block long, but it cut off a few minutes from the walk. It was in this narrow filthy French Quarter alley where I planned to kill Eddie Reece. It would be late at night and unobserved by any inquisitive eyes.

Another man might have been more careful about walking through the darkness in an alley late at night, but Eddie was a thug. He feared no man. His street fighter skills were well honed. Over the years, he'd left his share of men bleeding on the Quarter cobblestones.

158

Just as planned, I found a black ex-con working at Felix's Oyster House. I had been there several times, and engaged him in conversation once he opened my half dozen oysters. He used two oyster knives that were exclusively his. None of the other countermen used them. In fact, each of the men there at the restaurant had to buy their own fish knives and they differed greatly in appearance.

When he turned his back or walked away from the counter, I'd take one of his knives with a clean linen napkin and drop it into my coat pocket. It might take a second to accomplish. I could easily do it right under the nose of the other customers or the staff. I'd pay in cash, and there would be no history of me except for a vague recollection of some tourist at the busy counter.

The man told me he lost the sight in his right eye in a fight. I learned from one of the other men that it had been in Angola during one of the black-white riots. I'd bet Eddie Reece was somehow involved.

The counterman's history at Angola, and his fingerprints on the weapon that I intended to put in Eddie Reece's throat, would implicate him in this murder. The hapless man would be charged and had no defense. He became my sacrificial lamb in this madness even though I knew it was wrong.

Two days later, I did just that when he went into the kitchen to get me more horseradish sauce. He didn't notice his second oyster knife was missing and simply picked up the five-dollar tip I'd left lying on the wet counter.

In the few nights I watched him, I noticed Eddie Reece was drunk by the end of the evening at the club. There was a slight stagger in his gait as he threaded his way down the narrow Quarter streets. His drunkenness, and the element of surprise, would allow me to overpower this much stronger man. I could kill him with a single thrust of the broad knife into his larynx. He'd suffocate in his own blood.

159

As he made his way into the alley, I could hide in the shadows of a brick outcropping and trip him. He'd fall to the alley bricks. In an instant, I'd be upon him and thrust the knife into his throat. He would be dead within a few horrible agonizing minutes. After that, I'd disappear into the labyrinth of the streets and return unnoticed to my flophouse room.

I walked myself through the plan. I followed Eddie as he moved unsteadily through the darkened streets. He cut through the small alley as was his usual habit. He arrived at the alley maybe six, or seven, minutes after he left the jazz club.

Everything was arranged, and I readied myself for the death of Eddie Reece. I needed to repay the brutal murder of a beautiful and innocent young girl whose only offense was to love this human filth. He would die a painful death at my hands. Lizzie Connelly would be avenged: the vow fulfilled.

So, late that next night, Eddie put his trumpet in its case for the last time. He had two more quick whiskeys at the club bar and started back to his French Quarter woman. I moved quickly ahead of him and placed myself flush against the alley brick wall awaiting the heavy footsteps I could already hear in the hushed Louisiana night. My heart was pounding. I slipped on a pair of gloves and took the stolen broad oyster knife from my coat pocket. I held it tightly as I saw the large man come into sight.

As he took his third step inside that darkness, I kicked out my leg and knocked him off balance. He fell to the bricks on his back, stunned by the sudden impact of the fall.

In an instant I was on top of him. He tried to push me away with his strong arm but I batted it away. Now I had the oyster knife in my fist and it came down slowly toward his throat. It only needed a single thrust to end his miserable life. Within the frenzy, I quickly pushed the awkward blade downward though to no avail. A mysterious force prevented it somehow from entering his throat.

In that dim alley light, I saw a slim white hand on my wrist, a hand as fragile as a child's though with superhuman strength. I looked at the exquisite face of Lizzie Connelly. She held my wrist firmly as the man underneath me fought to move. Lizzie whispered, "You're not a murderer." With those words I dropped the knife on the bricks. My eyes filled with tears of love for this woman.

Eddie in his drunkenness saw me pause momentarily and glance upward mesmerized into the chilled New Orleans night. With a single motion, he grabbed the oyster knife from the damp bricks. Then with his massive strength, pushed it upward into my own throat, knocking me to the side with his knee.

Seeing and feeling what he had done, I lay on my back impaled. He moved quickly out of the alley as fast he could with his awkward drunken and murderous lurch, fleeing into the night.

In the silent alley darkness, I started to lose consciousness. I looked up and saw Lizzie Connelly on her knees right next to me. She was holding one of my hands in both of hers. She slowly leaned down to kiss it gently. I knew I was going to the other side with her. In the moonlight, life quickly left my body.

Within two months Eddie Reece was arrested for homicide. His prints were on the knife. He was convicted of murder and sent to Angola for life without parole.

Seven months into his sentence in the prison exercise yard, a black man with a cloudy blind eye pushed an oyster knife that somehow had found its way inside the bleak southern prison into his back puncturing his pancreas. Eddie Reece bled out in a painful death on the cold concrete floor before he was discovered by the disinterested guards. It was the third murder in the prison that year.

No funeral arrangements were made for Eddie. There wasn't any departing religious service said for him either. He was buried by a tired crew of unsmiling trustees in the prison cemetery in a pine casket the state provided. He was buried in the same cemetery with the graves of the unclaimed bodies of men who had been executed for murder by the sovereign state of Louisiana.

A letter had been sent earlier to Eddie Reece's mother in Nashville informing her of his death and subsequent burial. When she received that single page letter from the Angola authorities, she would shed a few motherly tears. She did love her son, though their life together had not been idyllic.

She hadn't seen Eddie for many years and didn't even have a photograph of him as a young man. She managed to locate a bent snapshot of Eddie on her lap in Centennial Park at the age of two years. He had been smiling widely, holding a melting ice cream cone and his boyish face smeared with chocolate.

While in prison, Eddie Reece had been visited twice by his dancer girlfriend, Darlene Jeffers. She made the trip from New Orleans by bus, and had found a taxi to take her directly to the compound. They had been allowed to talk via telephone in a visitor room for inmates separated by glass. She tended to cry during these conversations. She would remain in New Orleans for another year until she became pregnant after an affair with another musician.

After John Howard's unfortunate death in New Orleans his brother sold the Woodstock house to an insistent Midwest architect who was also a painter, and his former Broadway dancer wife. They were a couple of some curiosity to those in town who focus on such things, such as Stanley and his sweet wife Gayle, who subsequently welcomed the couple with several dinners, and cordiality.

It was strange to both that there was a twenty-year age gap between the architect-painter and his pretty dancer wife. Yet, there was something both Stanley and Gayle felt was familiar about the couple though they couldn't put their finger on what it might be.

Gayle told Stanley one evening before retiring, that the new neighbor had a striking resemblance to the neighbor who had died in New Orleans. Maybe they weren't physically that similar, but in mannerisms and speech patterns.

Stanley, who was more perceptive perhaps than his wife, said it was easily explained: both men were from Chicago. They had that Midwest twang which typically distinguished these natives. Gayle believed he was probably right and didn't think any more about it.

* * * * * *

Within this other world, there are so many separate rooms, incarnations. Lizzie Connelly and I returned to that life as different people. We were brand new individuals, though we were, at heart, the same souls as before. Dark-haired Lizzie, with her stylish boots and long scarves, drove our green Volvo too fast to the Hurley Ridge grocery twice each week. She gave dance lessons to local young women who had an interest in Broadway musicals at the spacious house. You see, the unseen world changes our perceptions as it will. There are no rules to which it must abide.

A few local people remarked on these similarities from that time when a divorced New York abstract artist lived alone in the house. It was that odd Chicago sensibility that East Coast people didn't quite understand and embrace, that's all.

Within the vast spirit constellation, the countless human souls don't go from bad to good. They remain what they were as humans. Elizabeth Connelly knew instinctively that this man, this painter she appeared to, had integrity and character. Even with the overwhelming obsession that he had toward her for the horrible death she'd suffered in life, she couldn't let him murder Eddie Reece in cold blood. She held his wrist with the unconquerable strength that only infinity can provide. It

163

was what the mortal David felt in Sinai against the mighty giant.

Eddie Reece murdered him with his own knife blade. Lizzie held his hand, ready to lead him into unknown Elysian fields, thereby fulfilling her vow of togetherness. It was the conclusion of her awful disappointment on earth, now finding this happiness within a far broader realm of the universe.

What exactly happened? Well, they achieved this new incarnation, into what they could've become in a gentler world, but they would be together.

In Woodstock, they'd be a beloved couple with many friends. They would do good charitable works throughout the small community. The house on Wylie Lane shone with glory as its lights flickered during the Christmas season. In the summers, music wafted into the surrounding flowered meadows.

Sometimes, the architect would paint, and once, he had an exhibition in New York. A critic had said his raw sensibility with lines reminded him of another artist he'd seen, though, couldn't remember who. There are so many talented artists.

No child was born of this union, and perhaps that was the legacy of immortality, we can only guess.

* * * * * *

Stanley, who stumbled on the architect's open studio one afternoon, noticed paintings against the wall, all turned to where you couldn't see them. Curious, he turned a canvas around. They were done in all blue with a white light aura that surrounded a single young girl, who seemed to be coming from that darkness into the light. They were powerful alright, but as he walked home, he couldn't remember anything about what he'd seen. It was almost as if they had been erased by some outside force from his consciousness.

164

He tried to describe them to Gayle later that night, though words failed him. For a man who was precise and intellectual in his approach, he could only stammer until she became concerned. Indeed, what poor Stanley had seen, no one else in this world would ever look at, it was far too metaphysical for mortal eyes.

As he and Gayle had a drink before the fire, he told her that he'd seen great art in the architect's studio, yet his mind had turned blank after seeing them. He could remember nothing about the paintings. Gayle feared that perhaps he had some short-term memory loss, but the following day he was himself again. They never discussed the studio visit at the architect's home again.

Not long after, Stanley had a strange seizure. His health became compromised, which was an unlikely outcome for a man who had been healthy for his entire life. A month later, he was dead. It was a sad time for the town as Stanley was much beloved. His funeral was attended by a wide circle of artists, many coming in from Manhattan. One of those who attended was Yvonne. She came with a man she had married the year before who was a businessman. They attended the interment at the Artist's Cemetery in the town which contained the remains of a hundred years of local artists who lived and worked there. It was a fitting tribute.

Later at Gayle's, she was introduced to the architect who lived in her old house on Wylie Lane. They'd talked for quite a while. He seemed rather nice and she told him about living in his house with her deceased former husband.

Driving back to New York, she remarked to her husband how that man had an odd familiarity. He had interrupted her when she talked in the very same manner her late husband had and that had shocked her. He even used the very same words to cut her off. He insinuated himself into the conversation as Johnny had. It was uncanny.

"I think that's a Midwest, or maybe a Chicago thing," her new husband answered. "They get a little anxious. Part of prairie life." Then he started to laugh loudly at his own quip, but all Yvonne could offer in return was a slight smile. It troubled her somehow. They didn't return to Woodstock for some time. When they looked for a vacation home they first searched Fire Island, where her husband's family had been for generations.

Strangely enough, Yvonne would continue to dream about Stanley's funeral. She saw the face of the man she talked with at the reception. The dream would come to her on certain clear nights when the moon was full. Because of these dreams, she was forced to seek psychiatric help, spending sessions with the same Jungian doctor her late husband had consulted.

In one of their meetings, this doctor suggested that she had been visited by Johnny's spirit. She dismissed that outright. It was absurd.

"We weren't perfect, either one of us. But we were good people, good to each other," she had told the Jungian. "There would be no reason for him to come back to haunt me. There was nothing to settle." The doctor had simply filled his antique briar pipe and remained speechless as his own mind wandered further into the cosmos.

Yvonne returned to Woodstock one more time. It was as a favor to Gayle who had invited her to show some work at a brand-new art gallery.

In fact, Gayle was a minority owner in the new gallery. She had arranged for their opening which had little fanfare or sales. It followed the Woodstock Film Festival which by the seventh year had established itself among the more important American cinema festivals. Although they were casual friends at best, Yvonne was invited to spend the night at Gayle's house, and she agreed without much reservation.

The night of the art opening, Gayle arranged for a small catered dinner at her house where there would be maybe ten guests. Two of those invited, were the architect and painter across the street, Peter and his wife, Jeanette.

With a nice crowd moving through the gallery and a lot of compliments on her fabric pieces, Yvonne felt good about the Upstate trip. She relaxed as she walked into Gayle's handsome home, readied for a fine dinner.

It was early September, and the weather was still warm. Her elegant dinner table was surrounded with Japanese lanterns lighting the back garden. Yvonne was seated across from Gayle at the table, and right next to Peter. His wife sat on his immediate left.

The conversation was generally about art as most of the guests were from New York, and worked either as artists themselves, or gallery owners.

Peter had talked about his own history and mentioned he had attended the Chicago Art Institute as a painting student many years ago. He only remained in the art school for two years before moving on to architecture at Northwestern.

Yvonne said, "That's interesting. My late husband was there around the same time as you. Perhaps you knew him, Johnny Howard?"

Peter smiled in the lantern glow at Yvonne, "Oh yes, I knew Johnny. We often painted in the same studio."

"My goodness," Yvonne uttered. "Small world! What's the chance of that happening? Out of ten people around this table. Amazing."

"Chicago is a such a small town in many ways," Peter answered, "particularly with something like painting. In architecture, it's much bigger."

"What do you remember about Johnny?" Yvonne asked. Gayle looked quizzically at her because of the tone of her voice, which seemed almost accusatory in a strange way. She let her eyes fall to her own half empty plate.

The architect laughed, answering, "Oh that was so many years ago. I can hardly remember what I had for breakfast this morning." He continued the mirth at the table, but there was something disingenuous about his forced laughter.

Gayle thought Peter looked uncomfortable as Yvonne became persistent with more questions.

"He was a colorist, that I do remember," the architect said, "He liked doing large canvases, and sometimes portraits too, as we both did. He'd rather paint dancers, to capture the motion. Freezing them in a sort of frenetic movement."

"That sounds like his big Paula Kantor show, before he died," Yvonne remarked to him and pressed onward. "You didn't stay in touch after the Art Institute?"

The architect obviously wanted the conversation to end. He shrugged his shoulders. "No, I never saw him again after Chicago. He moved to New York, I assumed, where you two met at some party."

"How would you know that?"

The architect said. "Maybe someone mentioned that at the show tonight. I don't know, or I had heard it from a mutual friend. I can't remember which."

He touched his young wife Jeanette's arm, and motioned with his head that they should go. He stated to the host and other dinner quests, "We must leave. Early morning tomorrow, I'm afraid."

Standing, he came over to hug Gayle who rose from her seat, and waved to the other guests at the table in acknowledgement of their pleasant company. With his hand at the small of his wife's back, he launched her gently toward the garden gate. In the road, he gave everyone a big wave to end the night's festivities and crossed Wylie Lane to his own house.

After all the guests had departed, Yvonne and Gayle sat together in the living room while the caterers cleaned up. Gayle asked her, "Why on earth were you so antagonistic with Peter? It started to sound like some kind of inquisition."

"Gayle, I can't explain what I did. I even surprised myself," Yvonne blurted out, "It's like I wanted him to tell me something secretive, something I didn't know, about Johnny."

"How bizarre," Gayle interjected, "Did you want to know if there were other women in his life? That sort of awful confession?"

"Maybe that was it, I don't know," Yvonne continued and started to pace around the room.

"There is so much about that man that's like Johnny, that it scares me, frankly," Yvonne confessed.

"What do you mean?" Gayle prodded, confused.

"Okay, let me back up, collect myself for a minute," Yvonne said. She stood at the fireplace where she could look down into Gayle's face clearly.

Yvonne slowly explained what she meant: "I watched that man eat dinner, and he held his fork in the same odd way that Johnny did for our entire married life. He had the same mannerisms: Like when he talked, he would rub his chin, and sometimes his hand would make it difficult for you to hear what he was saying. Johnny did that all the time."

"Oh Yvonne, that's ridiculous," Gayle blurted out. "Every human being has similar things they do. It's the human condition."

"When he was telling a story at the table, he'd reach back and touch his wife to make certain she had stopped her conversation, and was listening to what he was saying. That. It's fucking macabre, I'm telling you. Right now, I'm a nervous wreck. I'd better go to bed, sweetie. I'm sorry. Maybe it's menopause a little early."

Gayle got up from the couch and gave Yvonne a bear hug. She saw that Yvonne was crying.

"It's alright. These things happen," Gayle said. "Last week, I got up in the middle of the night and called out to Stanley. I thought I heard him crashing around in the bathroom. Stanley is dead. He wasn't in the upstairs bathroom."

Yvonne shook her head vigorously, quickly adding; "There's something about that man. Something so familiar about him, that it's almost like we were intimate. Even when I was talking to him at the bar, his smell was one I recognized. That's what my brain told me."

"You're in a state," Gayle offered, "Look, they may have worn the same cologne. Something that obvious, darling."

She proceeded to tell Yvonne about a man she sat next to on an airplane and by the end of the trip, he had remembered that they had met before. They had sat next to one another at a wedding reception nearly forty years earlier. That was the only time they had ever been together. Gayle had remembered so much about the man; it was rather disconcerting at first.

Yvonne expressed no interest in Gayle's rambling description of that long ago flight. In her agitated state, Yvonne began to move among the framed photographs sitting on the fireplace mantel until Gayle realized she wasn't listening and ended the rambling story.

Yvonne lowered her voice. "When that man first talked with me, he touched my arm in the same bizarre way that Johnny did, this soft pressure and then he'd let go, and he'd touch me again, making some point."

"Maybe he was attracted to you, nothing more than that," Gayle went on, not really believing that was the reason herself, but what else could she say?

"Did you see his wife? She's fifteen years younger than I am and absolutely beautiful." Yvonne continued.

"Well, some men like variety, I don't know," Gayle said, "and you're very exotic."

Hearing that word, exotic, brought a smile to Yvonne's face. She seemed to calm down a bit, though she was breathing irregularly.

"He had a very successful architecture practice in Chicago, and decided to come out East. He doesn't like the city," Gayle summarized. "That's all, except for the sweet wife who's very nice, but quiet."

"You said earlier she had dance students," Yvonne went on. "She was a professional dancer, on Broadway maybe?"

"No, she was a ballerina. That's what it was, yes. Well, the girls in town like her, and the mothers all tell me she's very good at teaching dance."

Finally, Yvonne could talk no longer and said goodnight. She found her way to the guest bedroom upstairs which faced her old Wylie Lane house.

At the window, she could see a light in the Great Room across the street. It appeared that the wife was dancing or making dance moves across the floor, but she couldn't see the architect anywhere.

Then in the corner, she saw him with a large canvas, and he was painting the dance movements, using an abstract language and bright color.

Yvonne pressed her nose to the glass to take a closer look. As she focused her eyes on his canvas, all the hair on her body seemed to stand on end. He was painting those same paintings that Johnny had painted for the Paula Kantor show that were so successful. He would abstract the legs of the figures he had moving across the canvas. What was more chilling was that his palette was the same as Johnny's, his reliance on four or five different blues, and white.

"Jesus Christ," she muttered to herself pressed to the pane. "He's using Lead White. There's no other way he can get the contrast with the blues."

The architect came into the light. The man had three brushes in his hand, and they were separated with his fingers like Johnny had always done. The way he raced back from the canvas in this sort of back pedal was what she had remembered of her dead husband in his studio.

Was she losing her mind? That thought had occurred to her. She might be on the way to a nervous breakdown. It had happened to other women friends. Perhaps she needed to get out of Manhattan. She was so sick of Fire Island and her husband's brothers and their cloying wives who only talked about wonderful Florida, or money. They were the worst bores she'd ever met, though her husband himself was a caring man, even

171

sweet to her. What could you expect from three brothers who spent their entire lives on Wall Street?

All the years she'd known her ex-husband came careening back to her in a moment: from that first party at her loft in the East Village to their moving in together, to how, that first cold winter, they'd get into bed after dinner for sheer warmth and read, and then make love until they fell asleep. She remembered his every movement, his animal musk, and how he never opened his mouth too much when he laughed. It was the architect across the street. It was him but with a little different face. Yet it was Johnny, alright.

The pretty young woman's face across the street seemed familiar to her too. Yvonne thought about those stark dancer portraits he had painted, and how after that, his painting career had taken off while their marriage imploded.

She needed to talk to a shrink. Yvonne needed more therapy to keep what sanity she had. All this unexplained mystery she had conjured up during the evening was purely circumstantial. It was as if her imagination had suddenly run amok.

Yvonne looked up at the bright moon, and saw that it was in Aquarius, which had been Johnny's sign. She then noticed how the Wylie Lane house was bathed in a cool white lunar glow.

In the dark winter heavens, she could see that the moon was in a straight line with a bright pinprick. Yvonne knew that this was the planet Saturn, and that meant magical powers were in the air.

Was it Johnny's tango that she watched in the muted light? Was it a clear message to Yvonne alone that she had indeed seen an unknown world, only her, and it was fine? She needn't worry.

She backed slowly away from the window, and undressed, crawling into the cool sheets. But with sleep, came the recurring dream of her late husband and the dancer she'd never seen. Had these two men passed that same young woman from one to the other? No, that was a trick of a troubled mind. Could this truly be Johnny's muse and mistress she'd seen tonight? Was this the same young woman who had made his paintings soar? Was she now the architect across the street's trophy wife? That same woman who had demurely smiled the entire evening at dinner with little to say?

She rose again from the bed and walked to the window. It was very late with only the waning moon for light as Yvonne watched. The couple appeared again, this time dancing on their half-hidden terrace, but without music, moving in familiar movements.

At that precise moment, she knew that somehow this was a force greater than her, and a slight smile came to her face. Yvonne let go of whatever fear had earlier troubled her thoughts. With a quiet resignation of fate, she walked back to the well-appointed four poster bed and climbed inside the laundered sheets.

Closing her almond eyes to sleep for what remained of the chilly mountainous night, Yvonne knew instinctively that the man living in her old house was her dead former husband. There could be no doubt. Perhaps this was beyond what could be rationally explained, or even known to such as her though she was certain it was Johnny.

Yet again, Yvonne was drawn to the window. As the architect danced in the Great Room across the road with his young wife, he stared out toward Gayle's house and into the upstairs window. Yvonne and his eyes met briefly. The man had stopped for that single moment during his nocturnal dance. He nodded his head seemingly with the understanding of what they both knew to be true, and then smiled again. For a split second, he silently mouthed the answer to her question of who he was.

Chapter Eleven

The next day, Yvonne and Gayle had lunch at the Garden Café before she caught the bus back to the city. It was a pleasant hour, and mostly they talked about art and how they should collaborate on more two-person art exhibitions. Their distinctive styles seemed to complement each other, plus they got on so well. There was no mention of the architect across the road. Yvonne let Gayle do most of the talking, anyway, since she was the more garrulous.

Gayle convinced her to return in two weeks and to stay for the weekend on Wylie Lane. They would use the time to visit local galleries with proposals. Yvonne had agreed telling Gayle she'd take an early bus from Port Authority so she could be in Woodstock by six in the evening. They could start planning everything over dinner.

Outside the restaurant with her bag, Yvonne told Gayle she'd people watch for another fifteen minutes until the New York City bus arrived, and waved goodbye.

On the two-hour bus trip, Yvonne's mind returned to the previous night at the window when she'd made the connection with the architect across the street. Their conversation at Gayle's dinner hadn't really meant anything to her. Yvonne remained uneasy about who this man really was. It was a conundrum.

She was convinced he had obviously mouthed the word Johnny to her then and given her Johnny's grin. The episode had made her almost deranged. Yvonne thought that she was gradually slipping into mental illness, a neurosis maybe, even full-blown madness.

Had Johnny faked his own death? Did he take on a new identity after plastic surgery? The other man didn't really have Johnny's familiar sharp features. Instead, he somehow inherited her dead ex-husband's mannerisms. He had the same quirky behavior, right down to the slight swagger when he walked. Johnny would keep his right arm stiff, an injury left over from the time his drunken father had broken it as a child.

Why would he fake his own death? There was nothing to be gained by it: no windfall of money or anything from the life insurance. He didn't believe in life insurance when he was alive, and the worthless brother inherited the Woodstock house which he promptly sold.

When Yvonne prepared to return to Woodstock, she called Gayle and asked her if she'd invite the architect and his wife to dinner. She'd like to repent for her earlier bad behavior, and they seemed like such a vivacious and interesting pair. In truth, she'd love to see what they had done to the interior of the house. It would be wonderful for her to visit it again.

Naturally, the older woman was taken in by it all, including the confession. She told Yvonne she'd arrange it, if she could, for Friday night. She'd prepare some salmon pasta dish the night before and just re-heat it. They'd have a marvelous evening.

The women worked in tandem to prepare the dinner. Yvonne arranged the flowers and set the table for their guests. As they busied themselves with the domestic tasks, they talked about art, and what new directions they might explore for the exhibitions. It was a lonely time for Gayle without Stanley. She was rather lost since his death, rarely entertaining and staying close to home with her sorrow. Yvonne made her feel alive again and she welcomed her younger presence. Her ready smile revitalized Gayle in so many ways.

Yvonne's present husband, the Wall Street banker, had little interest in his wife's profession. He referred to it as her 'hobby' in the company of his banker brothers, or other close friends. It was something the man didn't take seriously. In his reckoning, it contributed too little money to their lives.

He wasn't a bad man by most standards. Nevertheless, he had narrow interests and tended to judge people by their bank account or the value of their home. He was typical for his circle, and though certainly not without sophistication, he lacked real substance. This was Yvonne's second marriage, for better or for worse, and it offered obvious advantages. He had begged off on the Woodstock trip, citing his many business obligations during that time in the city. Yvonne was left alone, and relieved he wasn't along.

When the architect started walking across the street along with his wife, Yvonne stood at the kitchen window facing the street. Her heart was in her throat as she laid eyes on the man, watching his slow swagger across the asphalt. Every movement was that of Johnny Howard, including the stiff right arm at his side.

A shiver surged through her slender body as she carried things to the table. She was afraid that she'd drop a dish because of her nervousness.

Gayle greeted them at the door. Soon, everyone was in the spacious living room in front of the blazing hearth, drinks in hand, laughing and telling humorous anecdotes of their daily lives.

Peter spoke first to Yvonne, "Jeanette and I were hoping to see you again. We so enjoyed your conversation."

His pretty wife seconded that comment, with a distinct, though demure, head nod then mentioned the lovely seasonal decorations throughout the house. They moved en mass from gourds to pussy willows to fall leaf arrangements.

With the wife out of earshot, Yvonne moved closer to the architect, and summoned up the courage to speak candidly to him, "We've met before, haven't we? Before that last dinner? It wasn't our first time together."

The man didn't immediately respond. He looked deeply into Yvonne's dark eyes, then with the slightest smile, he took another sip of the scotch he had in his hand, and answered, "I don't think so. I'd never forget a woman as beautiful as you."

He continued to look into Yvonne's eyes with a piercing stare, as if he were reading her thoughts.

Johnny won't tell me what has happened to him, Yvonne thought. There is something so mysterious that there's no way of explaining it. Instead, he wants me to guess, and I can't. This absurd game will continue, but I refuse to play, dammit.

"Ah Peter, maybe you're right, though. After all, it's a big world, and we're all thrown together with tons of other people."

"It's the awful degrees of separation thing," he mentioned, laughing.

"Of course," Yvonne countered, because she had always been quick. "We're all only separated from a mirror personality often by mere degrees. As this earth revolves, we're intimately connected."

He talked about that whole 'opposites' concept at length. They discussed a new French play and film which had received critical acclaim in New York, and most recently nationally. His tone to Yvonne was that of conciliation along with some small tenderness that made him seem more human to her. She found herself starting to like this man. In fact, she became drawn to him in perhaps the same way she'd been attracted to Johnny.

Gayle dominated Jeanette's time as they moved around the house and talked about decorating and renovations, leaving Yvonne alone with Peter.

Peter recounted his abbreviated history. He talked about his practice in Chicago, his downstate Illinois roots. It all seemed rather normal. He was one of three boys and his father had been an architect. He had been influenced at an early age to pursue that craft, though he had a strong pull toward the fine arts. He still enjoyed painting.

"Are you left, or right, handed?" Yvonne asked him. While waiting for him to consider his answer, she picked up a glass ashtray and tossed it toward him.

Instinctively he reached out with his left hand catching it deftly in midair. He gave her a stare of surprise, followed by a quick grin.

"Left-handed, the same as my dead ex-husband," Yvonne added matter-of-factly speaking.

Finishing what was left of her drink, she added, "In fact, you resemble Johnny in so many ways. Not the face maybe, but in countless other ways. It's devilish."

To that remark, Peter gave her a forced smile, looking over Yvonne's head where he noticed his wife motioning them both into the dining room where dinner was about to begin.

Throughout the meal, Jeannette remained the more reserved guest. She would cheerfully answer questions, though provided little insight into her past life. Jeanette explained that she was from the Kansas City metropolitan area, actually Lawrence. Her father had been an economist. He had occupied an endowed chair in economic thought for twenty years at the state university until his death seven years earlier. Her mother had died in an automobile accident when she was twelve, killed along with her maternal grandmother. Jeanette had studied modern dance in New York at Julliard. She had danced briefly in New York City and then in Atlanta where she had lived for a decade.

Jeannette met Peter through friends in the Atlanta ballet. At the time, his architectural firm was finishing a building addition at the arts complex where the ballet and opera were housed. In time they had married. She joined him in Chicago where he'd spent most of his professional career.

Woodstock seemed a rather subdued town to her. It was unlike any of the other places she had visited or lived. However, they decided that they'd try country living. Its proximity to New York City also allowed Peter to continue his practice. It gave them the vibrant city and the mountains, the best of both worlds.

Yvonne then told them the story of her past and the connection to their home. She said she'd love to see what they'd done with it sometime. She left the invitation open. No one said anything immediately, though after a time, Peter confessed they hadn't made many changes

178

yet. He added that Yvonne was welcome to come over anytime.

She asked if maybe tomorrow evening might work. She stated that it may be her last visit to Woodstock for a while. They, or rather he, grudgingly agreed.

The next evening promptly at seven, Yvonne knocked on her old house's front door. She was greeted by Jeannette in a flowing Arabic outfit of blue silk and scarves. Jeanette led her into the Great Room and seated her in a leather chair in front of a roaring fire. She joined her sitting across on an uncomfortable looking Italian couch.

After a minute, Peter came down the stairs. He called out in his sonorous voice, "Yvonne," and her heart stopped. If she hadn't seen Peter, she would have thought it was Johnny.

His innate hospitality was warm and genuine as he took her from room to room to show her what he had done. The small design changes made the frame house far more elegant, and contemporary. It was as if the house was a center staircase colonial style home in the posh Greenwich woods.

He had connected the old garage to the main house through a walkway. It had become his architecture atelier with skylights, chrome and modern furniture. He saw Yvonne's mouth turn down when she saw the expensive furniture. Peter laughed, adding, "I'm a staunch post-modernist, Yvonne, not a renovator of farmhouses for second homes. It's who I am, right or wrong. Mea culpa!" He held up his arms toward the sky dramatically, almost posing for the camera.

Back again in the house, the only room Yvonne hadn't seen was the tiny room they both used as a studio when they first came here. She found her own way there as Peter was refreshing drinks. There were a half dozen canvases inside facing the wall. There were also some paints in an open cabinet and an easel that looked quite worn.

Yvonne walked inside the narrow room and turned on the light remembering where the wall switch had been. She slowly looked around. Curious, Yvonne went over to the canvases, and turned the closest one leaning on the wall toward her. She stared down at the painting. A shock like a bolt of lightning went through her body and she felt herself begin to faint. She managed to catch herself though leaning against the wall for support as she glanced down at the art.

It was a painting done in a range of blues and white. The canvas was of a young woman whose features had a striking resemblance to those paintings done by her late husband. This style, these same exaggerated brush strokes, the use of color and its various tones, all screamed out to her that this was Johnny's painting. It had all his signature icons. The composition was his alone. Feeling stronger, Yvonne reached for a second canvas and turned that over to where she could see the painting, and then she knew.

This was the very same woman Johnny painted. It was the identical model, whomever that woman was. Maybe her image came from a photograph. That was possible. The emotion in the face of this woman was painted from life. She was known to this painter; they had intimacy.

Peter had called out her name from the Great Room. He had made her another cocktail, and quickly she turned the two canvases to the same position against the wall, and flicked out the light.

'Sorry," she answered, "I was just looking around, memories, you know," and then she was in the spacious room to receive the new drink.

"I liked Johnny," Peter added gratuitously to the remark, "although I really didn't know him that well. Those were the days of detachment. Everybody was walking around in this self-absorption."

"That's awfully boring," added Jeannette who had been quiet as Peter did most of the talking about the plans for the house.

"You're teaching dance here summers?" Yvonne asked her, and walked around the spacious room in a sort of dance movement manner herself.

Jeannette answered with a smile, "Yes, only for a few girls who are more focused on contemporary dance, but have some limited experience, and ambition."

"Well, this house has a history of being a rather infamous dance academy," Yvonne reported. It was a purposeful statement, designed to learn more from these two.

"Did you know that a young dancer who was here, disappeared completely the following year, and was never found?" Yvonne continued. "The police believed she was murdered, and the body was hidden somewhere."

"Oh, how ghastly," Jeannette muttered, "Please Yvonne, you're going to frighten me with that kind of talk. I'm already starting to shake."

"It was something people told us about after we bought the house," Yvonne added, obviously well aware of what she was doing. "My ex-husband was more interested in that stuff. He found things around here from that same dead girl, her diary or something else when he was cleaning the garage."

"The poor thing," Jeannette said, and that seemed to end the topic of the missing girl for the moment.

"You're going to have a show with Gayle soon," Jeanette continued and got up to stoke the fire as she talked. Yvonne simply nodded.

"That's wonderful, we so love Gayle. She's made our living here so much better than it would've been without her."

Finishing her drink, Yvonne stood telling them she must really go as it was getting late. She turned toward Peter.

"I hope you don't mind, but I took a peek at your paintings in the little studio Johnny and I used when we lived here. They're magnificent, at least the two canvases I looked at. You've got the sensibility of real painter."

Maintaining his practiced nonchalance, Peter said, "Thank you."

Yvonne wouldn't stop: "I've never met an architect who could paint quite like that and I've known my share. Usually, they do dull cityscapes in the style of somebody else. Never a figure, and certainly never anything abstract. It's not in their DNA. You're different."

"Probably because I started as a painter," he said, with a grin to make it more real.

"Sometimes I might draw Jeanette, when she lets me, but that's not too often. And on the rare occasion, I might paint her."

"I'm a terrible model. I can't sit still long enough for anybody to paint me," Jeanette confessed, turning to him for his reassurance that she said the right thing.

Yvonne interrupted him as he was about to speak, "No, these weren't seated poses. The ones I saw were of some marvelous dancer who's captured in motion. You feel her intensity as she tries to move off of the canvas."

Peter cleared his throat, "You saw all that from two paintings, those quick studies?"

"I know fine painting when I see it," Yvonne repeated. Peter tried hard to make his response sound thankful, instead of challenging her. He didn't want to attack her taste, or worse, mention her intrusion in their otherwise cloistered lives.

Yvonne began to move, realizing it was time to leave. She graciously thanked Jeanette for showing her around, and commented on the loveliness the two had brought to the country house.

She stood in the doorway, directing her parting remarks to Peter. "Kevin and I are thinking about finding an old farm house, knocking it down and building something modern around Woodstock. I know you don't do residential architecture, but would you consider doing one, a very special house as a favor maybe? We've got the money to make it special."

"Oh, I don't know, Yvonne, I..." and she didn't let him finish before giving him a big hug and after the embrace held his fine hands in hers, looking into his otherwise blank face, saying, "Please, Peter."

Halfway outside the door, she called back to Jeanette who stood there mute, and added, "Convince him, Jeanette, to do it," then she was gone.

As she enjoyed a nightcap with Gayle, Yvonne blurted out her good news: She and Kevin planned to find an old farmhouse here in Woodstock, knock it down, and build something truly beautiful in the countryside, and she'd be up here all the time. They could be even closer friends.

Lying in bed that night, her mind raced. Yvonne schemed how she'd persuade Kevin to buy a house up here. They'd make it something magnificent for him to show off to his banker brothers, and their venal friends. She'd convince him. Tell him maybe it was time to start a family. Life for a child in Manhattan wasn't really enough. They needed the fresh air of the country.

True, she was almost forty, yet she could still conceive a child. She would get fertility treatments. He wouldn't have a choice if he wanted to keep her fulfilled and stay married. Kevin knew Yvonne loathed those family gatherings at Fire Island with the disgusting made-up wives, and their vacuous conversation. He hadn't missed her downturned mouth and bored eyes.

When she returned to the city, Yvonne wore him down, forever barraging him about a Woodstock house. She talked about it at dinner at home, in a dozen restaurants around Manhattan, at elegant Westchester homes, during those nights before they made love. She gradually broke down his resistance. In the end, Kevin agreed. It had taken her less than five months to achieve victory.

With their paintings and fabric art shown at several of the Hudson River Valley's better galleries, Yvonne saw Gayle more often. Gayle welcomed her company for those weekends. Kevin himself was comfortable with Yvonne's absences, because he had a full life with his businesses and friends anyway and was easily pleased.

With her near obsession, Yvonne began her campaign to get Peter to design her Woodstock home. At long last, he grudgingly agreed. She recruited his help to look for locations too. Together, they found a wooded lot on a dirt road below the Mount Guardian Buddhist monastery with magnificent views. They could tap into Ulster County utilities, so ready water and electricity weren't an issue.

Kevin came up the following weekend and the couples met. He gave Peter a fifteen thousand dollar check to begin the design drawings. They figured the house might cost three or four hundred thousand. The finished home would be a marvel of rustic architecture on the side of a Catskill Mountain, a mere two-hour drive from their New York apartment.

To celebrate, Yvonne invited the couple and Gayle to dinner at the Bear Restaurant on Tinker Creek. There, the infamous real estate deal became history amidst much hugging and toasted with a bottle of champagne brought to the table.

Quite naturally, Peter was rather urbane and poised at the dinner and more than held his own against Kevin's Wall Street mannerisms. In truth, he'd seen it all before, many times. He was far beyond the tedious wealth talk and into something far deeper. Jeanette, herself, could be charming and, of course, looked beautiful, so that meant something to Kevin's vanity. He found what little charm he possessed.

Peter wanted everyone to come to his house for another drink. He could build a roaring fire, and they could relax a bit more. After all, they would be spending more time together, and in fifteen minutes the caravan found its way to the Wylie Lane house where Yvonne had once lived.

Kevin had never seen the house Yvonne had lived in with her dead ex-husband. He was curious to know that part of her life and therefore eager for the invitation. Once inside, he looked around its Great Room, scanning everything with his moneyed eyes. He rapidly tallied up the cost of everything.

"So, this is where you lived as bohemian painter, Yvonne," he offered to the seated audience next to the sputtering fire.

"Only on some weekends, and in the summer, and I loved it," Yvonne told him, and gave him her false smile to punctuate what she'd said.

"I can see how you might," he added and got up to examine the rock in the fireplace closer, rubbing his fingers along the smooth outside surfaces.

"Where did these rocks come from Peter?" he asked, turning his head to the semi-circle of people in the room.

"River rocks from Kaaterskill Falls in the early forties when this house was built. The terrace on the side of the house has the same rocks, nice smooth stones, easy on bare feet." Then Peter laughed his familiar gentle laugh. He asked who needed another drink, and Kevin held up his empty glass.

When Yvonne heard Peter's lilting masculine laugh, her body stiffened. It was Johnny standing right in front of her with his strange Chicago mannerisms. They had been so different from anyone else's she had known, and quickly a smile lessened her discomfort.

"How about a house tour?" Kevin asked, and Peter reluctantly nodded. They started off, but not without Kevin first adding, "I guess you don't need a tour, Yvonne, since you've been here before."

On the landing above the Great Room, you could hear Kevin's voice meant for a tight-lipped Yvonne, "Ah, the master bedroom, how lovely."

The evening continued in a cordial way and Gayle graciously invited them to stay overnight. Kevin had wanted to stay in a nearby hotel, but there wasn't one he liked. This was counterculture Woodstock after all, not The Hamptons where he felt more comfortable. He

185

preferred the seaside dining in Sag Harbor and its elegant touch.

The Woodstock house deal was sealed. In less than a month, Peter had some preliminary design sketches completed. He had offered to meet them in Manhattan. Yvonne said no, instead she would rather look at them in Woodstock. Again, she became Gayle's weekend guest who was delighted for the company.

Yvonne told Peter she'd meet him Saturday at noon at the Garden Café on the Village Green for lunch, and they could discuss things comfortably. As she came in the café door, he had already established himself at the largest table, and spread out several of the architectural drawings where they could be easily studied and discussed.

Peter rose from his restaurant chair and hugged Yvonne when she approached the table. She sat down and ordered a latte and a chilled herb soup for later.

Amiable almost to a fault, he took her through his rationale for the Mount Guardian house architectural design. He spoke about how the organic environment of the Catskills should be reflected in this home. Not surprisingly, Peter had borrowed heavily from Frank Lloyd Wright's legacy and the Prairie School straight lines.

Since he shared some affinity with the Buddhist monks at the monastery above them on this mountain, he had created several rooms with a distinct Asian motif. He recommended Japanese screens to separate them.

What he had done was light years away from the second homes of Kevin's garish friends and their insipid wives. This was art and organic beauty that came from the drawing quill of a master. It was so exquisite she began to weep at the table, her tears falling on the drawings.

"Have I done something wrong?" Peter asked her, his brow furrowed and he reached over to touch her arm offering reassurance.

Tearfully Yvonne said, "Oh no. It's just that these drawings are so beautiful. It's a house I've always wanted, like those Japanese inks I used to do, you remember?"

He shook his head, but then caught himself, quickly adding, "What inks?"

"I'm sorry," she continued. "For a moment my mind drifted, and I thought you were Johnny," she confessed, and apologized.

Peter laughed, "It's that awful Mayor Daley Chicago accent. I'm afraid I can never get rid of it. You still hear the Southside Irish."

They both started to laugh loudly and couldn't stop, and tears of mirth filled Peter's round deep-set eyes too. People in the café started to look at them with dismay and that encouraged them to stop.

"I have a container for the drawings, so they'll be safe," he assured her, reaching behind him for a large plastic cylindrical tube with fiber handles used by most architects and developers to transport design materials.

"Did you drive?" Yvonne asked Peter, and he said no, he preferred the short walk. It was exercise he badly needed during the colder months since he was so sedentary at home and in the atelier.

So, they began a twelve-minute brisk walk, both with boots, warm coats, and gloves and started past the Woodstock cemetery to Wylie Lane.

"Would you mind a quick detour?" Yvonne asked him, and he merely shrugged his shoulders which she took to mean it was alright. They walked through the cemetery gates and climbed a small hill to a grove of elm trees where there was an odd circle of unusual gravestones.

"This is the Artists Cemetery and it's been here for a hundred years," Yvonne told him, as he followed her as she wound her way between the stones.

At last, she stood before a gravestone which was a luminescent black marble, carved in the design of a mountain range. She pointed to the name.

187

"That's where my ex-husband lies," she stated, her breath creating clouds in the frigid air as she spoke to him.

"Ah, that's the final resting place of the notorious Johnny," Pete added in a flat nasal voice. "He was one of a kind, I recall."

"Do you really?" Yvonne said to him. There was an unwanted sharpness in her voice as she turned to face him.

"What?" he answered, confusion on his face.

Yvonne moved even closer and now her voice was near a whisper as she spoke to him, "Johnny's not in that grave."

Peter stiffened, and answered quickly, "I'm not sure what you mean by that."

Yvonne turned and started to walk out of the cemetery. All she said to Peter as he caught up with her was, "Don't you?" They said little more to each other on the short walk up Wylie Lane from the main road going up to the monastery and the peak of Mount Guardian.

Yvonne would eventually learn what this twisted mystery in her life was. She became determined to find out the truth whatever it might be, or how painful. Yvonne and Johnny had drifted apart in their marriage as many couples do. The early passion that they had felt for each other from that first night dissipated. Nobody was to blame, or maybe everybody.

She shared none of this with Gayle. Their connection was a comfortable friendship. Their common bond was the world of art, but little more, and that worked.

As soon as the spring came, construction began on the new house. Peter selected the best of contractors. He chose men who were true craftsmen, and he made certain everything was done precisely to his vision. For some, it would become nothing more than another Frank Lloyd Wright style house sitting up on Guardian.

By the beginning of summer, the house was almost finished. Yvonne came up one weekend to stay

188

with Gayle to see her new house. Peter drove her up to the house together. They had the first walk-through to see if everything had been done.

Peter had arranged for a Japanese woman from the city to prepare a traditional tea ceremony for them. The two sat in the ornate Japanese tearoom surrounded by cherry blossoms and were served tea. It was marvelous.

"What do you think, Yvonne?" Peter asked her after the tea was served. Yvonne told him her house was the purest form of art. He was an artist. Her house was nothing like those over-indulged Fire Island glass boxes she'd come to loathe.

"Kevin's family will hate this," she said, and giggled for a moment in a girlish manner. She quickly brought her hand to her mouth to hide it. "It has too much grace. It'll be lost upon them all." She couldn't hold back the laughter any longer, saying, "And I'll love every minute."

She got up from the silk cushions he had found for the ceremony and walked to the floor to ceiling windows looking down the mountainside. In a hushed tone, she shared, "This is all I ever wanted out of life. From that shit tenement I grew up in, now to this."

He joined her at the large window. For some reason she grabbed his hand and held it, holding it the same way she had done with Johnny. For a moment Peter allowed the touch. Then he went back to the cushions to finish the tea and the balance of the afternoon was spent going over the rest of the house.

In New York, Yvonne made it a point to find the perfect imported Asian furniture for the house. She compromised with a few comfortable chairs for Kevin. She created a high technology office for him on the lower level where he was surrounded by Dow Jones flashing TV screens, and mahogany bookcases with all his company annual reports.

Kevin didn't particularly care for Woodstock. He had little use for the people he met there who were either artists, or simply people who made a little money in New York. As a rule, they were far below his own social circle. They were a little too crass, and without the Ivy League polish he'd come to expect. He met a gaggle of them at one of Gayle's civic soirees and was duly horrified.

On the way home, he complained to Yvonne, "I don't mind the artist types, they're OK. But those others, the Merrill Lynch brokers and what not, they're fucking insufferable."

Yvonne had snorted and chuckled. Kevin was so ridiculous, and incredibly proud of his own tiresome Wharton pedigree. But the man was kind, and kept his body fit; beyond that he was little more than ego.

Kevin tolerated Peter because he was smart, and successful. Consequently, they found enough common ground to spend time together as couples. Yvonne would always include Gayle too.

One night at Peter's house for a dinner he had run into town to get more wine. Yvonne managed to get inside the painting studio by herself as Kevin talked with Gayle and Jeannette. They didn't seem to miss her.

She had enough time to look through the paintings, and now there were half as many more. They were all variations upon the same brilliant theme, the woman dancer, whom he painted in blue and white tones, and sometimes with more portraiture, depending on the size of the canvas. The really large canvases had her face rather detailed. It was an ethereal stare, that somehow signified great pain and anguish. Yvonne looked closer at them. She touched one of the canvases and the paint came off on her fingers; the oil was still wet.

It was a monumental body of art for any contemporary master, and particularly for someone who called themselves an architect who would only admit to a Sunday afternoon watercolor for his own amusement. These were superb, the sort of top flight paintings only the best galleries in New York or London might consider showing. These were paintings that sold for a hundred thousand dollars. Yvonne was convinced of that. She'd

190

speak to Peter about it, since they'd become somewhat casual friends. Quietly, she turned out the studio light and found her way back to the others who were clustered around the fire.

Kevin didn't particularly care for Gayle. She was too old to be interesting. He did like the youthfulness and grace of Jeannette, who he knew had been a dancer, though that itself was of no importance in his assessment of any woman. Her professional life, or her accomplishments in pursuit of artistic journey, were meaningless to him if she were attractive. Jeanette was by all measurements. Kevin may have been a bit classier than his two banker brothers with their 'baseball wives', though not that much really. He would continuously leer if he found a woman attractive.

When the house was at last finished Yvonne announced to Kevin that she wanted to give a dinner party. She invited her closest Woodstock friends and went to the Guardian Mountain house to get it ready. She would select those people important to her in Woodstock who would be the usual three she did everything with.

Chapter Twelve

The house was decorated, and she had moved some of the pieces she wanted into the country from New York. She asked Peter to help her with organizing her own studio. It was a room he had designed on the north side of the house. It cantilevered out over a ravine, and was reached by a separate walkway that crossed over it. It had cost more, but Yvonne wanted an atelier feel to it.

She moved all her supplies from the studio in the city and was working in Woodstock, almost more than she had in New York.

When Yvonne heard Peter drive in, she added a scarf to her blouse, and put on lipstick. She had so many mixed feelings about this man and the strangeness remained unresolved.

As they took a moment together in the atelier, she fixed them both coffees. They relaxed looking out the large window at the wooded ravine filled with wildlife and birds. It seemed quite bucolic to her eyes, that hardwood forest below the house.

"So, what do you want as a house-warming gift? I don't know what to give the woman who has everything." Peter asked, relaxed with his long legs stretched out in front of him on the director's chair Yvonne had used in the studio.

"Maybe you won't give me what I want," Yvonne said, coyly.

"What? A new car?" Peter said, laughingly sipping his coffee.

Yvonne was standing at the window with her back turned to Peter. She spun around quickly saying, "I'll tell you what you can give me."

"Well?" he said, motioning to her to continue with his upraising palm.

She said, "I want one of those blue and white monochromatic paintings you've done of Jeannette, if that's her, or whoever she is. That's what I want, Peter."

He didn't answer immediately and it seemed telling to her.

Yvonne finally spoke again, and she was almost breathless this time, "Are you going to give me one of those paintings? Do you plan to sell them all? If you're selling them, then I'll buy one. Tell me how much."

Peter let out a long sigh, answering her with this seriousness in his voice, "I can't give you one of them, Yvonne."

"And why would that be?" she insisted. She wanted to know why, and her mouth hardened.

"It's too difficult to explain, and you wouldn't understand."

Now Yvonne was standing directly in front of him, and she said pointedly, "Understand what? What can't I understand? Do you think I'm stupid?"

"Yvonne, you know I don't think that for God's sake, please. I have my reasons. Can't you let it stay at that?"

"No, I can't, because you've deceived me already and now it's more of the same. Who are you anyway? You're a man who's more like my dead husband than he was, except for that face, and you could easily have had it changed."

She started to raise her voice.

Peter slowly shook his head, uncomfortable with the direction of the conversation.

"What's your connection with the Wylie Lane house? What do you and that woman do inside those four walls? Have human sacrifices, or what?"

Peter was now standing rigid next to the large window and said, "Calm down. What are you talking about? This is ridiculous."

Then he moved quickly toward the door, "I'm leaving. Get a hold of yourself and stop this nonsense. It's craziness. This isn't bohemian, or neurotic. It's bloody insane," and with that he started out the door.

Yvonne was right behind him and as he got to the front door, she spun him around. With a single grip of his expensive wool shirt, she ripped it down the front, and exposed a nasty red scar on his chest.

"Oh my God," she uttered, and Yvonne started to shake all over back pedaling several steps before she could find a piece of furniture to stop her from falling.

"You... you are him. You're Johnny," she cried out hysterical now. "That's where your drunken father shoved a screw driver into your thirteen-year-old shoulder, breaking the bone."

In a few seconds Peter was out the door. You could hear him hit the accelerator hard and spin out of the driveway down the mountain road.

This time Yvonne knew for certain. There could be no mistake. This man, Peter, was her dead husband. Everything had fallen neatly into place, and she wondered why.

For what ungodly reason would he conduct this charade? They had been divorced, true. He was a handsome single painter in a universe of pliable women. He had already achieved success with his paintings. His canvases graced the walls of museums and in the stark white mansions of wealthy collectors. Why would he pretend to be someone else? It was unmistakably him, that same man she'd married all those years ago. Now he lived under some alias in a house that he had already owned. Why would he do this? How did he become an architect, and when?

It was inexplicable. Yvonne continued to shiver as she found a bottle in the liquor cabinet and poured a full glass of whatever it was. She hadn't even bothered to look at the label. She'd just poured out the amber liquid.

She had to get to the bottom of this or she would lose her mind. None of it made any sense. Could she confront Peter again directly and learn what he'd done? Was there another way to find out why he'd done this? Maybe he had murdered Johnny for some strange reason, some vendetta, and this was payback time. He'd taken what he wanted from his identity and moved on. All these thoughts seemed convoluted and nonsensical. She became convinced that she was in the throes of a mental breakdown.

She was married to a man she didn't love, and only marginally liked, and for what, his considerable income? There was nothing else. Was this terribly different from other women? It was common enough across the entire country, probably the world, my God, who was there to judge? No one.

At last Yvonne calmed down, and smiled at her earlier antics. Well, he's been warned, she thought to herself. He knows that he'll see more of me in the future because it's not over yet. I'll give it a week, maybe. Then we'll find a way to get together, all of us, at some neutral spot such as Gayle's. We'll chalk it up to being overly emotional bohemians. I'll simply call him, or show up on his doorstep when the wife's out shopping and force him to talk. It's not over by a long shot.

She finished the last of the full whiskey glass. Calmed, she went to bed in her white-walled bedroom, designed by the man who coincidentally bore the same scar that her late husband had.

In bed, her mind kept coming back to how he had all the same mannerisms that Johnny possessed. What was more improbable was that he claimed to have known her ex-husband as an art student in Chicago.

I can probably stop that ridiculous lie dead in its tracks with a call to the art school and ask if they have any record of Peter. I'll use some benign reason such as an award for his prominence as an artist. I'll tell them we're making certain to have an accurate biography for the history books. Such nonsense ought to be enough for the alumni office student clerk who just looked at a long list, nothing more.

Then again, who knows if Peter's identity was taken from someone else. The FBI does that sort of thing in its witness protection program. Is it possible Peter was involved with the Mafia, or some foreign government who would kill him if he were found, such as the

195

Russians? That seems farfetched, but then again, there are too many coincidences to ignore.

Soon, Yvonne was fast asleep. It was an uneventful night, so she awoke refreshed. She drove into town to the Bread Alone café where many of the town's artists and eccentrics met for morning coffee. She liked talking to an old Broadway actor named Dean, who was half senile. He knew everyone in the town and their histories.

He was there, sitting at his usual window perch when she eased herself into the next chair. She gave him a bright good morning smile. They made small talk about the weather. She asked him if he knew the wonderful new architect who had recently moved to Woodstock, Peter. The craggy actor seemed a bit circumspect before he answered. He said he'd seen the man a few times. People around town claimed the man was a talented architect.

"Have you met his lovely wife?" Yvonne sang out, and put her hand demurely on the curmudgeon's arm for encouragement, again smiling.

"Can't say that I have," the ancient actor answered. He seemed uncomfortable, letting the conversation wane, and quickly gobbling the remainder of his English muffin.

"Doesn't she come here for pastries most Saturday mornings? Surely you must have seen her. Elegant and dark-haired, and she moves like a dancer when she walks across the street. I imagine a man like you has known a few dancers."

"Come to think of it, I have seen her," he recounted, suddenly remembering the young woman. He said she was always alone. Her husband doesn't seem to get around much. He's noticed her at the grocery and the hardware store, and at the florist too.

Yvonne asked if he knew Johnny the painter who used to live on Wylie Lane, but who had been murdered in New Orleans. He looked at her oddly and mumbled something inaudible as he headed out the door.

196

Few people in Woodstock knew either Peter or his young wife. Only the woman who ran the Garden Café had ever spoken with him. The conversation was only about the weather as he finished a roll on the terrace in the warm weather. Even Kevin, who was here so infrequently, had made an attempt to talk with various townspeople as he ran errands. He would have a coffee in town on Tinker Street to people watch, which he tired of after the first visit. Kevin was only comfortable with his banker tribe, or the Fire Island summer crowd from the city. He had no interest in people who couldn't be of use. No one here fit his expectations.

Two weeks after her meltdown with Peter, Yvonne was at the house. She had been cleaning the kitchen when she heard the doorbell ring. It was a local messenger service. After a quick signature, the young man handed her a wrapped package that appeared to contain a large painting.

Inside, she tore off the brown wrapping paper. There was one of the blue and white paintings of Jeannette, if she was the muse. The painting did resemble her facial features, though subtly. There was a note stuck on the back of the canvas that read: *All is never quite what it seems to be. Enjoy this, Peter.*

She propped the painting against a blank wall and sat down in a chair to take it in. It must have been an hour before Yvonne moved at all. She finally carried it up to her bedroom. There was an unfettered wall there, and downstairs she found a hammer and nails. She hung it opposite the large bed and chaise lounge. Stretched out on the silk-covered chaise, she grasped the note from Peter in her hand and continued to reread it, looking up at the magnificent painting.

Would he forgive her earlier behavior, or did it matter? She wasn't through with him quite yet. The man clearly had things to tell her and hadn't spoken up.

She had kept some of Johnny's early drawings of the dancers. They were in an art file in her studio. Instantly she ran downstairs and started to dig through

197

her folders. There were easily a hundred of them in three metal cabinets, representing twenty years of art practice. After an hour and a half and exhausted, she found one of his oldest manila folders. There inside, were two charcoal drawings. They were drawings that Johnny had done with his signature style and line of a dancer, but with a great deal of detail in the woman's face, almost portraiture.

As Yvonne held the drawing in her hand, she began to tremble, because what she saw was a face that belonged to Jeanette. There was no mistake in her mind of who that woman was. This young woman didn't just look like, or somewhat resemble Jeannette in the face. No, it was clearly her. There was no doubt. The second charcoal and pencil drawing had more of her figure in a fluid dance movement. Those arms and legs were of the same woman who had brought her drinks at the old Wylie Lane house, and had effortlessly glided across the Great Room floor as if it were a Broadway stage.

It was difficult for Yvonne to breathe for a minute. She picked up the two drawings and left the studio a mess then abruptly stopped inside the doorway. She quickly returned to the studio again and in a single motion pinned the two drawings on a blank wall where she usually painted her canvases. She sat in an old stuffed armchair facing the drawings looking at them for a long while. Yvonne might walk up to them, her face inches away, and study some part to determine if she might be mistaken about the identity of the woman. The woman in the drawings was without a doubt Jeanette.

Kevin remained in the city. She would stay in the house by herself for a few more days because he had clients from Europe visiting. That meant he was gone each night, throwing around money.

When night came, she lay alone in the bed with the dimmest of lights and stared at the painting. Uncomfortable for much of the day, she had drunk several whiskeys. One sat on her night table untouched.

Exhausted, she turned out the bedroom light. She lay in the darkness until the moonlight crept through the window and shone on the painting like a beam light. Yvonne looked at the painting carefully with her head propped up on a feather pillow.

It appeared in the mountain moonlight that the woman was alive on the canvas. She saw the kinetic movement of a ballerina from one edge of the canvas to the other. The long legs moved.

She said morbidly out loud to herself, "I'm losing my fucking mind. I'm going insane. They'll lock me up." Then she sat up ramrod straight in the large bed and yelled at the top of her lungs at the painting, "Stop dancing, dammit!"

Yvonne didn't flick on the bedside lamp, instead she continued to sit still in the darkness breathing heavily. Staring at the dark painting, it seemed as if that dancer had indeed stopped her dance movements. It was in the same position as if the model would forever hold that pose. To the world, it was a painting.

A little drunk and obviously upset, Yvonne got out of the bed and walked across the room for a closer look. She touched the canvas. It was wet as if it had been painted that very day. She felt the tackiness of the oil paint on her fingers. Instinctively, she rubbed the paint around her hand, and smelled it. It was indeed oil. She detected linseed that had been mixed with the color pigment. Yvonne knew that familiar scent after the hundreds of oil paintings she'd done over the years.

Inside the bathroom, she soaped her hands and with tissue wiped the paint off her fingers. This canvas had been painted in the last few days. There was no doubt in her mind. Was this some sort of magic that Peter conjured to drive her insane? What was the purpose of the gift? Would this mirror image of Jeanette leap off the canvas each night and run amok around the room, climbing into the bed with her? Ah, then perhaps they might have a meaningful conversation.

Once more in the large bed, Yvonne turned on the lamp but decided to return to the darkness and tried to sleep. Even with her head on the pillow, she could see the white dancer frozen in her dance. Her mind drifted back to those long-ago years with Johnny, and how happy they'd been as two young artists in New York. They had little more than the ambition to succeed. Without any money or even the smallest encouragement, they had continued to draw and paint each night. They filled their lives with color and images.

Johnny possessed an inner fire that his own artistic voice must be heard by the entire universe. Together, they'd huddle in that broken down bed, cold from the New York tenement chill. Feverish for a much greater purpose for their lives, they'd talk of the masters, and of swimming against the current. Together they created those breaking waves and surged ahead anyway in their youthfulness, undaunted.

They couldn't afford a real studio. Their paintings were on the walls of a single bleak room above a laundry. The two hundred and fifty dollar a month rent was tough to come by. They struggled each month to pay it, both working as waiters for a time. They never lost hope. A smile crossed her troubled face. With these thoughts, there was a feeling of serenity and loss. Sleep overtook her.

In the morning with her coffee, she returned to the bedroom and sat in a chair across from the painting. She stared at it in the bright sunlight. It was the work clearly of an accomplished painter who understood composition, and the emotion of color and line. No one could've painted that picture without first agonizing over the subject to capture its vitality and sorrow.

At last, Yvonne removed the painting from its new home and carried it down the stairs to her own studio. She put it on the blank wall. Then she found a large drawing pad and began to copy it, gradually attempting to recapture some of its content for herself, though it became impossible.

After three or four attempts to draw the dance movements, she gave up. Yvonne threw the new pencil drawings on the floor beside her. She then began a large painting, a portrait of the female dancer. She concentrated on duplicating her classic features, and the half smile.

Yvonne had always been a decent figurative painter and a portraitist. She found much within the face to express. Very early in her career, she'd shown her small oil portraits to some acclaim, but the art world didn't follow that path. Portraits weren't done by the important painters; well, unless they were of celebrities like what Warhol had done.

She sat down in the chair musing over what she'd done. Yes, there was something unusual in the dancer's expressive face. It was an unspeakable agony she must have suffered, but couldn't speak of. This young dancer was like a wounded small bird, that an unknown youth had shot from the air with his slingshot. The result of too much evil in a world that had accepted its awful inevitability.

Yvonne used the same colorful palette that she had always used. It began to come to life, the eyes and the mouth which couldn't or wouldn't speak.

Making another pot of coffee and some buttered toast; she went back into the studio and continued to paint all morning and into the afternoon. Yvonne only stopped as the sun sunk in the winter sky. When she finished, her hands were covered with wet paint. She sat down again in the big chair with cold coffee, staring at what she'd done.

It was a stunningly emotional painting. Yvonne moved closer to the painting and for the first time in years, she liked what she'd expressed on canvas. The brushstrokes were true, and the mixed colors sang out with the authenticity of the emotions she had felt.

She went into the bar, and made herself a straight whiskey. She stood at the large picture window and looked out over the mountain sunset. Yvonne was somehow at peace with her life in that moment. Art was the most important gift she'd been given in this life. It took her to a far better realm than the disgusting Brooklyn household where she'd been raised.

The yellow of the evening sun slowly changed to a magenta as night fell. In her imagination, she held a large brush and moved its expressive colors across the gigantic sky canvas, mixing the richness of tone on a flat plane. It was how painters thought. It's how they took the bounty of this flawed world, and made it their own, and celebrated the majesty of life. What was the act of creation all about anyway, but God's gifts spread across the heavens?

Tonight, Kevin would arrive from New York. The routine they'd come to embrace as a couple would no doubt continue with its dull predictability and its relative comfort. She sighed deeply at the prospect of it all, and went to pull some dinner together.

She put Peter's stark painting of Jeanette back in the same spot on the cream-colored wall across from their bed. That night, Kevin would take no notice of it because it was invisible to him as all art was. He was a man of commerce, at the heights of high finance. He may have a passing interest in politics or New York sports teams. His company had a skybox at Shea Stadium for its customers to enjoy the Giants. Kevin rarely went there. He left the tiresome entertaining to the junior members of his investment banking firm who enjoyed the spectacle.

Slowly, Yvonne found herself back within Peter's trust again. Whatever truth he might confess, he didn't. Their earlier cordiality had returned, however, it made her warier of her boundaries with the complex man.

Gayle hosted a festive holiday dinner at Thanksgiving and invited Peter and Jeanette to join them. At first, Kevin had balked. He wanted to include his own family in some way, though the geography made that difficult. He finally relented.

It was going to be a potluck Thanksgiving with the first course presented at Yvonne's house. They would enjoy fresh seafood, a panoply of appetizers, and mixed drinks. From there, the party would move on to Peter's for the soup, fresh baked bread, and salad course. They would finally arrive at Gayle's to share the traditional Thanksgiving turkey, and the many vegetable dishes. To top off the dinner, Gayle had ordered three delicious pies from the chef at the Garden Café, including a gourmet cream cheese and pumpkin pie.

When everyone arrived at Yvonne's, it was the first time they'd all seen the house finished and decorated in its glory. It had an amazing eclectic mixture of Asian influences and the contemporary New York art world in the design. It was perfect. Peter beamed at every design decision Yvonne had made. It was all done with great sensibility and impeccable taste. With drinks in hand, the guests moved from room to room. They admired the view of the mountainside in this late fall Hudson River School landscape set before them.

Peter and Jeanette curiously wandered into Yvonne's painting studio. They were hypnotized by the large painting of the dancer. When Yvonne joined them, Peter spoke first excitedly, "Yvonne, you're such a fine painter. This is so like Elaine De Kooning. My God, it's beautiful."

Demurely, she answered: "Oh, I don't know. I was inspired by a painting Johnny did years ago of a dancer. I kept a few of his drawings."

Yvonne pointed to the two small drawings together on the far wall. They captured the wonderful innocence and beauty that had been Lizzie Connelly. They were of Jeanette, too yet slightly different. The eyes were larger, and the mouth was often turned down.

After a beat, Jeanette walked over to the drawings standing next to them. "Do they look like me, Peter?" she asked, with a knowing smile on her face and offered a momentary dance pose.

"Vaguely," he said, "but all dancers are beautiful. They're God's best creation for man."

"Smart boy, you remember your Balzac," Jeanette sang out. That was the first time Yvonne had ever heard her attempt anything witty. It surprised her.

They all laughed at that remark. Slowly they returned to join the others at the vast living room windows. They looked at the outline of Woodstock in the distance with its white Dutch Reformed church spire puncturing the clear blue sky.

"Kevin, your wife is a fine artist," Peter had remarked to him as he finished a story about his boyhood summers to Gayle.

"I guess," was all Kevin could muster for the compliment. You could catch the faintest strain of disdain that had brought to Peter's eyes. As a rule, Kevin appeared more diplomatic with most people, but this time he hadn't bothered.

The strange Thanksgiving caravan moved to its next way station on Wylie Lane. The soup and salad course soon appeared on the large slab table in the narrow dining room, and the conversation covered many familiar subjects.

Jeanette had suddenly become this vivacious woman. She told dance stories from her Broadway days, and how incestuous Julliard was in those first years, mostly from its ballet beginnings.

"No one at the school cared for modern dance, it was only ballet, and if you didn't like that you could go elsewhere."

Then even more animated, she stated, "Well, Alvin Ailey had been a dancer with the New York ballet, but the man wanted to do something else. The people that ran Julliard forced him out. Told him to get out."

"Is that when he opened his company?" Gayle interjected, trying to contribute to the conversation in her small way.

"It took him another two years," Jeanette added, confident of the history of the New York arts landscape.

Yvonne showed her interest with her body language, leaning toward Jeanette, and then asked, "Did you enjoy dancing? It must have been wonderful."

For a second Jeanette stopped and looked at Peter. "Yes, but my life is finally complete now." She smiled affectionately at him.

As Lizzie, she had died a painful, unfair death, and came back to live a fruitful life, as she would have if she had not been murdered.

* * * * * *

No one suggested a visit to the small studio that Peter had used in the past. The door was closed to the room, and it may have been locked, for that matter. The Wylie Lane house hadn't been changed much considering a successful architect now lived there. Peter had sophistication far beyond the typical Upstate vacation home designers. They redid the wood-framed farm-houses for young Brooklyn couples with little feel for, or even knowledge of Frank Lloyd Wright, or the master before him, Louis Sullivan. Taliesin was a word they didn't know in their limited vocabulary. They were mostly the offspring of Pratt's feeble attempt at architecture, where at best, they designed fire doors for those new high rises in Robert Graves' atelier outside the Princeton campus.

Yvonne would remain undaunted with Peter. She pleaded with him to let her see his newest paintings. After the continuous back and forth that had wrinkled Kevin's brow with consternation, Peter agreed and led her to the small studio. Only Yvonne had any interest in the paintings because the rest of the guests encircled the warm fireplace and talked of the town. Once inside the tight space he had chosen for painting, Yvonne saw several large canvases which hadn't been there before.

She grabbed one, and turned to him to ask, "May I?" He had nodded for her to go ahead, so she awkwardly spun the canvas around.

What she saw on the dark background of the canvas was a strong likeness of herself. It was her sharp nose and tiny mouth painted carefully. Yvonne was enveloped in a white aura. It surrounded her standing figure as if it had been a vision of Saint Paul, or another of the Apostles, or Mary before the crucifixion.

Her slender blue-draped arms were splayed at her sides with the palms facing outwardly. Inside those pale womanly hands were two bloody wounds from the nails the Romans had employed for the crosses. It was identical to the stigmata of Christ. Without words, she backed up from the single painting she observed. She thanked Peter, and almost in a run retreated to join the others near the fire.

For the rest of the time at Peter's house, and for the Thanksgiving dinner itself at Gayle's, Yvonne said almost nothing. She offered little in holiday season conversation at the table. The others were garrulous enough. The evening belonged to Kevin and his continuous flow of stories about past holidays and the marvelous things that had happened to him in New York. Nobody talked about art. Gayle told a story or two about the local eccentrics she'd come to love. Few people in the small town tried to hide anything from public view. Woodstock continued its counterculture appearance despite the more conventional citizens who were coming there to escape the craziness that was New York.

Saying goodbye, Yvonne had a moment alone with Peter and whispered to him, "I don't know what to say about the painting." In response he merely shrugged his shoulders and smiled at her wordlessly.

Before long, Yvonne was in the BMW passenger seat climbing to the Mount Guardian house. Kevin extolled the fine evening, though not the company whom he had found 'a bit odd,' and too unorthodox for his taste.

The bloody stigmata stayed firmly in her mind. She paid no attention to Kevin's rantings, tuning out whatever he was saying as if he weren't there. Why had Peter painted such a strange piece? What was its meaning? Did he intend to harm her? Was this simply part of his metaphysical musings that he hid from everyone around him? Were they in some sort of cult? That might explain some of their strange behavior, and perhaps the history with Johnny.

Her ex-husband hid some of his life from her. He may have been involved in a coven or pagan group that worshipped devils. In that last year together before his death in New Orleans, he had been secretive. There was that woman, the so-called model he painted. A woman who was some obscure dancer in New York that Yvonne had never met, and he denied even existed.

"I make up the people I paint," he had told her, "Take them from magazines, and let my imagination run wild."

The painting that Peter had done frightened her. Could he be an unknown serial killer posing as someone charming, who with his wife, might murder or torture unsuspecting women?

Chapter Thirteen

As they walked into the Mount Guardian house, Kevin went immediately to the bar, deciding they both needed a nightcap. He was mixing a whiskey with water, and called out to her, "Johnnie Walker, OK?" She didn't answer him. He said it again, with the same result.

He yelled across the room at her, "Are you with me tonight, or somewhere else?"

Yvonne turned to him and apologized. She said that she was tired from all that nonstop 'holiday cheer' but had enjoyed the long evening.

"They're all nice people," Kevin admitted. "But Peter and that zombie wife are too weird." Then he started to laugh loudly, thinking that his comment on the Woodstock couple was hilarious. He had quite liked that unexpected 'zombie' reference. Kevin thought himself clever in so many ways.

"Peter's a fine painter, but he's such a distant man," Yvonne went on, "They're a strange couple to get to know, too secretive."

"Really," Kevin said, sounding uninterested. "He's just some architect with a nutty wife. What's the mystery there?"

"Oh, I like them both, but they're difficult to be around," Yvonne added.

By now, Kevin had finished his drink and was ready for bed. He motioned with his head to Yvonne that he was going to the bedroom. She smiled, "I'll be there in a minute."

What Peter had meant in the painting of her was known only to him. As an artist herself, she knew it could be nothing more than strange irony that only he embraced. Nothing more than an image he had deftly manipulated.

On a shopping trip into town several days later, she called him. He encouraged her to come by the Wylie Lane house if she wanted. They could talk. It was fine with him.

Knocking on the door, there was no answer, however, the door was open so she walked in. She looked around and noticed him sitting in the makeshift studio, this time with a drawing board and charcoal.

"Yvonne, I was waiting for you, because I'd like to draw you, if you don't mind," Peter said, and his tone was matter-of-fact. There didn't appear to be any hidden agendas that were obvious to her.

Yvonne said, "OK, but no crucifixion stuff," laughed and sat in the chair he had reserved for her. "Hair up or down?"

"With you, I'd rather it be up. With Jeanette, it's different," he said.

Quickly, Yvonne tied up her hair and put a paint brush through it to hold the knotted bun in place, which she had always done from the age of twenty onward as sort of her artist's persona.

"Where's Jeanette?" she asked Peter, and he hesitated before adding, "She's out of town for a few days. Family things."

"Nothing serious, I hope." Yvonne said and looked at his face for some clue as to the reason for the separation, though none was given.

"Oh no," he responded, and started to sketch the oval of the face. His fingers moved quickly and expertly to establish the boundaries of the face.

"I do like Jeanette," Yvonne said. "But sometimes she seems hard to get to know. We'd love to see more of her." After saying what she had, she thought about how disingenuous it sounded. She blushed slightly.

Peter made no response to what she said. Instead he seemed to give his full attention to the drawing itself. Suddenly he had stopped looking at Yvonne's face for the features and nuances. His hand seemed to find its own path as he drew quickly with a surprising precision.

209

"We should do this more," he added. "Jeanette has tired of sitting. To be fair, I need the challenge of newness in the subject for any drawing or painting to mean anything."

"Yes," Yvonne agreed without much enthusiasm.

Peter's hand was now smearing the charcoal to shade her cheek on the drawing. He stated, "Of course, you don't have to agree. Your experience may be much different."

"It makes sense," was all Yvonne felt like saying about the process.

Peter threw away the piece of vine he had been using, and found a thicker piece, then continued with the facial shading.

"I typically don't draw for drawing's sake," he explained. "It's just the first step before I paint, and usually I'll do pen and ink, not charcoal."

Yvonne could only muster a slight, "Oh," and remained deadly rigid with all the discipline of a former artist's model in her history.

In forty minutes of sitting, Peter had completed the drawing. Stretching Yvonne stood up and walked over to his easel and looked at what he had done. A sigh passed through her lips, perhaps in some sort of self-discovery.

The drawing was ultra-sharp and perceptive. The single thing it shouted out to her was her 'doubt' of most everything in her life thus far. It expressed her insecurities in her own considerable talents, her questionable beauty, her intellect, and emotions she'd never quite had mastered.

"Yvonne, I can bring out those things you hide from everyone," Peter said to her calmly. "It's my gift, and it has nothing to do with art. It's something far deeper and more mysterious than you can imagine. I can bring out ultimate truth, the truth of who you really are. Not who or what you want to be, or some ridiculous fantasy connected with Kevin. All that means nothing...no, less than nothing,"

She didn't know exactly what to say to him, so she remained silent. For what seemed like forever, though it was probably only one or two minutes, they said nothing but looked into each other's eyes.

It was as if Peter was a shaman or a seer. He could inhabit your very thoughts without any effort or judgment. Perhaps he came from a different place, somewhere spiritual she didn't know about. He understood the human experience. The mind was his to manipulate. These were only silly, fleeting thoughts that she entertained sitting there in Peter's small studio. She felt physically attracted to the man, so maybe all this amounted to little more than her sensual cravings.

Her present marriage was empty of deep emotions like those she had with Johnny. Perhaps that feeling could never be reborn with anyone else. It had been a wildflower that had blossomed, and unfortunately died nearly as quickly.

"If you want, I'll sit for a painting," Yvonne told Peter to which he gave her the slightest of smiles, and nodded.

"It would be an honor," he responded bowing his head in this chivalrous movement.

"I paint slowly, not like this," Peter explained motioning to the drawing. "It would take weeks, perhaps two months. Would you be prepared for that kind of commitment?"

"Yes, let's do it."

"It'll be a journey," Peter warned. He said nothing more of the painting agreement and changed the subject.

Kevin had little interest in whether Yvonne sat for the portrait, or not. To him, the practice of art was simply a waste of time. He was schooled enough not to express his callous opinion. It never occurred to him to feel a jealous twinge if his wife sat for hours with a handsome man alone. She was clothed for the formal portrait, and that's all that might have concerned him.

Yvonne had explained to Kevin that it wasn't a conventional portrait of a bank president in a dark pinstriped suit, or the New York mayor at Gracie Mansion. Artistic liberties, whatever they were, should be expected.

"What the hell do you mean?" he asked her, confused with the rambling explanation.

"It might not look like me, that's all," Yvonne reported., "The artist can interpret the figure how he wants."

"Alright," he said with a smirk on his over confident face. "This guy paints a picture of you that doesn't look like you. I get it." With that, he walked off to refill his watery drink, and forgot about the conversation.

Peter had asked Yvonne to dress simply for the sitting and maybe bring a few outfits she might consider wearing. They'd choose the best one for what he wanted to accomplish with the painting.

When she got to his house for the first sitting, there was still no evidence of Jeanette's presence. She asked after her. Peter dismissed her question with a word, or a gesture so she didn't pursue it.

They chose a white silk blouse and a dark skirt. He wanted her to be bare footed. He wasn't certain what the pose might be; they would experiment. The first thing he did was move her into the atelier where there was more room to maneuver. Peter put her on a chaise lounge with her legs pulled up underneath her. This was the preferred pose.

Once she was in place, he produced a board with drawing paper on it. He sketched with India ink using a fine quill pen. As Yvonne sat there with her thoughts racing, she could hear the distinct scratching sound on the thick paper. It was the method most of the European portrait masters such as Lucian Freud used. Peter considered himself a classicist.

Peter sketched three different poses of Yvonne. The drawings took almost two hours to complete. At that point, he suggested they quit for the night. He would study what he had done later. Then he would have a better idea how the body should rest in space.

After the session was over, he made drinks for them, as they sat by the fire to relax. A portrait process is an arduous journey for both model and artist.

"How old are you, Yvonne?" Peter asked as if he were inquiring about the time, so it appeared to have little import.

"I beg your pardon," Yvonne snapped back, put out with the temerity of the question.

"Well?" he continued, and turned an upturned palm toward her in gesture.

"If you must know, I'll be forty this year," Yvonne said, with some irritation present in her tone of voice.

"Good, that's a perfect age," Peter commented without explanation. He nodded his head in agreement with his own reasoning several times.

"Too old to pose nude, don't you think?" she spat out, thinking that she had trapped this man at his own game.

He laughed. "No, I didn't mean it that way. But if you'd like to pose nude, we can, that's strictly up to you. We can do a second painting. It will be faster."

Then Yvonne turned a bit mean, hissing, "If I'm nude it goes faster, you mean. You get generous with the wrinkles, and the saggy skin, do a little abstract touch here and there to cover them with the brush."

"Yvonne, you're too much," Peter laughed, "You're fine, perfectly formed, a classical woman. Stop it."

"Thank you," she answered, and it was her turn to smile.

Gradually they became closer and nothing untoward happened at the sittings which went on for a month. A second month passed before the portrait neared completion. It was painted with a rather loose hand. It was unmistakably Yvonne. It had brought out a part of her that had been hidden from the rest of the world.

The portrait was on a five-by-five-foot linen canvas. The colors at first glance appeared muted, though they weren't. It featured yellow-whitish light on her face, and dark shadows on much of the rest of her reclining figure. Her perfect female face stopped whoever looked at the canvas with her caramel skin and her piercing black eyes. It was, in fact, a modern-day odalisque, though with a sharpness of tone and color.

Peter hadn't captured Yvonne's essence with the painting. No, he had gone far beyond to uncover her very soul. With it, the viewer couldn't miss what the painter found in this woman; it was there to touch, to savor, and to celebrate.

As Yvonne looked at the completed work, she moved around it slowly from side to side for several minutes without comment. Then she sat down on the bench in the atelier and wept. She cried softly for her joy and sorrow, and for all of humankind which were represented in these brush strokes.

She walked over to Peter who was standing against the wooden doorframe and kissed him as hard and passionately on the mouth as she could. She breathlessly said to him, "I've never seen a better painting."

"I'm glad," he said, his own handsome face a vacant canvas itself.

Their connection together deepened. She pressed him the next week to do a nude of her, before she became a 'grotesque woman' as Yvonne put it. Peter agreed.

The first portrait had been shown to Kevin who said he liked the painting. He complimented the architect on his painting skills, which was as far as Kevin's interest in art went. Kevin strove to be painfully cordial to the usual people in their Woodstock circle. Sometimes, that would challenge him.

They found a place in the living room to hang it even if it meant moving the couch to a less convenient location. This portrait of Yvonne became a part of their lives.

The portrait had also spurned Yvonne to spend more time in her own studio. For days now, she had been drawing botanicals, finishing them with a mix of charcoal and watercolor. They became ready exhibition pieces. Yvonne talked about another joint show with Gayle who had returned to her original wall-size fabric and assemblage art where she'd first made her reputation in New York after she had met Stanley.

The association with Peter broadened. It seemed Peter had left his architecture practice and was focused on painting. Most of the people who knew him in Woodstock figured that a man of his age and considerable talents had made enough money over the years to pursue what interested him.

It was now several months since anyone one had seen Jeanette. The ugly rumors started to spread. Finally, one day Gayle, who perhaps was the closest person to Peter, asked him what happened with Jeanette?

Careful with his few measured words, Peter told her that they had been troubled for some time as a couple. They decided to separate. In fact, only this week Jeanette called him and asked him for a divorce. He had agreed that it was the right thing to do. There, it was finally said, and Gayle hugged him to assure him that she understood his pain.

Later that same day, Gayle called Yvonne, and told her what she had learned. She said little else because she suspected Yvonne had already known of the marital rift between the two.

The artist and model continued their close association. Yvonne posed nude for another large canvas. It was cordial as before, even friendlier. After each session, they'd retire to the fire where they'd talk, mostly about art and other things, though never about Peter's past or Johnny.

It was inevitable that they would fall in love. They were attractive and vital people who had a fierce passion for everything around them. Her comfortable life with Kevin amounted to nothing. Deep inside her bosom, the artist's soul finally repudiated it, and drove her toward Peter.

Peter knew how she felt, and so the night when she took his hand, naked and led him up the bedroom stairs, he wasn't shocked. It came naturally to both, and they became intimate. Yvonne was perhaps the aggressor, and her passion had led her on this path though Peter tacitly agreed.

In the bed afterward, or in front of the fire, they'd talk for hours. Yet Peter never told her of his history with Jeanette, or really of anything else of his past. Urbane and intelligent with an affable charm, he volunteered nothing of those inner thoughts to her. She learned only what she already knew of the man.

She tired of asking questions he never answered. He deflected those topics with deft maneuvers. Yvonne never knew Peter to rise to anger. He didn't have fiery and uncontrollable emotions like her own. He was mildly irritated with things that displeased him. He was a calculated and cool man.

Giving themselves the luxury of time, Peter continued to work on the nude. At last, spring came to the Catskills, and Yvonne could no longer stand the voice nor touch of Kevin. She announced one night that their life together was a charade, and she wanted out.

A rather emotionless man, Kevin saw too that it was time to get out of this unfortunate marriage. Truthfully, it had brought him little real pleasure. The entire experience was misguided from the beginning. They had been two ill-suited people.

Yvonne could keep the Woodstock house. He would get another vacation house on Fire Island, where he wanted to be anyhow. The lawyers would do the divorce deed. Before long, Yvonne found herself spending most of her time at the Wylie Lane house. It was inevitable. She gave herself over to her emotions.

She asked Peter if he thought she should move in the Wylie Lane house, or did he want to live in the house he designed? He said he really didn't want to be in the Mount Guardian house and that the Wylie Lane house worked better for him. Yvonne shrugged her shoulders and let the decision stand.

The latest nude of Yvonne was nearing its completion. One morning when Peter was out running errands, she called Gayle and told her to come over quickly for a secret peak at the painting. Gayle hurried across the street with excitement.

In the house, Gayle marveled at the style of the large nude. Her older eyes watered up because she knew she was in the presence of a master. She sat with a thud on a nearby chair in the atelier.

"There you are for the ages!" she said to Yvonne once she composed herself, "It belongs in the Whitney."

"I know," whispered Yvonne who was so comfortable around this woman she'd known for so long, and together had come through so much.

Yvonne got up and moved closer to the large canvas, staring intently at her own face with awe. She quickly turned toward Gayle, announcing, "I'm thinking of selling the house, and moving in here," to which her friend simply nodded her own acknowledgement.

"I thought as much," Gayle offered in response.

The two of them talked of what this uncertain future might bring. Then, as always between artists, the conversation found its way to their own work, and what they expected from it.

When Peter returned he came into the house with his usual cheerfulness. As he stood in the foyer, he could look at the nude of Yvonne and that's where his eyes went.

"I'm pleased with it," he said to Yvonne as he walked closer to the large canvas. He touched the surface with his long fingers in some sort of reaffirmation of what he'd accomplished with paint, and smiled.

Turning serious, he said, "I saw Jeanette today, the divorce is final. She told me she's moved on, that she served her purpose. She said she had to leave because it was time. Something about how in soul renewal there is no time. There are no boundaries. I'm sorry that she had to go. I love her, but I also love you.

The mere mention of Jeanette again had slightly taken Yvonne aback. She didn't know what to say. It was very strange.

Peter continued, "She said she wanted one of her paintings since she was the model. Unfortunately, it's the painting in your bedroom. Do you think you could part with it?"

"I really don't care about that painting. She can have it. I have this now," and she motioned to the nude in the atelier. "That's enough."

"Can you bring it to me tomorrow? I think she is going to stop by to get it." Peter said.

Yvonne replied that she was spending the night at her house anyway. When she returned tomorrow, she'd have it with her. The uncomfortable subject had been settled without harsh words, or unnecessary hand wringing.

Back at the Mount Guardian house, Yvonne prepared herself a late evening coffee which had never inhibited her sleep. Sitting alone in the living room, she looked out over the wooded ravine and saw the moon rise in the chilly heavens.

In two weeks, she'd be forty years old. Yvonne had come so far since her half-baked childhood, and its mean streets. The circuitous path had been strange and uncharted. Looking back on it all had made her smile at the serendipity of everything that occurred within her life.

She had always loved the bitter taste of coffee and savored the last of the cup. That was the single thing her troubled mother had done right. She always made the best coffee.

Now she sat in the darkness, and didn't mind it. The hazy moonlight filled the room with its silvery presence. Yvonne relaxed, thinking that Peter would now fill that emptiness inside her that Johnny had left. Yvonne was a woman who lived in the moment; it was the legacy of her upbringing. You took what was in front of you, because if you didn't someone else would. It was a basic law of survival, nothing more.

There was time when she thought she'd birth four screaming kids in some crowded Queens bungalow. Maybe going out for Chinese once in a while, and that would be her whole life. A better life than her mother had. Though those wild years at Pratt had changed all that with its bohemians. It had been for the better. Her life would now be about meaning, not money or false security. It would be what she could find with Peter, the commonality of purpose they shared.

Those forty years went through her memory as if they had been frames in a motion picture. She saw them being played out before her. Yvonne saw her fifth birthday party at the kitchen table. She saw her father on the windy night he had abandoned his family. She had heard him go down the building stairs, heavy-footed. The breathy alcohol scent lingering in the dirty hallway.

She remembered when her brother had come home with bruises on his face from a fistfight. Proudly, he had announced that he'd joined the Marines. Juan was only seventeen. There was nothing else out there for him, only some laborer's job, or easy money on the streets.

After a while, Yvonne felt tired. She walked the few steps up to the bedroom, undressed and climbed into the sheets. With rays of moonlight illuminating the room, she looked from her pillow and saw the stark painting Peter had done of Jeanette. A smile came to her face, as she uttered the word 'bitch'. Then she laughed loudly to herself and got comfortable within the bed awaiting sleep.

At first, she expected sleep to come quickly, though it didn't. She raised herself again up in the bed, pushing more pillows behind her head. Again, she stared at the stark painting.

"Who the hell are you, Jeanette?" she spat out. "The figment of someone's sick imagination. Because you're not real, are you?"

Then Yvonne rolled around once or twice and soon was fast asleep. As the rhythm of Yvonne's steady breathing filled the room, the moonlight on the painting became a theatrical spotlight. The sparse figure began to dance in slow movements, ending in a crescendo before bowing to the imaginary audience.

Yvonne returned the dancer painting to Peter. As far as she was concerned, she was happy to see it go. It hadn't brought her much pleasure. Yvonne always had this rather eerie feeling about it anyway from that first horrid nightmare.

Summer passed, and fall. Peaceful months, maybe the best of her life. Yvonne divided her time between both houses. That was fine with Peter who knew she needed to spend time on Mount Guardian just to make certain nothing went wrong with the new house. That magnificent house really shouldn't sit up there without someone in it because something might happen. It always paid to be vigilant.

Peter didn't want to stay in the Mount Guardian house for some reason. Maybe he was superstitious of his own work. Perhaps all that had gone on in their lives only served to complicate things. Yvonne didn't make an issue of it. She was perfectly at ease dividing her time between houses as they were both comfortable. Frankly, she particularly enjoyed the pride that Peter felt for the Wylie Lane house and his painting atelier.

He had started another nude painting of her. She enjoyed the prolonged process. This canvas itself was enormous, over seven feet tall. It was a challenge to him with the figure perspective.

She teased him unmercifully. She mused that only the Sistine Chapel ceiling was left for him to repaint. Maybe he could paint some cartoon characters or even Batman.

With Christmas coming around the corner, Yvonne agreed to help with a holiday party at Gayle's house. The two of them had great fun decorating the house, each trying to outdo the other with novel twists on the season.

The short cold winter days moved ahead in a wondrous manner, with the marvelous white Christmas snowfall. They prepared for the open house at Gayle's. Peter had a small Christmas tree, well, a decent size for the Wylie Lane house. He found a ten-foot Douglas Fir for the cathedral living room of Gayle's house. They had to cut ten inches off the top so it fit the room.

One winter night, they all congregated happily in Gayle's country kitchen and made trays upon trays of cookies. Peter found his old recipe for mulled wine he remembered from a Michigan uncle's farmhouse.

Everything was wonderful and Yvonne felt serene as they returned to Peter's house; until she found the painting of Jeanette behind some blank canvases in his atelier.

"I thought Jeanette was coming back for her painting?" she asked Peter whose face showed no reaction to the remark.

"Obviously she didn't pick it up because it's in your studio," Yvonne said, a little too pointedly.

Now Peter smiled, but it looked forced. "Oh, she was going to come for it, and then something happened, and she cancelled."

"Look, why don't we just send it to her? I'll go down to UPS this afternoon myself and ship it off to her. It'll be my pleasure," Yvonne had added, trying to force the issue.

Peter balked. "She's moved around some, and I don't have her address. She'll call, and we can get rid of it. OK?"

The answer hadn't pleased Yvonne, and she quickly asked, "Don't you have her cell number? We can call her right now."

"I deleted it because it was someone else's phone. She had borrowed it to call, so we could meet."

Yvonne believed none of what he'd said, yet she held her tongue for the moment. She was angry with

Peter's obvious deception, but she would let it rest. She didn't want the misunderstanding to career into anger and an awful shouting match. She understood that separating from a marriage wasn't easy. It always included so many conflicting emotions.

"Well, the next time Jeanette calls, please tell her it's no trouble to ship the painting to wherever she is. It will take two days by air. My Christmas present for her."

Peter listened in silence merely nodding that he understood, but not necessarily that he would do anything about the problem.

Perhaps it wasn't a problem to him, Yvonne thought. She now had the nagging suspicion that Jeanette wasn't entirely out of his life. This upset her. Less than a week later, the dancer painting disappeared. When Yvonne asked Peter about it, he told her that Jeanette called. He had shipped it to her to at an address in New Mexico and the subject was closed. Jeanette said nothing.

They continued as they had been and had a marvelous time as the hosts, with Gayle, for the Christmas bash. It included singing carols, and making a snowman in her yard, complete with black coal for eyes and a carrot for the nose. Gayle had tearfully put one of Stanley's old cowboy hats on the snowman. When she looked at it, she had started to cry on Peter's shoulder.

Later, when the guests had departed, Gayle and Yvonne teamed up against Peter and they launched a vicious snowball battle in the front yard.

It had lasted for fifteen hectic minutes in the cold until Gayle slipped in the snow falling on her face. Alarmed, they both had turned her over assuming Gayle was badly hurt. They only got her laughter for their efforts. It had been a fitting conclusion to the warm friendship the three of them shared. Yvonne skipped back to the house. Her expensive Fifth Avenue boots were soaking wet from the slush. It was such a festive holiday gathering. Later, Yvonne fell placidly asleep in Peter's arms believing that all was well with the world, certainly the one she occupied.

Snowing again that same night, Peter lay awake next to a sleeping Yvonne. He watched the blowing snow outside the frosted panes. He remembered another night like this long ago when he saw a strange white apparition in the moonlight that became Lizzie Connelly. What might Yvonne ever learn about the people surrounding her? Why so readily had she had become a part of this illusion, these faces without reflections?

Even in the soundest of sleep, Yvonne was restless. She reached out to touch Peter beside her but the bed was empty. Now awake, she heard voices from the floor below. It had sounded like a woman speaking, and then Peter's voice as he answered her in a hushed conversation, all spoken above a whisper. She got out of the bed and grabbed her robe, quickly wrapping it around her nakedness. She stole quietly down the stairs and listened again for the voices.

They seemed to be coming from the atelier. Although there was no light inside that room except for the moonlight, she thought she'd seen figures move slowly in the shadows. Walking silently on her bare feet across the floor step by step, Yvonne found herself near the half open door where she halted, hidden by the same door.

She heard a young woman's voice say, "You need to finish with her. You need to bring her to the other side." Yvonne thought that she had recognized Jeanette's girlish lilt. Peter had responded with, "Soon."

Still hidden, Yvonne moved ever slightly until she could push her head beyond the closed door and glance into the darkened room. It would only be one more step she needed to take to clear the wooden door. She moved forward with that last step.

Inside in the darkness, she could make out Peter who sat on a chair facing a painting up on the easel. He was facing the painting of Jeanette which had been on her wall at the Mount Guardian house. He spoke to it in low, muted tones.

Yvonne saw no one else there except for Peter. Carefully she moved another step trying to position herself for a better view. Now she could see the room in its entirety, and Yvonne saw there was only one person inside the atelier, Peter. Perhaps he was talking to someone on his cell. Maybe he had just activated its speaker function, because his hands had been free as he gestured with them in the stale room air.

That must be what I heard, Yvonne thought to herself. I feel so foolish. He'll think that I'm spying on him, that I don't trust him, and we'll have harsh words. Slowly she backtracked and crept up the bedroom stairs without a sound. Soon she had removed her robe, and slid back into bed where she would wait for him to return, but sleep came to her first.

Peter had stayed downstairs in the atelier for hours. He didn't return to the bedroom until the morning when he surprised Yvonne with coffee and croissants. His thoughtfulness had erased the suspicions of the night before. She literally purred contentedly on his shoulder as they sipped the hot coffee.

He would repeat this same behavior on several nights, though Yvonne would not be awakened. Only the one time had she found him downstairs speaking into his telephone in the darkness, or to the painting.

Chapter Fourteen

When spring came, Yvonne decided it would be easier to have only one house to maintain. She put the Mount Guardian house on the market. It sold within two weeks. It was elegant, tasteful and completely different than everything else in Woodstock and its surrounding villages. A Swiss banker who recently moved to New York City purchased it as a second home.

Soon, Yvonne was the mistress of her former Wylie Lane house once again. The past easily blurred into the present, and possibly the future. Peter talked of marriage as he was a traditional man.

However, one night it all radically changed. Peter confessed his secret. He admitted that he was not who he appeared to be, but someone else. He said after this present identity as an architect, he'd be yet another man. This charade would continue. He wanted her to follow him. Peter believed that they couldn't continue in this same manner because Peter himself was not a normal man. He had a deceptive appearance of normalcy.

He called it incarnation, and told her it only came through the spirit world. He was part of infinity.

Peter said to her, "When I died in New Orleans, I was Johnny. It was the only way to release me. Jeanette took me through that journey. We'll rejoin the others soon. You see, Jeanette was really Lizzie Connelly who I met right here in this bedroom."

Now Yvonne became frightened for her life. She was convinced that this man was a fraud, a con man, or worse, maybe a serial killer who would murder her.

"It's too much for you now, but with time, you'll understand." He reassured her with a gentle tone. Then left her, disappearing into his atelier where he stayed for the night.

Yvonne didn't sleep all night. The next morning, she called the real estate agent in a panic and cancelled the house sale. She returned the Swiss banker's money.

By ten that morning she was out of the Wylie Lane house, taking only her own clothes with her, and speeding away in her BMW sedan.

Her furniture remained in the Mount Guardian house. It was all readied for packing and a move within a few days. Everything was now halted. Now frightened, Yvonne barricaded herself in the modernist house until this initial fear subsided.

She thought about telephoning the local police. But honestly, Peter had not actually threatened her life. He had talked about things that only madmen discuss. It was a psychotic rant about other worlds.

Yvonne stayed at her mountain house and didn't speak to anyone in town. She finally went to the city and stayed with friends where she talked about moving back. She told her closest friends she missed the frenetic Manhattan pace and needed to get back into the art world.

She cut poor Gayle off completely without explanation. Yvonne hadn't returned four of her voice mail messages. She assumed that Gayle had probably discussed this whole matter with that madman across the street. She was over them all.

"Return to infinity, please!" she said out loud to herself at an elegant Upper Westside café. The man at the next table had turned, inquiring, "I beg your pardon, were you talking to me?"

It took two weeks before Yvonne could bring herself to drive back to Woodstock. She would put her affairs in order and find a loft to rent in New York. She would divide her time between the two places until she was ready to unload her modernist house.

After leaving the Wylie Lane house, she had heard nothing from Peter. Yvonne had finally called Gayle. She admitted that she and Peter had encountered these serious differences they couldn't resolve. She had decided to end their relationship. It was painful to do, but there was no other choice. Yvonne apologized for her prolonged silence. She said that as far as she was concerned, her friendship with Gayle remained as strong as before. It had been such difficult period for her to work through. She needed that solitude to muster her inner resources. She knew Gayle would understand.

Throughout the weeks in the city, Yvonne had forced any thoughts of Peter out of her mind. Yet the passage of time brought those thoughts back. What unearthly nonsense had he been talking about that night? Was he high on some kind of hallucinogen? It wouldn't surprise her. Peter was such a peculiar man. He admitted no past, and rarely spoke about himself, let alone share his emotions.

Peter never once told her he loved her. He had been close-mouthed before and even after their nightly lovemaking. It was Yvonne, who had done all the talking and shared the overwhelming feelings she had for him.

Even Kevin had made some pathetic show of emotion. Of course, he had always lied with such un-convincing impunity. That all came from Wall Street.

Yvonne believed there was no choice but to sit down and have a forthright conversation with Peter. She needed to talk rationally and openly about their feelings. If he's half-crazy, she'd at least know it. She was resolved to do just that, and so she called him.

He answered the telephone. His baritone voice sounded much the same. He had the same pleasantness as always. Peter said he had missed Yvonne, and he couldn't wait to see her again. He told her he wanted to cook her a gourmet dinner. They could discuss whatever she wanted, and most of all, Peter said he wanted her back in his life.

He wanted her to be completely at ease with him. He wanted both of them to be comfortable inside their own skins. That was the awkward and unsuccessful way he had tried to express it. Yvonne let him talk without interrupting. She genuinely believed what he told her, and wanted to make it work, this last time.

That Friday afternoon, she drove her BMW to Woodstock. When she pulled into her mountain house driveway, she felt relieved. There was no point trying to escape what she doesn't understand. No, she'd face it head-on. She would learn what these mysterious things were that he had talked about, and then get to the bottom of whatever it was that she didn't understand. If it didn't make any sense to her, she'd abandon everything with a clear conscience. She planned to get on with her life, but on her own terms.

The first night back in the house, Yvonne slept soundly. There were no dreams that upset her, or any that she remembered. In the morning, she had her coffee at the large picture window watching the sunrise over the forest below. She felt serene, and empowered. She appeared ready for whatever the next few days would bring.

She had arranged to meet Peter for dinner the next night at the Wylie Lane house and drove into his narrow driveway on time. He met her at the door giving her a bear hug, and he gently kissed her cheek.

Yvonne had brought one of the expensive wines Kevin had left in the house for his brothers on their infrequent visits. Peter thanked her. He looked much the same as before, but more handsome. The grey at his temples gave him a distinguished look. His smooth skin and blue eyes were enhanced by his colored linen shirt and his creased khakis. He was effusive with his compliments on her appearance. Yvonne had worn an outfit that made her look both youthful and attractive.

There was a roaring fire and Peter poured the wine. They sat quietly staring at the flames, not speaking for the longest time. They became reacquainted in those subtle ways that only lovers knew.

* * * * * *

Six months later, they would both die in a nighttime automobile accident. They were driving down the curvy Mount Guardian Road when her car left the road and overturned in the wooded ravine. Peter was driving. It had been a clear summer night with the half-moon illuminating the dark trees alongside the deserted highway when the accident occurred.

In a subsequent investigation of the fatal crash, the Woodstock police could find no reason for the car going off the road. There was a lack of tire skid marks on the asphalt pavement. It was as if the couple had left the highway voluntarily and launched themselves into oblivion.

A Buddhist monk from the monastery had discovered the wreck. He had flagged down an approaching car whose occupant in turn had summoned the police. The first police officer on the scene asked the diminutive monk what he knew about the car crash that claimed the lives of the man and woman. He only shrugged his shoulders.

Placidly, the monk stood near the overturned car where he could see both victims inside quite clearly. The fingers of the dead woman's hand were intertwined with those of the man.

"See," the orange-clad Buddhist said to the tall Woodstock cop as he eagerly pointed to the two corpses, "He takes her with him into the next life. There are other rules in the spirit world unknown in this dimension."

His wide smile seemed to linger forever while he remained silent to the policeman's few further questions. The officer wrote down the monk's confusing words about the accident. Moments later sitting alone in his police cruiser, the cop ripped the page out of the small notepad and threw it angrily to the floor, chalking it all up to craziness.

* * * * * *

On a Friday night two months later, Gayle noticed a car she had never seen before pulling into the driveway at the Wylie Lane house.

A young olive-skinned woman got out of the car. Her attractive face was clearly illuminated by the street light. She looked vaguely familiar to Gayle who thought she'd met her somewhere before. Maybe she was just another of many artists who had crossed her path over the years. In the hushed darkness, their eyes seemed to meet as Gayle stood at the living room picture window. She noticed a smile slowly crossing the woman's face.

For a moment, Gayle's heart skipped a beat. She thought the woman in the car might be Yvonne. She reassured herself that this was impossible. She left the window to continue with the needlepoint sampler that had been occupying her for the past hour. It was a homespun craft that Stanley had always admired.

The next morning, Gayle went out to get the mail a little later than usual. She saw the woman from across the street looking around the front garden. The woman was the first to speak, and waved her hand in friendship saying, "Hello, you must be Gayle. The realtor told me we'd be fast friends. I'm Diana."

"Oh, hello," Gayle managed to say as she looked closely at her beautiful face and dark eyes.

When Gayle recovered from her initial surprise of meeting the mysterious woman, she asked her if she'd come over for coffee. Diana quickly agreed, nodding with enthusiasm. They started down the few steps to Gayle's fieldstone walk, and into the light filled house. Over the coffee, Gayle was cautious to not appear too forward with questions. Diana carried much of the early minute or two of awkwardness that people experience when meeting others for the first time.

Gayle laughed, "Are you Spanish, Diana? You talk with your hands." And she laughed again at her own forwardness.

"You mean the dark skin?"

"Oh no, I..." Gayle stammered, embarrassed.

"Gayle, please, that's fine. Truth is, I'm half Asian, well, Filipino."

"My father was born and raised in Manila, then he went to medical school in New York. But he took his residency in Charleston, West Virginia. That's where my parents met. My mother was a young nurse at his hospital. She's Scotch-Irish, with red hair. "

"Oh, that's interesting. Would you like more coffee?"

Diana handed Gayle her mug and Gayle filled it.

"My dad is small and dark. I ended up with a skin color lighter than his and my mother's straight longish nose, and her height. She's almost five inches taller than him." As Diana spoke, Gayle thought about how she had a faint resemblance to Yvonne. Maybe it was just the skin and her exotic looks.

For an instant, Diana's face showed seriousness: "It wasn't the best family to grow up in. My father was brilliant. He's a surgeon who could've gone anywhere in the world, but he liked the mountains around Charleston. It must have reminded him of the island where he lived his entire childhood before the university."

Gayle kept silent and shook her head in acknowledgement of the confession.

"We had a big house in the hills, and lots of maids coming and going, but my father was a hundred percent Filipino. He acted like a strange kind of chieftain. Oh, he slept with the young nurses and resident women doctors for as many years as I can remember. Didn't have any remorse, because his island culture sanctioned that kind of behavior for a man of his power."

"It must have been hard for you to see," Gayle offered with a downturned mouth, shaking her head with disapproval.

Diana's eyes started to water but she wiped them quickly with her slim hand.

"It killed my mother inside. Made her this shell of a woman. She went through the motions of the dutiful wife at parties, and at country club dinners."

Diana continued: "He never changed, even on the day he died three years ago. Collapsed in the hospital parking lot after a five-hour operation on ten-year-old boy with a malignant brain tumor. He saved the child's life. He was walking to his car. He was with a nursing student that was twenty who he expected to spend the afternoon with at her apartment."

"We don't have to talk about this, Diana. Take a deep breath and think about the spring flowers you see outside," Gayle said, acting like a confidante.

And they talked more, comfortable with each other. Gayle decided to share some of her life, her own pain, believing it might help Diana deal with her past.

"I grew on the end of Long Island before it was a destination for celebrities, a long time ago," she recounted. "My father left when I was seven. My mother was so hurt that she just stopped living. Well, she never really worked much. We had no money or owned anything as basic as a house. We rented rooms."

Pausing to drink from the tepid coffee in front of her, Gayle went on. "My mother had to do something though, and she found work as a clerk in a shoe store in the largest village near where we lived. We moved from these rooms to even smaller rooms above a clothing store. She'd gone to high school with the owner, and he felt sorry for her. The man let us stay there for almost nothing. We survived from day to day, year to year. And because I could draw, a teacher in high school told me to apply to Pratt as a scholarship student so I sent them my drawings."

Gayle paused to compose herself for this long ago recollection. "Pratt called me in for an interview, and I took the train. By some miracle they admitted me and gave me a half scholarship. They taught me how to get a student loan. So, art really saved my life and gave me strength to go on."

Her lip quivered for a moment before she continued.

"After I graduated from Pratt, a few friends and I moved into a dirt-cheap place on Avenue A in the East Village. I waitressed and did office work, paid my share of the rent, and this wonderful and crazy artist's life became mine. Then of course, I met Stanley."

Diana got up from her chair and went around the table to hug Gayle.

"Thank you for sharing that with me," Diana said, her own eyes full of tears.

"What is your husband like?"

Diana smiled and said, "Well, Alex is a lot different than my father. I'm lucky."

"I'm sure," Gayle added with a reassuring smile.

"He's from Chicago originally," Diana informed her.

Gayle felt a quickening of her pulse at the similarity. Was this synchronicity at work? The earlier conversation had changed so dramatically within a moment's time that it was as if Diana had read from a script as she moved from one emotion to the other at the snap of the fingers.

"He's head of one of those large advertising agency spinoffs but started out as an art director before he put the suit on," Diana continued. "I've only known the suit side of him. We met six years ago, when I did work for his New York agency."

"Are you a writer then?" Gayle inquired.

Diana laughed again, "Oh no, I went to Parsons, and later worked in fashion on Seventh Avenue. Alex's company was doing the ads for Annabelle Carsen's lines where I worked. We got thrown together over a half dozen meetings."

Diana said she was a painting student at Parsons for two years. At one point she got caught up in the glamour of the fashion industry, working as a model for one or two of the new emerging fashion houses. She said she thought about modeling as a career, but she felt that she couldn't stand the pressure.

"I could draw, and I had ideas, so it was easy to find a place assisting someone who'd already made it. I was doing all their dirty work, cranking out the drawings from their sketches on cocktail napkins at lunch."

"Oh, I know how that goes," Gayle added, "I worked for a big-time potter for a year in New York right out of Pratt. All I ever did was carry the clay from the storage locker to the studio, then clean up the mess around the wheels. It was drudgery. But I was launched into art. We'd go to the parties around town. There were plenty of them, you know, at those studios of painters who already made it. They liked pretty girls admiring their canvases and exciting lives."

Diana shook her head in ready agreement.

"And sure, you slept with a couple of them. The nice ones, that is," Gayle stated matter-of-factly, and a laugh came from deep inside her.

Then they both started to laugh almost uncontrollably.

"Bad girl," Gayle said jokingly and slapped her hand.

The atmosphere had slowly changed. Now both women seemed to be comfortable with each other just a little.

"Tell me," Diana wondered, "what's the story on that house of ours? Alex bought it because he wanted to get out of the city. He made this quick deal with the broker that held the estate and bought all the furniture too."

"You didn't at least drive by yourself, once?"

"No," Diana admitted, adding that Alex was insistent. He has such a good business mind that she simply went along with the purchase.

"He showed me a bunch of photos that the realtor gave him, and we had lunch with her a few days later where she filled me in on the town. We just felt drawn to it. We're going to create great art here. Didn't it start as a dance school for young women who wanted to be on Broadway?" Diana asked.

Gayle started at the beginning with the Russian ballerina and dance school director Katrina. Then she went off on that tangent, filling Diana in on the quirky Bolshoi nature of the woman, and her ever present drama.

"Katrina was such an amusing dinner guest, and I know Stanley adored her stories of Moscow, and that world. His parents came from there during one of the Jewish pogroms in the twenties, I think," Gayle explained.

"The woman always dressed like those old photographs you saw of Isadora Duncan. She wore a long flowing scarf, trailing five feet behind her as she came in the door for dinner. Never failed to bring an exotic present for me, or the both of us, that had some relationship to Russia, or her days in Paris as a prima ballerina. Katrina was strictly old school. She was this tight-lipped stern European ballet mistress. She gave no quarter to these teenage girls."

"How exciting."

Gayle smiled as she continued, "It was the Summer of Love, that crazy time."

She leaned closer to Diana as if telling a secret. "There were two girls there who became caught up with rock musicians."

Gayle's smile widened as spoke. "And because they were in love for the first time, Katrina could forgive them. She admitted it. She herself had a wild affair with a middle-aged commissar when she was seventeen."

Diana laughed. She reached across the table and grasped Gayle's folded hands in a sort of solidarity of familiar emotion.

"So many years ago." Diana added with a sigh. "Since that time our house has always been owned by artists, I've heard."

"Oh, we'd need a day and a night for me to tell you the whole story of that house and the people, believe me," Gayle volunteered. "You'll like it."

"We still have the New York apartment on Central Park West, and I'm not so country-oriented, even though I come from a bunch of hillbillies. I don't know, we'll see."

"You're a painter?" Diana asked and glanced around the living room at some of the small paintings displayed on the walls. Then she walked around slowly, looking at them, and asked, "Which are yours?"

"The two to the right of the fireplace are mine, the still life's, which is really my thing, though I've done some landscapes of the Catskills too," Gayle admitted.

"I like landscapes. Alex not so much."

"Both my husband and I are... were painters," Gayle said, catching herself in the familiar trap she'd never learned to escape since his death.

"Those in the den, the figurative paintings, are all Stanley's. He had his own unique style, working mostly with a pallet knife, and sometime brushes too," Gayle pointed out with pride.

"Alex is a damn good painter, but he only thinks about money these days," Diana said. "He did a big nude of me though last year."

Her hair was dark and lustrous like Yvonne's and cut almost the same way just touching her shoulders, Gayle noticed.

"Yikes, I've got to run," Diana shrieked, rising quickly to her feet, thanking Gayle for the coffee before scurrying out the door.

As Gayle stood on the small porch, she watched the young woman literally skip across the street to the old house. She wondered what sort of people they really were.

The next morning around ten o'clock, Diana knocked on her front door and asked Gayle to come over for a simple dinner. "Please come. Alex is so anxious to meet you," she gushed. "I told him all about you."

Gayle agreed mostly because she was curious about the husband. She brought a bouquet of flowers, fresh yellow jonquils from her back garden as a small housewarming gift.

Inside, the house looked no different than when Peter lived there. His modernist furniture was still situated as she remembered. But to be fair, the couple had just bought the place furnished. They hadn't had any time to really change it at all to reflect their own individual tastes. Well, this was a second home for them. Most summer people in Woodstock took their time getting comfortable in the country environment, first locating grocery and hardware stores, and then maybe the cafes and restaurants around town.

Gayle was greeted at the front door by Alex. He was an attractive man around fifty with thick sandy hair and greying temples. He was probably fifteen years older than Diana. The man was gracious and well spoken. He told her he hoped that they'd have a wonderful time together as neighbors.

He brought Gayle a glass of red wine and then they all sat in the living room, and the spirited conversation went from one to the other. Alex told Gayle about his upbringing in a Chicago suburb called Lake Forest. Gayle had heard of it from friends who lived there and knew it was the city's best address, going back to its wealthiest families at the turn of the century.

Alex and Diana had been married for two years. They loved the city art scene, particularly theatre in Alex's case. They attended Lincoln Center dance performances often. Diana was particularly interested in dance and had at one time thought about a career as a ballerina.

"I was in a car accident at sixteen in Charleston, unfortunately, and broke a leg in four places, and it took a year to heal,"she lamented. "I think I have a slight limp, actually."

"Nonsense," Alex said, "you can ski, skate and ride horses. Hardly the life of a crippled girl."

"Not crippled, just a slight turning out of the right foot. You can't have that and dance, so that was the end of that dream."

"Diana said you painted portraits," Gayle said inquiringly. "Are there any here you'd feel comfortable showing me?"

There was a moment of silence from the couple. Alex shot Diana what appeared to be a look of disapproval. It was as if she'd crossed some imaginary line he didn't approve of and had said too much about their lives.

He recovered his earlier jovial demeanor quickly, "Not yet. I'm working on a couple. I do enjoy painting. I lose myself. It's like someone's painting through me. You understand, you're an artist yourself."

He told her he'd started as a commercial artist in Chicago with small and large ad agencies. He was his best as a conceptual thinker in graphics, focusing on the more boring aspects of the trade like designing logotypes for consumer products.

"For years, on the way up at Leo Burnett, I was the go-to guy for designing cigarette packs for our tobacco clients. My claim to fame, if anything, was Kent's when they went national. The same cigarette package and not a thing changed on it since it left my drawing board."

Soon, they all sat down to dinner and the lively talk continued unabated, with Gayle telling them more of her own life, and describing some of her own art.

At the table, Gayle noticed that Alex wore a fine light blue shirt and a patterned silk ascot, which she hadn't seen worn since her first gallery visits in the late Fifties in New York. As he stretched across the table to grab a basket of garlic bread, Gayle saw what looked like a scar on his throat. He wore the ascot to cover it. Poor man.

Compassion for his past suffering from probably a horrible cancer swelled in her generous heart. She understood why he'd want to hide his wound.

As she was leaving their house, she called out to Diana who had disappeared for a moment to say goodbye. She saw that she was inside a little anteroom off the great room which Peter had used as his painting studio.

"I must go, Diana, and I can't thank you and Alex enough for the hospitality and delicious dinner," Gayle said at the open doorway,

Diana seemed to rush to prevent Gayle from entering the room, and quickly shut the door. In that split second, Gayle saw a large painting on the far wall that she recalled. It was a bluish dance scene that Peter had done, or so she thought, when she'd visited the house six months earlier. She remained silent.

Alex insisted on accompanying Gayle across the dark road to her house. Diana waved from the lit doorway as he started across narrow and windy Wylie Lane walking next to her. As they trod slowly together, he told her he adored painting. He confessed that his life in advertising was only about money.

"I hope to see some of your paintings soon, and Stanley's too," Alex said with a genuine affection in his voice.

He laughed, then quickly added, "I did go to the Chicago Art Institute, and it was a beehive of crazed but dedicated painters in those years.

Almost at her door, Gayle turned to Alex and asked, "Did you possibly know Peter who lived in your house? He went there for a while around the same time?"

"Oh yes. Everybody knew Peter. He was a force of nature with his big abstracts, the blue nudes. I was amazed that this used to be his house. It was a strange occurrence, that accident."

Gayle touched his arm, and said, "Stanley and I both liked him. He was such a fine painter, but he could be thorny. You know, distant."

"That would be him. We never became friends, which was unusual for the kids in those days, all the hippie stuff, and the music. But not Peter. It was as if he came from a different world."

"Well, goodnight. It was such a wonderful evening, and I know we'll become fast friends."

Up in the bedroom, she turned on the light and walked over to the far wall where she had a small drawing that Peter had given her.

Standing in front of it, she saw the swirl of his line and the emerging form of this female drawn in clear movement. He certainly had an evocative style, masterful.

Gayle enjoyed the new couple so very much. Yet, there was something about them which she couldn't quite fathom that was slightly discomforting. It was if they were hiding something.

Diana mentioned they had been married for two years. They probably lived together for a few years first. This was probably his second marriage judging by his age. With Peter and Yvonne, they both had been on the rebound, anxious to find someone else quickly. It felt the same.

That's what Gayle reasoned anyway, and she was usually right with her instincts. She'd always been a people person even as a very young girl. She had this unique sensitivity to those unseen things people have about them and was rarely mistaken.

She thought about her coffee with Diana and how she seemed to say all the right things to win her over. It almost seemed too calculating. Diana acted vulnerable and uncertain at the kitchen table. It appeared to Gayle when she thought about it more, that this behavior was undoubtedly an act on her part. Fool the silly old neighbor lady, that sort of thing. That made Gayle angry. She went downstairs to make a hot chocolate, or she knew she wouldn't sleep.

Gayle slowly sipped the sweet hot dark liquid when she returned to her bed. She remembered how Stanley was always so good at seeing through people's charades. You couldn't fool him. It came from growing up on the hard scrabble streets of the South Bronx.

240

"Don't sign on with this gallery. I'm warning you now," he once said to her after they'd first married. And he was right. Predictably, the fancy gallery owner talked a good game, and made a ton of promises she didn't keep. In the end, she cheated Gayle out of a few thousand dollars. It was a lesson in deception.

Now in a state of agitation, Gayle uttered out loud to herself, "It's that crazy house over there, and what it attracts," and she chuckled a bit. But, she thought, life here in the country outside of New York was bound to attract unusual people.

Looking again at the framed drawing, she felt that it could be the work of a renaissance painter. Peter had been mistaken not to follow that muse, devoting his life to art. Architecture seemed the easy way out. You had a safe profession that would bring in enough money to live a decent upper middle-class life, and so you sold out. Sure, there were a few stars at the top who designed those glitzy towers in the big cities, but everyone else did those boring vacation homes for equally boring stockbrokers.

Stanley had admired Peter's artistic talent from the very beginning. He knew genius because he was one himself. In fact, he told her many years ago that Warhol was a genius before anyone else did. Gayle remembered clearly the night he had come home after walking unannounced into Peter's studio. He saw those large paintings when Peter had stepped out for a moment, and had left the door open. Later, Stanley staggered into their kitchen and became speechless, sitting down at the kitchen table as if he'd seen a ghost. Such was the impact of historic painting.

Snuggled warmly under her comforter, Gayle thought about the evening with Alex and Diana. It was a bit perplexing. At first, she couldn't sleep at all, because there seemed something familiar about both of them. It was as if she'd known them in the past and there was something she couldn't quite put her finger on.

241

What could it be that bothered her so much? This uncomfortable feeling confused her. It was these inexplicable similarities they shared. Perhaps it was a damned house. Maybe it was one of those bizarre places whose very walls were filled with supernatural mysteries or powers. Maybe it affected seemingly normal people who lived or worked there. Yet, there was nothing about Katrina that wasn't simply the result of being Russian and foreign.

Gayle turned seventy this year. Honestly, this could easily be the time of life for senility to take hold. It had for her ailing mother who had heard strange voices from the past toward the end. She had rambling conversations with long dead people who sat on the single chair in her bleak nursing home room.

A well-regarded astrologer analyzed Gayle's birth chart at Mirabai, the local New Age bookstore. The man predicted events which had happened. He saw some of the future. Did her constellation alone provide him with an ability to ferret out this circuitous path in her life?

Gayle believed that there were those who were indeed intuitive and could see what others didn't. Over the years in Woodstock, she met several enlightened people. They had convinced her that there was a thin line between this world, and any other.

He had said of Stanley that he was always an agreeable man, "But only when the party was going his way." How she had laughed at that, because it was so true. Stanley was intense, he was an artist, and a complex though generous, man.

Gayle had a piece of quartz on her night table she'd had for years. She kept it to erase negativity she sometimes felt by rubbing its rough surface. She hoped to absorb its healing properties and feel the electric energy move through her body. It offered comfort. She grabbed the sharp-edged mineral again holding it firmly in her small hand. She offered a prayer for deliverance from evil and from all that troubled her.

Gayle said to herself in a whisper, "I'm not crazy," and stared out at the light coming through the upstairs bedroom window from across the street. She saw there was a faint shadow of a woman, which must be Diana.

The shapely woman moved her hands as if to reach upward and then spun around. Was it a dance? Were they having fun together as any couple might who were in love? Oh, how she missed Stanley's touch, and wrapped her own arms around herself in a sort of embrace. She tried to see him clearly in her thoughts, yet she couldn't. He had been such a thoughtful man. He had adored her and she him.

Before he died, he had said to her that he had never seen paintings such as he had of Peter's. He didn't comment on the color, strokes, or the female nude, but something else he had no words to describe. He was such an intelligent man, never usually at a loss for words.

He had told her, "They weren't soulful, no, not that. What I saw was naked and raw and violent, and it made me shake with fear. I felt disarmed."

"Look," he had said at the time, and ran into the room they both used as a studio and came out with a tablet and a piece of charcoal.

"I want to show you how it was, as close as I can." Stanley bent over the tablet he had put on the kitchen table.

"It starts in the upper left corner. The woman's arm reaches out above her head which is lowered, but you can still make out her features, well, barely. The face, it had this look. It wasn't anything I'd ever seen, even the eyes were real. God, the eyes, they looked straight at me. Even blinked, I know they did."

"Stanley that doesn't seem possible, but maybe it was, you know, some kind of assemblage," Gayle pointed out. "You'd see mechanical stuff in galleries."

He shouted no and started to draw even more fiercely than before until he was almost finished with the charcoal nude. His hand had moved the charcoal in a zigzag motion across the buff paper to where he created

243

the upper torso of a nude woman. The faintest of breasts dropping alongside her chest.

"The face was distinct. It was her, from over there, the same girl, the one who disappeared," he had said excitedly. "Then there was an inhuman twist of her body like this. I can't get it right, dammit."

He had spittle on his lips as he spoke of the painting, and had tried to draw it in the air first with his hands, showing her the mechanics of the dance.

"Danse Macabre, that's exactly what I saw over there, some spawn of the Devil," Stanley stammered out. Gayle became worried with his continued agitation.

"It's a painting, nothing more. A painting, please," Gayle besieged him for some calmness. She laid her hand gently on his shoulder patting it. He shook it off quickly and glared back at her. In a rage, he tore off the half-drawn page and threw it on the floor. Gayle dutiful bent down to retrieve it and put it back on the far side of the table.

Quickly he started to sketch again, and this time, his lines were more accurate. He began to shade the woman as the upper and lower torso took form. He erased what he done earlier to the face. This time, he attempted to create what he'd seen but his charcoal vine was too thick. Beside himself with frustration, he put the black chalk in his mouth and bit off a piece. He spit it onto the table, all to give it the sharp edge he needed. The point of black charcoal gave him a face, expressive and rather human, but it was wrong. He rubbed it off with his fist, shouting.

Visibly upset Stanley walked around in a tight circle in the kitchen and attempted to speak incoherently several times. The words wouldn't come. He'd become unduly emotional, and for what, she couldn't understand.

At last, he calmed himself and looked intently at his wife seated next to him. "Gayle, I saw things that I should not have seen, that are forbidden to look at. By God himself."

"Darling, isn't that a bit farfetched? We're artists, and everything goes. We've seen it all in New York," she reminded him.

"There are no words for what that man has painted. There will never be, and do you know why?"

She could do nothing but sigh to what he'd told her, and fought to be supportive. "No, why?" Gayle reluctantly asked.

"They're evil, that's why. It's like looking into death."

Although she didn't want to, Gayle laughed. This had gotten to the point of silliness with him. It was a ridiculous fantasy that neither one of them had ever believed in.

"Don't you think that's a bit extreme?" Gayle said then, seeking to erase her earlier laughter which she hoped hadn't offended her husband.

At the time Gayle figured that it was only that familiar babble that painters sometimes use to describe work with magnificence or cache.

Yet, Stanley persisted in his description of what he'd seen. She let him talk. She nodded when she felt she must. Now and then, she asked a question which might assuage his discomfort. At the end of the evening, he had talked himself out, drunk four straight brandies, and Gayle helped him up the stairs to bed. There was nothing more to say about Peter's nude paintings, satanic or not. Stanley never spoke of them again as long as he lived.

Stanley attempted to recreate the dance figure painting he'd seen of Peter's, but it became impossible. She remembered him rigid in the kitchen chair with fright and anxiety. He wouldn't speak, but stared out into space, and never attempted another drawing of Peter's nude after that.

Gayle thought that because of his age, this sort of episode could possibly be an aneurism, or a blood clot. She made it a point to calm him down. She gave him hot tea with brandy, steering him away from the trouble-some nude recollection. For her, it was a frightening time,

245

so unlike any she'd had before with this man that she'd married, who was always confident.

He died six months later of a stroke. Gayle believed she saw the first seizure that night of what was to come. Why did he get so upset by the painting? He was such a sensitive artist.

At first there was hardly a sign that Stanley had gotten ill, not even those little things that a wife might notice like coughing at night, or a difficulty with words, or a loss of appetite...nothing. Stanley acted as he always had, and painted in his studio. He had his coffees in town with friends. They continued to entertain as before.

Within two months, there was a slowness in his step as he walked back from town each afternoon. She'd badgered him to see his doctor, and he had. All his signs and blood work were normal. Still the decline continued. By the fourth month, he became a mere ghost of himself, without energy or direction. His ability to carry on an evening conversation disappeared.

The doctor came to the house repeatedly, but could find nothing which pointed to Stanley's decline. He urged Stanley to go to Sloan Kettering, or maybe Colombia in New York for more tests. Stanley steadfastly refused. It was almost as if he knew his time had come and accepted it. He'd readied himself as the end came peacefully in his sleep.

There seemed to be nothing that Gayle might've done to reverse the outcome. Their family doctor certified the death as a natural one, brought on by un-expected heart failure.

These bittersweet memories made Gayle hum a song they both adored. She softly sang some of the lyrics, thinking of those days of their youth and its fierce passion.

"You're a silly old woman," she muttered to herself, and turned on her side.

She was still pretty with an aquiline nose, and a gentle chin. She had always been slim, almost boyish, and those few extra pounds she'd gain were really indistinguishable. People on the street in Woodstock, or in galleries, always would say she was a truly handsome woman. Maybe she could find a mature man with whom she had things in common. But the grief of Stanley's death had been too much to bear for her. Gayle disappeared into herself.

Finally, tired from the hectic day and night, sleep came to her heavy eyes. The moonlight overtook the lace-curtained room while the tiny figure in the drawing on the wall spun in silence.

Across the street things were quiet. Nothing was going on in the other Wylie Lane house that was out of the ordinary. There was a light on in the upper stairs master bedroom and also another in the downstairs studio.

One might call Alex Pontius a dedicated and fierce painter. It was evident in the approaches he took toward the large half painted canvas on his easel. He moved back and forth with almost malicious intent, and passion, as he painted. He was one of those singular artists who only worked at night, and rather late at that.

In the studio, Alex had been painting now for almost two hours. The model, Diana, was tired. In her nakedness she walked from the raised platform where she stood and came to him at the easel. She stroked his face with her long fingers, and said suggestively, "It's time for bed. I'm going up."

She walked to a nearby chair putting on her silk robe that was laid there, and then started out the door. He could hear her bare feet make slapping sounds on the wooden stairs as she climbed to the second floor. Quickly he cleaned his brushes and covered his oils on the glass palette. He wiped his hands on a nearby cloth then turned out the studio light before heading upstairs.

Behind him in the studio, moonlight filled the room, illuminating the half-painted figure of a woman. It was clearly Diana's fine Eurasian features to the casual observer though there was much more. In the painting, there were other women against a dark color field of blue-black, which seemed to have no beginning or end.

You could look at the dark void around and behind the standing women caught in a strange dance movement. It wouldn't end, there was no horizon. The eye and brain can't comprehend that unique spatial relationship because it's infinity.

Like most couples, the two of them sat in bed for a few moments talking about ordinary things men and women discuss. They talked about the business of everyday living such as household bills, errands and friends.

When Diana at last turned out the bedside light, she kissed him hard on the mouth. Then they started into that familiar connection with great passion, and its fulfillment in this late hour. Afterward, they talked more of plans, and what they hoped to accomplish. There was no discussion of the future, and what their lives would be in ten years, fifteen, or thirty, it hardly mattered.

"I must finish the painting," he said.

The full moonlight enveloped the bedroom from the two large windows to the bed itself. Its inhabitants were bathed in a luminous sheet of whiteness that seemed to change their very features. It was hard to determine exactly how, but there seemed to be subtle differences.

Those differences moved from one to the other's faces until it appeared that they might've been separate characters in a film, all moving in and out of the frame. This went on for a time, though it was difficult to measure exactly how long. Was it a single second, or an hour? There was no real way to determine time. When the moonlight dimmed, the couple embraced again and fell asleep.

The sounds outside the window were those of the mountain night. The wind picked up as the temperature dropped. The next morning, Alex had left early for the first Trailways bus to the city. Diana slept in the otherwise empty bed until 7:30 and then went downstairs to make coffee.

The morning was crystal clear with the hint of oncoming spring with warm sunshine. The dew dried quickly on the outdoor furniture on their side terrace. Throwing on a pair of denim shorts and a jersey, she set her breakfast on the table to welcome the glorious day. She leaned back comfortably as she stretched her arms. She heard a small dog bark and saw the woman from the last house down the road walking her French bulldog Henri.

When she came in view of the stone terrace, Diana waved to her, calling out, "Good morning." The woman dutifully returned the wave. She continued her morning regime to the far end of Wylie Lane where it opens onto Rock City Road into the town.

Gayle appeared on her porch to retrieve the New York Times and waved.

"Gayle," Diana shouted out to her, "Have you had your coffee yet?" When Gayle shook her head no, Diana added, "Please come on over and keep me company. There's plenty."

Gayle gingerly started across the road and was soon on the terrace seated at the table.

"Up early, I see," she announced, and took the hot coffee that Diana had gotten for her.

Diana gave her a wide smile in response.

"Perfect in the Catskills. Best of time of year," Gayle said. "You'd better enjoy it because it's short. Alex is in the city, I imagine."

Diana nodded, "He had one of those afternoon meetings he dreads, a contingent from Winston-Salem coming in." She held up two fingers to mimic holding a cigarette.

"Oh my," Gayle responded, "that would be those vile tobacco people."

"And his biggest customers, who spend fifty million dollars a year, so he must march to their drumbeat."

Gayle shook her head, "He's better than that. He should just leave, retire, and paint up here for the rest of his life."

"I wish," Diana interjected. She told Gayle that they had discussed when he could finally leave that life, which took a toll on everyone.

"I just love it here. I feel so at home and content. I never want to leave."

Gayle felt so relaxed with the young woman, even more so than with Yvonne, whom she had liked a lot. That first woman of Peter's was entirely too standoffish and strange.

"Is Alex painting or drawing anything?" Gayle inquired, almost ready to go. She had picked up her newspaper off the table and held it in her hands.

"Funny you should ask. He begged me to pose, and after the third time he pleaded. I finally did it."

"A portrait?" Gayle prodded, curious.

"No, more of an abstract thing with some hints of the figure."

"Can you give me a peak?" Gayle asked.

With that, Diana sat up almost rigid. "He'd kill me. He made me promise to never show his work to people, until he tells me it's alright."

"C'mon, one little look. Pretty please," Gayle beseeched her. "I'll only look in the room for a moment."

For some unknown reason Diana agreed. The two of them walked into the house, and over to the studio door. It was locked. Diana had to remember where he kept the key. After rummaging through most of the drawers in the living room furniture, she recalled that he had put it in a Buddhist begging bowl on the small table against the far wall.

She retrieved it and walked to the studio door which opened easily with a single turn of the key. At the open door, Gayle didn't do what she promised. Instead she walked inside past a surprised Diana.

Gayle moved around the room in a quick swath. She looked at the paintings and finally at the easel where the painting of Diana rested. The woman's figure, and the other figures around her, seemed to meld together as memories of so many standing together. Sharing infinity. A long line of souls.

Gayle stood in front of the half-finished canvas. "He's a master." She let out a prolonged sigh as she looked closer at the paint and the meticulous brush strokes.

As she walked to the door, she kept staring at the painting, and stopped in the doorway.

"You remind me so much of Yvonne, the other woman who lived here." Shaking her head, she said, "My, how things blur together and come full circle."

She turned and walked across Wylie Lane toward home thinking that what she saw is hardly ever offered to human eyes. The two people in that house weren't ghouls. This crossing of dimensions doesn't only produce monstrous things.

Bruce Colbert is the author of fifteen novels and poetry collections, most recently *Canary in the Dark*. A Navy veteran and ocean sailor, he lives in coastal Alabama.

www.ingramcontent.com/pod-product-compliance
Lightning Source LLC
Chambersburg PA
CBHW070926260626
47162CB00007B/2810